Burn Point

Newman Fire Dept Series

Rae Fields

HEA Books LLC

Developmental and Line Editing: Jessica Snyder, HEA Author Services

Copyediting and Proofreading: Marie Edits

Cover design: Kari March

www.raefields.com

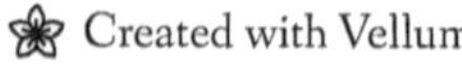 Created with Vellum

*To first responders everywhere - the men and women who
put their lives on the line, and meet us on or worst days -
thank you for your unwavering service.*

Chapter 1

Jordan

"Jordan Ashley, I swear. It's like pulling teeth to get you to talk to me sometimes."

My mother's voice pierced my ear. Thank God she couldn't see my eyes roll through the phone line. Conversations with her were a test of my nerves.

"Mom, I don't have anything to say. I don't want to talk about Gerry. We've been broken up for months and still, he's all you want to talk about." I gritted my teeth in frustration.

The late March evening air was thick with humidity and unseasonably warm as I relaxed in my favorite rocking chair with my feet propped on my front porch rail. I sipped a much-needed glass of wine, studying the high white cirrus clouds in the bright blue sky. On the horizon, lofty clouds melded into a deeper, darker blue-gray, but the neighborhood was alive with people enjoying the break from cold rainy days, out walking dogs, enjoying a late run. The squeals of children echoed in the distance.

The green of fresh spring grass provided a vibrant backdrop for the last of the jonquils that had been in full bloom since I'd moved in last month. But all the beauty surrounding me couldn't override the frustration that a conversation with my mother brought on.

"He's a good man, Jordan. You should try to work things out with him," she continued, ignoring my request to drop the subject. Her ludicrous statement sent me right over the edge.

"Mom, are you serious right now? He cheated on me." I threw my free hand up in disbelief. This was why I kept my conversations with my mother to a minimum.

She was delusional.

I drained my wine to calm down, then took a deep breath to gather the right words.

"Mom, a good man is one who takes care of the people in his life. He doesn't cheat, or lie, or try to place blame on anyone else. A good man takes responsibility for his actions. Gerry is not a good man." I hated the tremble in my voice. Why was it so necessary to her that I have a man in my life?

She huffed into the phone. Of course, she didn't agree with me. My mother had relied on men for most of my life, each choice she made based on what they could provide for her.

"Well. At least when you were with him, you had a stable income and a place to live, instead of renting some two-bit shack in the backwoods. I swear. You are just like your father. Taking off at the drop of a hat, with no backup plan. Just living your life by the seat of your pants."

Not this again.

How many times had I heard this? If I'd thought she could be reasonable, I would've told her the truth about my move.

Coming to this small town south of Atlanta had been a last-ditch effort to start over. A safe place for me to sink into something peaceful while I figured out my next steps after coming home to find my fiancé in bed with another woman. Quitting my day job as a copy editor for a marketing firm in Washington, DC, had come next, followed by moving to the one place that had been constant in my childhood.

Growing up as a Navy brat had meant lots of moving around and no lasting friendships. Starting over in a new place was normal for me. But visiting Grandma in Newman, Georgia, had been the place I could always return to and know that life hadn't been rearranged.

In the weeks I'd been here, I'd concentrated on building my freelance editing business. I had a couple of new clients, and my calendar was filling. I still had enough money saved to last a bit longer before I needed to worry about getting a part-time job to supplement my income.

I had a roof over my head, transportation, and enough business to keep me busy. Things were finally looking up and through hard work, I'd made my dream a reality. Why would I want to get back with the man who made me feel like total shit? Who'd brought me so low? How could my mother even suggest it?

"Mom, I need to let you go," I said flatly. The sooner I could end this call, the better.

"I just worry about you, Jordan. You shouldn't be alone." And that was the crux of her issues, because the woman had never learned to just...be alone. "What're you going to do if something bad happens?"

"I'm fine, Mom. If something happens, I'll take care of it. Look, I've got to go, I'll talk to you soon." I hung up quickly, cutting off her goodbye.

I hated this push-pull feeling I had when I talked to her. I loved her, sure, but she was hard to talk to because she always overreacted. Our disagreement over my independence didn't help matters much.

She didn't understand my need for independence, and I never understood how she could jump from man to man, without ever living her own life. Just once, I'd like her simply to be proud of me—of the strong, independent woman I'd become.

Regardless of her opinion, I was happy living on my own.

Looking for a distraction from my troublesome mother, I scrolled through my Instagram feed, clicking on photos from my favorite van-lifer. How awesome would it be to have that lifestyle, to work from anywhere? To see and experience so many new and wonderful places?

Setting my phone on silent and placing it on the chair next to me, my gaze landed on a sweet labradoodle puppy learning to walk on a leash.

"Good evening." His owner, a cute older woman sporting short, curly hair, waved at me as she passed.

"He's doing much better," I called to her, waving back.

"He is. Thanks!" She paused at the end of my little sidewalk and her furry buddy dropped into a proper sit, his attention solely on her. I rose and met her in the yard. We'd gotten into the habit of chatting during their walks, a way for her to make sure the sweet boy, Nelson, learned his manners. I still didn't know her name, though.

"Nelson is doing such a good job," I repeated and immediately cringed at sounding like a goober.

"It's a great night for a walk," I tried again. Social grace was not my thing when meeting new people.

"It is." Her curls bobbed around her head as she looked up, "Although, it does feel like it's going to storm. The evening just has that feel to it, you know?"

I nodded.

Nelson, obviously bored with sitting still, popped up and lunged after a butterfly. I patted my legs. "Come here, buddy."

I bent and cupped his little snout, rubbing my face on his soft fur. "Who's a good boy?"

"Make sure you have your weather app on tonight," my nameless friend said while Nelson licked my nose. "We're supposed to get storms later."

I stood and looked around, then returned her smile.

"I will. You guys be safe too."

I watched them walk away and made my way back to my porch, resuming my post. Now that Nelson's mom had mentioned it, the evening did have an eerie quality to it. No birds were singing. A haze hung in the air. The hair on the back of my neck stood in warning.

Maybe she was right. Maybe I should make sure I had a flashlight somewhere.

It had been years since I'd been back in the sleepy town of Newman, since I'd spent my summers with my grandma, but I hadn't forgotten how rapidly changing Georgia weather could be. And springtime in Georgia was chock full of pop-up thunderstorms.

My grandma's voice played in my head, triggering old preteen memories of tornado drills. She had a habit of packing what she called a bug-out bag. She'd toss supplies into a bag and have it ready to go at a moment's notice. Since her old house didn't have a basement, we'd climb into the tub, and she'd tuck us in under a blanket or pillows. Thankfully, nothing had ever come of those drills, other than creating a scared girl.

This little place I was renting didn't have a basement either. The similarities between her home and my rental were disconcerting, and what had brought me comfort suddenly felt ominous.

I shrugged off the lingering unease. Likely, there was nothing to this weird weather and I was just remembering old fears.

Four hours later, my phone alarm jolted me awake. I sat up on the couch, disoriented after falling asleep with the television on.

"What the hell?"

The wail of a distant siren, barely audible inside the house, sent my heart racing. I glanced at the TV where the meteorologist gestured animatedly at a radar with arrows pointing directly to my location.

"If you are in the Newman area, you need to take cover now!" His excited voice broke through the last of my sleepiness. "We have a confirmed tornado on the ground."

Outside, the night was ablaze with flashes of lightning, coming one after another. Thunder rumbled and shook the walls.

Oh, shit.

I jumped from the couch and grabbed my laptop bag and cellphone, making a mad dash for the hallway bathroom.

I tossed my stuff into the tub, dove in after, and pulled the heavy "just-in-case" quilt I'd placed there over me as the lights went out.

Rain pounded hard on the roof, the sound intensified by the quiet of the house. My heart raced, blood pumping through my veins. Tucking my head between my arms, I curled into a ball and tried to catch my breath.

The rain grew more intense as the wind howled. Was it hailing now?

Glass shattered nearby, and I screeched, ducking deeper into the tub, pulling the quilt tighter around my shoulders. Something—wind, rain, something more?—battered the outside of my rented house. The terrible noise grew louder and louder and louder still, like a train barreling down on me. The pressure in the room rose, making my head hurt.

Fear gripped me as realization struck. Clenching the quilt in my fist, I buried my face and screamed, "Oh my God!"

I was in a tornado, and I was going to die.

A sudden cracking sound ripped through the room, the bathtub shuddering around me. I flinched and squeezed my eyes shut, curling into the smallest ball possible, and for the first time in a long time, I prayed.

"Please, please, please stop," I whimpered.

A horrendous crash shook the house, and the quilt pressed down heavily, trapping me. Flashes of lightning brightened my hiding spot while debris pelted the room and me.

This was bad.

This was so incredibly bad.

Then, just as suddenly as it had started, the storm moved past. The wind quieted, and the rain slowed. My labored breath against the heavy quilt was loud in the deathly silence that followed.

I shifted to lift the quilt off me, gasping as pain burned hot and bright when I tried to move my leg. The pressure of the quilt and whatever was holding me down was too much. Claustrophobia kicked into high gear. I had to get out.

In a flail of arms and elbows, I battled that damn quilt until blessed fresh air kissed my cheeks. I sank against the side of the tub, panting, gulping in huge mouthfuls of burnt-wood-scented air, slamming my eyes closed as if, somehow, I could avoid whatever nightmare this was if I didn't actually see it. A cold, wet drop of something hit my cheek with a splat. I blindly reached out, my hand brushing the rough bark of a tree limb. My eyes popped open and I glanced up. The night sky displayed back-lit clouds where my roof should be, the view framed by leaves and branches just above my head.

Oh my God.

There was a tree in my bathroom.

And where was my roof?

I felt around for my laptop bag, wishing beyond anything that I'd remembered to put a flashlight in the bag. My fingers grazed the rough fabric, and I gripped and tugged, but couldn't budge it.

Maybe I could find my phone and call 911. I thought I remembered grabbing it, but after a brief feel, it was nowhere near me.

The wail of sirens and robotic bleep of home alarms going off sounded in the distance. The house groaned, and the tree snapped and popped, paralyzing me. If I moved, even an inch, would this thing topple and crush me? I sat frozen in place, scared to move, staring blankly into the inky darkness of the remains of my house.

What was I going to do? How was I going to get out of this?

Voices of my neighbors calling to each other broke my trance.

I was alone in this town. Other than the dog walker, would anyone know to look for me? And where would I go if someone did come?

A whimper escaped.

Stuck in a collapsed house, with no way to call for help, I used the only thing I had, and began yelling.

❖

Nate

Sitting in the firehouse bay on the edge of the storm, watching as it passed over our town, knowing lives and homes were in danger, had been a grueling exercise in patience. We'd been listening to radio traffic, ready to move, ready to do something, anything, just waiting on the storm to pass. The crackle of the radio was a constant hum as I pulled the engine out of the safety of the Station Four bay and hit the button to close the big red sliding door behind us.

"Which way are we headed, LT?" Cal Johnson, lead firefighter in the jump-seat next to me, asked in a strong, sure voice. Cal and I had worked together for a few years. He was filling in at our station for Big Mo, who was out on medical leave. His normally goofy attitude was on the shelf, and he was all business. Like the rest of us, he was ready for action.

"I don't know, but I'm done sitting here waiting. We can at least head toward where we know it hit." Sitting by with confirmed reports of a tornado in downtown had been excruciating for the entire crew. Knowing that people needed us and being unable to act had gone against everything I was as a person.

"911 to NFD." The radio operator's voice cracked with tension.

"NFD, go ahead 911." Captain Mac Collins's gruff voice floated through speakers. I checked the rearview to make sure he was following the engine in the pickup truck.

I took a left out of the station and headed toward town. Knowing that we were at least rolling eased the helplessness churning in my gut.

"We have several calls and our CAD system is down. How would you like to proceed?" Looked like we were going old school without the benefit of having a computer mapping system.

Cal stared wide-eyed out the front window. "Oh shit, Nate. This is bad."

He'd never worked without a computer system in the truck and looked scared to death.

"We'll take down the addresses when you are ready, 911," Collins answered.

I glanced at Cal. "Grab a pen and start taking notes."

The 911 operator began, "Respond to the area of 2900 Lagrange Street. Caller advises collapsed roof with entrapment."

"10-4, go ahead with your next address." Captain Collins was all business.

"Respond to the area of 5 Colonial Drive. We have multiple calls of trees on houses. The caller states a tree is on every home."

I glanced at Cal. "Let's get ready to rock and roll, boys."

The streets through the quaint downtown area were quiet, littered with debris. Where there were normally white twinkle lights shining over sidewalks, even in early spring, now limbs and leaves were scattered across the dark, wet pavement. The streetlights were dark and the engine's headlights cut a beam through the inky black of the night. We crested the hill at the courthouse square and looked beyond. The landscape was unrecognizable in the moonlight.

The downtown area of Newman included a series of two-lane, one-way streets around a historic copper-domed courthouse. Around the square, brick buildings housing everything from boutique shops to coffee shops, even a brewery and a butcher, were part of a years-long revitalization project that had been successful. On any given night, the streets were filled with citizens out enjoying the local art, or having a picnic, listening to local musicians camped on street corners, sharing their gift to all.

Tonight the idyllic scene was disturbing. What lay on the other side of town? What tragedy had happened? It looked all wrong. This landscape that I knew, even in the dead of night, was now foreign to me. Where the downtown area had been spared, three blocks away had taken a direct hit.

The awed voices of my crew filtered around the cab. "God damn, where are the trees?"

"It looks like a war zone."

This was the single worst thing I'd ever seen in my career, and we weren't even at ground zero yet. Trepidation at what we might find when we hit the scene weighed heavily.

Ahead of us, huge hundred-year-old trees had fallen across the road, blocking our way. Their branches spread out across two lanes and into the neighboring yards. Their massive trunks had crushed vehicles parked along the street.

We stopped next to the rescue truck, and I got out to meet with the other lieutenant on shift.

"We can't get through? How are we supposed to get to these people?" He blinked wide eyes at me, his voice high and tight with panic.

"You got a jump bag? And an air tank?" I barked, frustrated at his flailing leadership. He'd been promoted ahead of guys with more seniority and skill. His lack of experience in crisis management was crystal clear, and it looked like I was going to have to lead for him.

"Yeah." He swallowed, and I bit my tongue to keep from tearing into him more. Now wasn't the time to deal with his bullshit.

I pointed to the guys on his truck and called, "One of you take the jump bag, and the other take an air tank and hit the road on foot."

"The address is two miles away!" the fucking new guy called. This was not the time for his bullshit either.

I leveled my glare on him. "You better get to humping then, Rook."

Rook was the nickname of our newest hire. So new, I didn't know his name. And calling him Fucking New Guy didn't sit well with the higher-ups, so Rook it was.

I looked back to the LT. "I'll take my crew to the other side of town and approach from that direction." I climbed back into my engine and set off. A long half-hour later, I finally made it to the other side of town. I got as close as I could to the devastation and stopped the truck.

"Okay guys, we're going the rest of the way on foot."

Picking our way through a mountain of rubble and debris, I paused where I thought the intersection of Lagrange Street and Colonial Street should be. There were no street signs. Landmarks and homes I'd seen my entire life were destroyed.

I pulled out my phone and hit my Google Earth app to confirm my location. All around us, residents were exploring the exterior of their trashed homes. Live power lines lay everywhere. If we didn't get electrocuted, it'd be a fucking miracle.

A woman carrying a puppy caught my attention, shuffling my way with a frantic look on her face.

"My neighbor, I haven't seen her yet. I heard her calling earlier, but I couldn't get to her."

"Which house is hers, ma'am?" I'd add it to the list of ones to search.

She pointed toward the end of the block. In the moonlight, all I could see was the downed tree.

I turned back to her. "We'll check it out."

Cal was helping an elderly woman into a pickup, so I grabbed my jump bag from the bed of the truck and called to them, "I'm headed to that house at the end of the block. Possible entrapment. One of you come help me when you get finished here."

It took another thirty minutes of navigating debris and picking my way around downed power lines to finally get close enough to really see the house, which was mostly buried under a massive tree.

Fuck.

The tree had collapsed most of the exterior wall, and most of the roof was torn off. If anyone was alive in there, it would be a miracle.

"Hello!" I called, then waited.

"Hello! Is anyone in here?" I stepped onto the porch, testing the boards as I inched forward. The tree groaned and popped. The building shuddered under my feet. I paused to assess which route to take, realization dawning that this house was about to fully collapse.

"Hello!" I shouted a last time, then listened intently.

A rhythmic noise caught my attention, followed by a muffled, "Here."

Adrenaline raced through my system as I picked my way into the unstable structure.

"Keep talking to me. I'm trying to get to you," I ordered, scanning a flashlight across the area, looking for the best path. Who could survive this destruction?

"I'm here," came a shaky voice, a little louder this time. It was high-pitched, exhausted, definitely female.

"Ok, I hear you. Keep talking, sweetheart. I'm on my way." My response was unprofessional, but who cared.

I braced myself on a beam, treading carefully through the remnants of a hallway. My pulse raced, my muscles hurt, and my lungs heaved, but by God, I was getting this woman out of here.

"Can you walk?" Maybe I could talk her into meeting me.

"I don't know. I'm sort of —"

I rounded the doorway, the beam of my flashlight landing on a slight figure buried under a large branch. Her arm rose to cover her eyes.

"— trapped," she finished.

I shined the light over her, trying to see where she was pinned. On one end, she might be able to crawl through.

"Are you injured, or just buried under this mess?" With any luck, she'd be able to assist me in getting her out. But since she was still here, hours after the tornado had been through, I'd probably need to pull her free.

"Well, my leg hurts pretty bad," she said with a shaky voice.

I crept closer, shoving debris out of my way. The walls and floor of the house creaked with each movement. Fuck, we needed to hurry.

When I got close enough to reach her, I dropped my bag

and offered my hand. "Take my hand. I'm going to pull you this way. Can you do that?"

"I'll try."

She took my hand, but with my tug she let out a piercing cry.

"Stop! My leg is caught."

I stopped pulling and leaned back, studying the situation. The tree groaned and popped around us.

I leaned over her to find a two-by-four fragment protruding from the quilt covering her, blood staining the edge of impingement.

It was going to hurt like a bitch to move her. And I didn't have enough time to truly assess the situation and stabilize her.

I needed to get her free because we had to move.

Now.

"What's your name, sweetheart?" I had to keep her talking while we did this. Maybe if I distracted her enough, I could tug her out.

"Jordan."

"Okay, Jordan. I'm Nate. We are going to work together to get you out of here. You up to helping me?" There was no reason why I told her my first name. It wasn't a normal part of protocol, but this was unlike any other scene.

"Yeah," she said softly. "Can you see my laptop bag and phone anywhere?"

I scanned the light over the tub, found the bag, and pulled it free. There was no phone in sight.

I set her bag down next to mine and reached for the board.

"Okay, Jordan, I'm going to pull this board away. I want you to bite down on that quilt if you have to, but try to keep still."

There was a soft rustle as she shifted and then she said, "All right, I'm ready."

I gripped the board and gave a test pull. A slight whimper rose from Jordan.

"I'm sorry, sweetheart. Normally, I'd be a helluva lot easier about this, but I'm afraid we've got to get out of here, like now, before this tree crashes on us. So, here we go. On count of three. One, two." I tightened my grip. "Three."

I tugged with all my might. Jordan let out a piercing screech and then fell silent. I flashed my light over to find her slumped, her breath shallow. But she was free.

The tree creaked, and the house shook.

Time to go.

I grabbed our bags, tossing hers over my shoulder messenger style, then reached in to pull her from the tub. With a grunt, I lifted her deadweight over my shoulder, then spun around, retracing my path out of the house.

I cleared the porch and laid her gently on the ground in the solitary patch of untouched grass. Behind me, the tree shifted, a part of the house collapsing in a horrible crush of cracking wood and destruction.

A sharp gasp drew my attention back to Jordan.

"You okay?" I asked, crouching beside her, aware that my own voice shook now.

"My leg hurts, but nothing else. What happened?"

I did a cursory assessment now that I had better access to her. Blood ran down her leg, but otherwise, she seemed to be relatively all right. Or as all right as one could be when their house had nearly collapsed on them.

"You passed out when I pulled the board. We need to get you out of here." I said, swiping the sweat off my brow with a shaking hand.

"Sorry about passing out on you," she said as she stood, gripping my arm as she tested her injured leg.

I tucked her under my arm, her hand gripping mine, and led her toward the pickup truck waiting at the end of the block. We'd navigated a couple of downed lines when my flashlight batteries finally bit the dust and we plunged back into darkness.

"Shit!" Jordan jolted as she took a step, clutching my hand tighter as she gasped.

"Hold still, let me see if I've got a backup light."

Pulling my phone out of my pocket, I flipped the light on. As it blazed through the dark, I realized the poor woman had walked a hundred yards or more through the debris filled street barefoot.

"Jesus," I muttered. "Why didn't you say anything about your feet?"

"What?" I felt her turn toward me.

"Your feet are gonna get all kinds of buggered up out here in this mess. There's all kinds of shit on the ground and you aren't wearing shoes."

"I didn't even notice."

Shock and adrenaline were for sure flowing through her veins if she didn't feel the crap she was stepping on.

I handed her my phone. "Here. You're on flashlight duty." Before she could get a word in, I whipped her up into my arms and got us the fuck out of there.

Chapter 2

Jordan

One minute I was standing, trying not to notice my feet. The next, I was pitched a cell phone, lifted into a pair of strong arms, and being carried through the destruction that had once been my quaint neighborhood.

He jostled me a bit, securing his grip, and fire shot through my injured leg. I cried out in pain, and he shifted me slightly, then the pressure eased.

"I'm sorry, hon. I didn't mean to hurt you. I just need to get us out of here."

The pain returned to a manageable throb. I slipped an arm over his broad shoulder. "What's your name again?"

He wobbled a little as he stepped on something, and I flung my other arm up around his neck.

"Nate."

Nate, my rescuer. My own personal hero.

Something about his low voice resonated with me. His utter control amid chaos. This man had saved my life. A few minutes later, and I would've been in that house when it collapsed. The reality of what had just happened sank in, and I buried my face in his neck to hide my tears.

Everything I had was gone.

My house had crumbled.

My car was probably totaled too.

I had my laptop, thankfully, and the clothes I was wearing. I didn't even have a pair of shoes. But at least I was safe in the arms of this kind stranger.

Though I couldn't make sense of the words he was saying, just the tenor of his voice and the strength of his arms soothed me.

At this moment, I wasn't alone in the world.

I took deep breaths, trying to calm myself. He smelled like clean laundry mixed with the scent of burning wood. Was there a fire? Odd how it smelled like a campfire.

"I've got you, but I need you to focus and hold the light for me. Can you do that?" His deep voice cut through to the rational part of me.

I lifted my head and released my hold on him to look around. He'd paused and was looking down at me with concern. I offered him an embarrassed smile. "Sorry about that. I just needed a moment to fall apart."

I turned the phone so the light shone on the ground ahead of us. At least I could try to be helpful in this situation. He started walking again, picking his way through a massive pile of debris.

"It's all right to fall apart, but I need you to trust me, and I need you to help me get us out of here."

"I can do that." I tried to sound confident as I aimed the light farther ahead.

Nate took a few steps one way, then backtracked and headed another direction, then paused again.

"Shit, there are fucking power lines down everywhere."

A radio on his shoulder crackled with a transmission, though I couldn't understand what they said.

"Well, that's one thing going our way." Nate's body relaxed against mine just the slightest.

"What did they say?"

"They shut down the power grid for this area. That's good news. That means we won't get electrocuted trying to get out of here."

"Oh, yes. That's a good thing," I replied stupidly.

He chuckled. How could he chuckle at a time like this?

"How far do we have to go?" I asked, trying to adjust to make sure I directed the light where he needed it.

He nodded ahead of us. "Just there. See that pickup truck?"

I swiveled my head, taking in the littered street. Ahead, little spots of light bobbed in the dark. Beyond, the end of the street seemed well lit with the headlights of vehicles. Someone had a spotlight shining on a relatively clear path to the vehicle. We just had to get to the path.

I focused on his labored breathing rather than the eerie sounds of the night. He had to be exhausted from carrying me all this way. It must've been a good quarter mile, mostly uphill at that. Finally, we reached the area where several vehicles idled. Other storm survivors were being loaded into trucks and four-wheelers.

"Thoren," my rescuer called. "Open that door for me, man." A dark-haired, bearded man turned, caught sight of us, and hurried to open the back door of a large pickup truck.

"You got her, Nate? You need help?"

"Yeah, I'm good." Nate leaned into the truck and set me gently on the seat. A light flashed over us, skimming down my legs, then over Nate's torso.

Thoren stopped the light on Nate's arms, covered in dirt and blood. "That hers or yours?"

"Hers," Nate responded, tucking my feet into the truck. "This is Jordan. She's going to need a ride to the hospital to have her leg examined."

The door on the other side of the truck opened and a woman with a cap of dark brown curls climbed in. She leaned back in the seat, turning to reveal a bundle in her arms.

Nelson, my furry labradoodle friend, wiggled at the sight of me, struggling to get out of his owner's arms. He got free and climbed into my lap, licking my face.

"Nelson! You're okay!" I cried, wrapping my arms around him, burying my face in his soft fur. I choked on a sob at the realization that they were both alive. Despite the horror of the night, we were all still alive.

"Thank God." My curly-haired neighbor's reply was soft, relieved. We clasped hands as the firemen closed the door on the terrible scene.

The ride to the hospital had been a miserable test of patience. Trees and bystanders blocked the roads, and by the time we got there, my adrenaline had crashed. Exhaustion weighed me down. Everything hurt, and I had to pee.

After a quick examination, a few stitches, and clean-up by an older nurse, I found myself sitting on a bench outside the hospital entrance next to Jules, Nelson's owner, while we took turns cuddling the sleepy pup. We'd gotten to know each other better on our long ride to the hospital.

"So where are you going to go now?" I asked her.

"My brother is on his way to pick me up. He's got a

houseful with his five kids, but I'm sure he has room for a few more. Do you have a place to go?"

I combed my fingers through Nelson's fur, trying to find the answers to her question. No. No, I didn't have anywhere to go. And even if I'd had a phone, there was no one I wanted to call.

Instead of speaking that bleakness into the universe, I simply shrugged a shoulder and gave Nelson another scratch.

"We should exchange numbers," she said, pulling a phone from her back pocket.

"I lost my phone in the storm, but I can give you mine and write yours down. Maybe if you text me, I can get the number from the cloud on my laptop once I get it charged." I rattled my number off to her, watching as she typed it into her phone. She only asked me twice how to spell my name. I guessed we were both still out of sorts.

"I'm sorry it took a tornado for me to properly introduce myself," Jules said as she slipped the phone back into her pocket.

A Suburban pulled to a stop in front of us, and a giant red-headed bear barreled out of the passenger seat, running to swoop Jules into his arms.

"Oh my God, sis! Are you okay?"

Nelson wiggled out of my arms to bounce in circles around the man, excited to have a new playmate.

While Jules reassured her brother that both she and Nelson were fine, I busied myself by fumbling through my laptop bag. I had a random pack of crackers, my laptop with no charger, a pad of paper, and a couple of pens.

"Jordan, this is my brother, Steve. Steve, this is my neighbor, Jordan." Steve released her, and she bent to gather

Nelson. "Steve, do you have room for one more?" she asked with an armful of wiggling puppy.

"Oh, no...I couldn't impose," I blurted, hating feeling like an intruder.

"I'm sorry, sis. We've already got nearly all our floor space covered with storm victims. There are sleeping bags and air mattresses in every square inch of my house."

Jules looked like she might argue, so I offered them both a semblance of a smile. "It's okay, Steve. And thank you for thinking of me, Jules."

"But where will you go?" she asked, concern etched on her face.

I shook my head. "I'm not sure just yet. I heard the nurse say they had a temporary shelter set up somewhere. I'll be fine."

Her brow furrowed, then she stepped close, wrapping an arm around me in a hug. "I'll text you in a couple of days and find you."

I nodded, swallowing against the lump in my throat at the thought of being alone. Even though we weren't really friends, the trauma of the night had forged a bond of sorts. That she had family and friends nearby while I remained alone was a reminder—I needed to get my shit together and take care of myself.

Hadn't my mother questioned this very circumstance earlier? I refused to prove her right.

I patted Jules's back and nuzzled Nelson. "I'll be fine. I'll try to find you soon."

Four a.m. was such an odd hour of the morning. My body knew it should be sleeping, but my mind was racing, and my awareness was high.

With my heart in my stomach and nerves frayed, I'd walked back into the emergency room lobby after watching Jules and Nelson leave. Since I had nowhere to go, I'd planned on camping out in the lobby of the ER. No sooner had I gotten situated on a hard double-sized waiting chair, the security guard approached and told me I couldn't sleep there. Instead, he'd led me to a waiting area, then loaded me on a transport bus to a local church that had opened a temporary shelter.

By the time I arrived, the shelter was full, and since I was one of the last arrivals, I'd had exactly one choice of cot, next to a scruffy man that smelled of pickles and onions.

Thus, I found myself perched on my cot, with my back to the wall, laptop bag next to me. I shifted, trying to relieve the pressure on my leg, draping it over my laptop bag to ease some of the throbbing.

Four a.m. passed to five, then six. Every time I tried to lay down and close my eyes, the storm raged in my mind. Giving up, I finally stared at the ceiling. Waiting. Wondering what would happen next.

At seven, a couple of volunteers arrived with a warm breakfast. I stood in line, waiting to receive my portion, heart heavy and mind void.

I wandered away from the crowded hall, outside to sit at a wooden picnic table in the church courtyard. The sun was just rising, the air crisp and cool. The day promised bright blue skies. In the trees beyond the courtyard, songbirds greeted the day with bright melodies. In the distance, the whir of chainsaws cut the calm of the morning.

The church that housed the temporary shelter sat on a hill a block off the courthouse square. The historic three-story marble building boasted Gothic-style spires, stained glass, and a massive bell tower. As each hour passed, the bells played hymns. Supposedly a sign of hope, but in my post-storm haze, the sound was haunting and melancholy.

I opened the wrapper of my meal to find a chicken biscuit, which looked and smelled amazing, but somehow, also turned my stomach. I pinched off a corner of the biscuit and peered out at the scene below.

Where once had stood huge, hundred-year-old trees, there now was nothing. Workers secured tarps over holes in roofs. Four-wheelers and utility vehicles ran among the streets. The remaining trees had been snapped off midway up the trunk, their spindly stalks standing naked, while their vibrant green leaves lay in piles on the ground.

Though I hadn't been in town long, it had begun to feel like a place to call home. At first, I thought maybe I was imagining the magic of the area, but just the short time I'd been here had cemented my love for this sweet, small town. From the quaint homes and historic buildings, to the modernized metal art sculptures in the park, even the painted sculptures that peppered the corners of the downtown streets, all of it was inspiring and heartwarming.

And now the entire landscape of this city I loved had changed in a matter of minutes. Beyond the desolation and destruction of the town, everything I had worked so hard for, everything I'd based my success on...was gone.

Sorrow for all that had been lost threatened to overwhelm me.

Though my stomach wanted to revolt, I forced myself to swallow a bite of biscuit. The view of the destruction wavered as I fought the threat of hot tears.

I had no home.

No car.

No clothes.

No steady job.

No way to contact my clients until I could get access to email.

I'd walked away from the security of a home with Gerry. Walked away from a stable career and established my independence, thinking my life was changing for the better. Only to be slapped back down.

The reality of *rock bottom* descended around me. I dropped the biscuit, unable to eat more. What in the hell was I going to do? Was my mother right? Was I a fool for being so independent? Had I really isolated myself so much that I didn't have a single person to call in my time of need?

For a long, long while I sat at that table. The courtyard filled with people, and then it emptied, until I was alone once again. The world outside continued without me while my mind shied away from deep thoughts and the truth of my situation.

Trucks filled with chainsaws passed by, going one way, and then back again full of limbs and debris. Four-wheelers with boxes of food, water, and supplies made round after round. All of them passed through my periphery, yet never drew my full attention. I was aware but removed.

Exhaustion hit and I laid my laptop bag on the table and folded my arms over it, then dropped my head on my makeshift pillow and closed my eyes. I needed some sleep, then I'd figure out my next step.

Nate

I was six hours into overtime after my twenty-four-hour shift and had gotten approximately one hour of sleep. There were another six long hours to get through before the end of shift. A steaming-hot shower and an ice-cold beer beckoned like it never had before.

Captain Collins pulled his pickup next to the UTV I was loading with water. "Which way you headed, Williams?"

I slipped a case of water into the last open space on the cart and dropped my jump bag on top of it. On top of the shitty scene, we had a handful of radio equipment suddenly die on us. We resorted to using our personal cells, but could've done without the added frustration.

"I've got sector two with GSAR."

The Georgia Search and Rescue Squad had deployed to help us assess homeowners. We'd split the city into quadrants and were going door to door checking on people. If no one answered, we searched the house. If there was no house, we searched the rubble. As we entered, we spray painted half an X, on the structure or the drive, some place easily seen, to indicate there were personnel inside. Once complete, we finished the X and listed the number of occupants, or dead bodies, found.

Thankfully, we'd found no casualties—a miracle given the utter devastation of the storm.

I was loaded up to deliver supplies to the other SWAT medic before joining the search and rescue team again.

"Check in when you get there and make sure you get something to eat. There is a food truck out, serving tacos to everyone."

"Will do." I rounded the back of the vehicle and climbed in. What I wouldn't do for a fifteen-minute power nap right now.

Between running calls and busting up fights amongst the newer guys, I was toast. And that thought reminded me... "Hey Captain, did you hear about the incident with

Rook last night? He was wired. I had to get rude with him a time or two. I guess he flipped under the pressure."

Captain Collins's brow dipped. "What happened?"

"He got into it with a guy from A-Shift in front of some civilians. I had to grab both by the shirt and get in their face a little."

Collins scrubbed a hand over his face and sighed. "That guy."

"I handled it. But in case you get any complaints on us, thought you should know."

"Right. Thanks." He dropped a hand to the gearshift, and the metallic clunk of the transmission engaged. He bent his arm in the window and regarded me for a moment.

"You all right?" Captain Collins was a good boss, a good man. Way more perceptive than he let on. He was also the hardest working captain in the department. Admitting that the events overnight had worn me down felt like admitting to failure.

"Yeah, boss, I'm just tired. It was a hell of a night."

Hell, we were all running on fumes at this point.

The memory of a set of long legs, curly hair, and the sweet feel of a soft body in my arms had kept me going.

I usually didn't think past a call. But I couldn't shake the memory of the woman from the collapsed house. Which was stupid. She was fine. She'd never remember me anyway. I was just the guy who pulled her out of a horrible situation, and I was just doing my job. She'd forget I existed, and life would move on.

And they still needed me on the job, no matter how tired I was. I'd push myself to the limit if I knew there might be someone else out there stuck in the rubble.

Collins watched me a moment longer then slapped the door of his truck and with a nod to me, he pulled away.

A man of few words, and an old-school veteran of the fire department, he'd been a part of the brotherhood back in the day when all we ran were fire calls. I had started just as the department switched over. Now we ran both fire and medical. All the damn time.

I took the nearest route to my post, stopping to grab some tacos along the way.

Giant root balls stood tall out of the ground, the trunks of their trees laying wherever they'd fallen. People working now filled the streets. Neighbors helping neighbors salvage what they could, hauling away debris. The sheer amount of clean-up needed was overwhelming.

There were two distinct types of people out. Those who lived in the destroyed area, moving slowly with shell-shocked expressions on their faces. And those who were there to help with the clean-up.

I eased my way to my post and met up with Thoren. I handed over a box of tacos because I knew he hadn't eaten either. We'd spent most of the day together. He had to be as exhausted as I was.

"Thanks, man," he said, tearing into the tacos like he hadn't eaten in days.

I kicked a leg up on the dash, opened my box and took a huge bite.

"You talk to Bunny?" I asked around a mouthful. They'd been dating on and off for a while. She wasn't my favorite person, but it wasn't my place to judge who the guy spent his time with.

He nodded, swallowing his own mouthful and making a backhanded swipe over his mouth. "Yeah. She's good, I guess."

"I bet she was scared shitless last night."

"She said she took the dog to her tornado spot and

hunkered down. I got all of two minutes to talk to her and she bitched the entire time because I wasn't home. Kind of left me with a guilt trip." He shook his head, frowning. "To hear her tell it, she's a strong, independent woman and can handle herself. But she let me have an earful and made me feel like shit for doing my job." He shook his head, studying the remnants of his food.

Relationships in the fire service were a touchy thing. It took a special kind of person to understand the drive required in this line of work and to support someone who chose this profession. The long shifts, the emotional impact of calls, and the day-to-day bullshit of people abusing the system placed a challenge on even the best relationships. Add in that most stations included members of the opposite sex, and that was fuel to the fire for anyone with jealousy problems. Most of the guys I knew were either single or divorced.

I'd avoided relationships, choosing to date casually, for that very reason. Why start something that was just going to end anyway?

Again, my mind filled with images of the woman I'd helped from that collapsed house. Jordan had been on my mind most of the night. I marveled over how close we'd come to being caught in that house when it caved in.

Did she make it to the hospital? Was her leg okay? And out of all the people I'd helped over the last twenty-four hours, why was she the one that kept piquing my curiosity? Maybe being so close to death ourselves is why I kept thinking of her. She had been alone for hours, literally pinned in the bathtub. Plus, she'd lost everything.

I felt sorry for her.

Thoren slipped his sunglasses off and rubbed them on the hem of his shirt. "You ready to get back to it?"

I wadded up the trash from my meal and set it in the empty seat next to me, jumped out of the seat, and grabbed my gear. "Let's do it."

A couple hours later the sun was blazing down on us, the humid air thick, soupy. We'd walked for miles, checked every home, and amazingly, everyone had been mostly okay. One guy'd had a heart attack and another had fallen off a ladder during the day, but for the most part, the only losses had been structural.

Thoren and our buddy Mike, a Newman police officer, met me at our four-wheeler. Mike was the latest addition to the fire department. Technically Mike was still a cop while he worked his notice with the police force, but soon he'd be joining us as our Fire Marshall.

"You headed back to the station?" Thoren asked.

I grabbed a bottle of water from the cooler, dousing my head to cool off. "Yeah, you?"

He shook his head. "Not yet. I'm going to run by and check on my buddy and see if he needs help."

"I'd heard that a guy from the county fire department had lost nearly everything." Mike said.

Thoren pointed behind me. "That's his house."

I turned to look in the direction he pointed. "The brick one without a roof?"

The yard was filled with pickup trucks, and people filed in and out with rubber storage bins. At least the family had something to search for.

He shrugged. "Yeah, I just need to check in, you know. See if I can help."

I clapped him on the shoulder. "I get it, man."

We were all feeling pretty damn grateful to be alive. And supporting those who'd been impacted was the least we could do.

"You mind running this case of water by the shelter at the church?" Thoren nodded at the remaining case in the bed of the UTV.

"No problem."

"Speaking of," Mike started, "we hear that some of our troublemaker regulars have been vying for space at the shelter. They're harmless, but they've harassed people from time to time. I'm hoping they will all behave, given the circumstances, but let me know if you hear anything. Mostly, I'm on watch for the guy that was exposing himself downtown last week. I don't know where he ended up."

I knew the regulars he was talking about—we'd all dealt with them at some point. Some were homeless, some were just down on their luck and needed a meal, but for the most part they didn't cause problems other than to ask for food or money. Occasionally, a business owner would complain if their customers were being harassed. When I ran into these folks, I tried to make sure they had what they needed. Most of the police and fire department personnel did. This town took care of their own, though the one guy was troubling.

"Well, at least for the time being they have a place to stay."

I tossed my trash and clapped hands with Thoren and Mike. "I'm headed to the shelter, then I'm headed home to sleep for as long as possible."

"I heard that."

"Catch you later."

The drive back to the shelter took me out of the way of the station, but what was a few more minutes? Though my bed *was* calling my name. How long had I been on duty now? It had to be going on thirty-six hours.

So much had happened in such a short period of time. I

was moving on autopilot at this point, long past the point of sheer exhaustion and running on fumes.

At least it had been a nice, sunny spring day. And wasn't that the way after a big storm?

As I passed by the south end of the church, movement in the courtyard caught my attention. Likely some refugees hanging out. Were they refugees? What was the right term for them? Victims? Survivors?

I slowed down to check out of habit, just like I'd been checking in with everyone I'd passed all day.

"Hey, you doing okay? Need anything?" I asked. What a stupid question. These people probably needed everything right now. Why else would they be here?

A woman approached from the edge of the courtyard, and when she stepped out of the shadows, there was the face that had been haunting me all day. The sun lit up her blonde curls, framing her face like a halo.

"Jordan?" I called, hope lacing my tone.

She gave a small wave. "Nate, right?"

I nodded, stunned that I'd found her here, of all places. "Wow...I don't know why, but I'm surprised to see you here."

Even with her dirty shorts and t-shirt, messy hair, and bags under her eyes, she was the prettiest woman I'd ever seen.

She rested both hands on the iron fence and leaned in with a tired smile.

"I don't really know anyone in town, and my family is far away. I didn't have anywhere else to go." Her voice held the sweetest hint of southern twang.

I wanted to bathe in it.

I turned off the UTV to hear better, suddenly not in such a rush to get back to the station.

"Have you been working since I saw you last?" she asked.

I nodded. "I have. We've been running search and rescue, and we set up an emergency post since the trucks can't get through."

Crossing her arms over her chest, she gazed at the destruction in the general direction of her house.

"Have you been here this whole time?" I asked.

She gave the smallest nod.

Jesus Christ. She had to be miserable. "How's your leg?"

She dropped her arms and turned to the side, baring her leg to me. The long creamy expanse of skin was marred by a gauze strip.

"Not too bad. They cleaned me up and gave me a few stitches." She paused and glanced at me quickly, then away. Her gaze locked on the ground at my feet. "Thanks for being there for me last night. I don't know how I would've gotten out of there if it hadn't been for you."

I studied her face, the dark circles under her eyes. Even in her disheveled state with her shoulders hunched, and her clothes rumpled and hanging off of her, she was so pretty.

With her soft smile and gentle manner, she looked like an angel. Like the sweetest gift to come from the destruction.

I hated the thought of her being in some makeshift shelter. She should be at home, or in the finest of hotels. Somewhere comfortable and cozy and safe.

She probably hadn't slept at all.

And she didn't have a home to go to anymore.

I squinted against those troubling thoughts, because why was she any different than anyone else? Why was I so concerned about her? Of all the people I'd helped over the last twenty-four hours, why did I feel the most responsible for her? "Are you staying here again tonight?"

She wrapped her arms around herself and peered over her shoulder at the church. I didn't miss the slight shudder that ran through her.

"Yeah," she said with a sigh. "Do you know how creepy churches are at night?"

A smile tugged my lips. "I can imagine."

She shifted her gaze back to me, her lips tipped up in a small smile. "Red Cross says they can put us up in a hotel, but only for a few days."

"Do you need anything in the meantime?" I gestured to the remaining supplies. "I've got some supplies here if you want to go through and see if there is anything you can use."

"You have a spare laptop charger or a spare cell phone?"

I grinned at her. "No, but I have a toothbrush and some hand wipes."

"Oh my God, yes! I could use a toothbrush," she blurted, pink creeping up her cheeks.

I dug one of the individual toiletry packs out of a bin and handed it to her through the fence with a smile. "There's even a travel shampoo and conditioner in there." I'd given these bags out all day but handing one to her was humbling.

Her blush grew brighter. Adorable. Even in the aftermath of trauma.

"It's the little things," she murmured, her fingers brushing mine as she took the small ziplock bag I offered her. Tingles shot up my arm at the contact, and my eyes locked with hers.

She took the bag and took a step back. "Thanks, Nate." The sincerity in her voice rocked me.

Suddenly, I didn't need to get home so badly. My bed

and a long sleep were the least important things on my agenda. I was a selfish bastard for even having a bed to go home to when she had lost everything. Compassion for all that she'd suffered filled me.

I gripped the fence, wishing it were her hand. "I'm so sorry about your house, Jordan."

She blinked rapidly and gave me a small smile. "Thanks Nate, I'll be okay. I lived through it, and things can be replaced." Hugging the bag to her, she cleared her throat and said brightly, "Well, I bet you're tired and ready to get home." She shook the bag at me. "Thanks again for the supplies and for, you know, saving me from a collapsing house."

She was dismissing me, giving me the perfect opportunity to wish her well and head home.

And I wasn't ready to say goodbye.

It was rare that I ever ran into the patients I helped. I mean, I'd see them in passing along the way sometimes—it was a small town, after all—but it wasn't often that I got to spend any significant time with them.

I wasn't ready for this to be our last chat. I wracked my brain, trying to figure out a way to keep her here and talking to me.

"Can I check in on you in a couple of days? See how you are, see if you need anything?" It was unethical for me to ask, but I didn't give a fuck at the moment. I just knew I couldn't tell her goodbye and never see her again.

She shook her head.

No?

She was seriously telling me no? Did that mean she had a boyfriend? Was she married? Was she not interested in me? And why was I worried about her being interested in me? She'd just lived through a nightmare. It didn't matter what her reasons were.

"I was serious about the cell phone," she said. "I lost mine in the storm."

Oh.

"Okay, well how about this..." I whipped my field notes pad out of my pocket and wrote my number down, then tore out the slip of paper and handed it to her. "Here's my number. Keep in touch and let me know you are okay. Please. And don't hesitate to call if you need anything." I pierced her with a look. "I mean it. Call if you need anything."

She took the slip of paper, staring at her hands as she folded it in half. "Thanks, Nate." Her voice was barely a whisper. "I appreciate it."

Those emotional eyes met mine. "See you around."

I waited until she'd backed away from the fence and turned to go into the church before turning the UTV back on. I dropped the water off at the loading area, taking a quick peak inside the large hall, row after row of cots lined up. Jordan would spend her night on one of those uncomfortable bastards. With a bunch of strangers. With my heart in my gut, I drove back to the station.

Chapter 3

Jordan

Losing everything really hammered home what was important in life. Like being safe, having a roof over your head, warm clothes that fit, a place to rest your head, and food to fill your belly.

I was being a little dramatic, but as evening settled and the sun went down, so did the temperature. It had dropped to near freezing, and though I had a roof over my head, I was still in a pair of shorts, and it was damn cold.

The spacious room, usually used for church activities, had been converted to a temporary shelter. Rows of cots filled the space. The industrial black-and-white checkered flooring—I didn't know if it was laminate or tile, not that it mattered anyway—and the high ceiling did little to stop the chill creeping through the room.

What I wouldn't give for a pair of sweatpants. And a sweatshirt so that the creepy guy next to me would quit studying my T-shirt. He was hoping for a nipple shot, no doubt, or maybe he was using his imagination.

Blech. I shuddered.

A pair of socks that fit would be welcome, too. One of

the volunteers offered me a pair of his from his gym bag, and though I wasn't too keen on the idea of wearing used socks, he'd sworn they were clean, and after a sniff test, that proved to be true. Beggars couldn't be choosers though, and at least my feet were covered.

I'd found a cot by a wall, so I didn't have to keep watch on both sides of me. Tonight, there were more people looking for respite from the cold. I'd been lollygagging around outdoors and missed the opportunity at having a blanket, or maybe someone had taken two. Regardless, I had a place to lay my head, and I was not sleeping on the street. So, it was a small win for the day.

Most of the storm victims had been moved to alternate locations during the day. Some had friends or family offer homes, some got lodging at hotels.

But I didn't have any local friends or family to call. And I didn't have any money or funds for a hotel. My purse and wallet were buried somewhere in a collapsed house, along with my phone.

I had no ID, no credit card... I had nothing. Literally, I had the clothes on my back, and my useless laptop.

The weight of everything I didn't have lay heavily on me. Where did I even start to pull my life back together? I'd spent the better part of the day pondering my situation. As I stared into the distance to the soundtrack of buzzing chainsaws, I sat in a slump of self-pity, caught in a loop of indecision and inaction. Every single decision and necessary step seemed insurmountable.

Cross-legged on the uncomfortable cot now, I dug out the slip of paper Nate had given me. I had no idea of the time, but it had to be at least midnight if not the wee hours of the morning. The fluorescent overhead lights had been turned out, and the room was cast in a weird darkness, lit only by the lights of the front door lobby area and the red glow of the emergency exit light. At least power had been restored to the building during the day and there was a security light tonight.

I'd been sitting on this cot for hours keeping vigil, afraid to drift off, stuck in a mindless, exhausted state. My sore leg ached, along with my shoulders, hips, and back. I fingered the scrawling numbers Nate had written like the simple scrap of paper was a lifeline. One single solitary connection to another human being.

He probably didn't really mean for me to call him, but it was nice knowing I could. Maybe I would at some point, whenever I got another cell phone. Just to thank him again for saving my life.

I was being all dramatic again.

The guy in the cot next to me made a garbled sound in the back of his throat and then spit on the floor beside his cot. He noticed me sitting up and turned to face me, his hand landing somewhere near his crotch. His arm moved in a telltale way.

Gross.

I kept my eyes on the slip of paper, trying not to let on that I knew he was watching me. What I wouldn't give for Nate to come rescue me from this nightmare.

A noise at the front door drew my attention and I hugged my bag closer to me. This bag, though useless, held my sole possessions at the moment, and I for damn sure was not about to let it get away from me.

In the dim light of the front foyer, I made out the shape of a tall man. Broad shoulders, boxy frame.

I blinked. There was no way. Could it be?

I cringed inwardly. Was I so lonely and pathetic, I was

conjuring images now? Wishfully thinking that Nate had come back for me?

And why did I even want him to?

I didn't know the guy aside from the two times we'd met in very unique circumstances. I had some serious hero worship going on if I was imagining him now.

The tall man followed the night security guy, winding their way through the cots. The two men got closer, and something about the way the tall guy moved had me rising and calling out, "Nate?"

He whipped his head toward me, then was moving in my direction. "Jordan?"

A cry of relief ripped from me. "What are you doing here?"

He stopped in front of me, glaring at the disgusting guy so hard the dude grunted and rolled away.

"Let's go." Nate's voice was a low growl that had the hairs on the back of my neck standing on end.

I took his outstretched hand, the warmth of it engulfing mine. The simple act filling that hole in my chest that the storm seemed to rip open. At this moment, I didn't really care where he was taking me. I was grateful that my own personal knight in shining armor had shown up once again when I needed him most.

I slipped my bag over my body with my free hand as he tugged me through the room and out the front door.

Outside, the frigid night air was a slap to the face, instantly waking me fully and setting off involuntary shivers. The warm yellow-orange glow of decorative lights lit the path of the sidewalk down a set of stairs to a lone four-door pickup truck sitting at the curb.

Nate led me to the passenger door, opened it, and helped me inside. Afraid that I might be dreaming, I kept an eye on him as he slammed my door and stalked around the front of the truck and climbed in next to me.

The engine growled to life with the push of a button. He punched a couple of knobs on the dash, and a flood of warm air blasted over my frigid toes, eliciting an involuntary moan from my throat.

I couldn't take my eyes off him. His scruffy jaw clenched, his brow furrowed. He looked pissed. I couldn't tell if he was mad at me, and I couldn't help but wonder why he'd come if he clearly didn't want to.

"What are you doing here?" I broke the tense silence.

He shook his head and huffed a small breath. "I'm not sure."

Well, that didn't make me feel so great—not that I wasn't grateful for the warm air and the feeling of safety. "Okay, then why are you here?"

So it was the same stupid question, but I was too exhausted and dumbfounded to think of another.

Draping one hand over the steering wheel, he turned to face me, leaning his shoulder into the seat. A lone street-lamp broke the darkness of the night. Inside the cab though, there was barely enough light to see by. It lent an intimacy to the moment that made my breath hitch.

Feeling all kinds of self-conscious, I tucked a lock of hair behind my ear and forced myself to meet his gaze. His eyes swam with some emotion, probably pity, or maybe disgust at the mess of my current state. Either way, the hard set of his jaw and flaring nostrils weren't giving me the warm fuzzies. The hand on the steering wheel fisted, as if he wanted to punch something.

I flinched and shrunk back a little.

His expression softened at once. "I'm sorry. I didn't

mean to frighten you and steal you away, and I'm not trying to make you uncomfortable now."

I nodded even though I still didn't understand what was happening.

"Let's start over. Pretend I just found you again." He stopped abruptly and his jaw flexed. "Maybe without the part where that asshole was jerking off next to you."

Realization dawned. He was mad at the shelter guy, not me.

"Okay." My voice was small and tiny in the cab of the truck. Tentatively, I stuck my hand out and offered him a small smile. "Hi, Nate. It's good to see you again. Thanks for saving me."

One side of his mouth tipped up in a half-grin as he took my hand, rubbing his thumb over the skin on the back of mine. His fingers were warm, and I wanted nothing more than to cuddle up to him and see if the rest of him was just as toasty.

"Hey, Jordan. I'm glad you're okay." Instead of releasing me, he held on, lowering our clasped hands to the console, his thumb still brushing softly.

An unruly curl flopped over his handsome forehead. My smile grew until I was pretty sure all my teeth were showing. I kept my voice light and flirty, like I would if I were hitting on him in a bar, rather than in his own pickup truck outside of an emergency shelter for storm victims.

"What brings you to the local shelter in the middle of the night when it's freezing cold?" I asked.

The grin grew as his gaze wandered my face. His attention shifted to the area outside the truck in the direction of the tornado destruction and his smile fell away.

He studied the same area I'd been gazing at all day.

He was silent for a few moments. When he finally spoke, his voice was gruff. "I was at home, sort of coming down from the last two nights, processing all that's happened." He paused, throat bobbing as he swallowed. His grip on my hand tightened. "A buddy of mine mentioned some trouble with some of the homeless people earlier. There are a few who do some pretty ugly things sometimes."

The line of his jaw worked as he stared into the night. After a moment, he turned to me with an expression I couldn't read. "I couldn't stop thinking about you. I needed to know you were in a safe place. The shelter wasn't answering their phone, so I drove over to see if you were still here."

The rhythmic way his thumb rubbed my hand settled me a bit, and my shoulders relaxed. Was this man for real? This was some next-level romantic shit.

"That was awfully kind of you. But isn't it kind of late?" My voice was soft and timid.

"It is. And I'm sorry if I woke you. Are you okay? How is your leg?"

My leg? What leg? All my attention centered on where our hands met.

"I'm fine. A couple of stitches aren't a big deal. And you didn't wake me. I was up, pretending not to notice my neighbor."

He studied me in the soft light, obviously pondering something. Abruptly, he let go of my hand, as if he'd just realized he was still holding it and leaned back against the door.

He opened his mouth to say something. Closed it, cleared his throat, and tried again.

"Why aren't you at a hotel or something?"

I slipped my hands between my legs and hunched my

shoulders. "So, it turns out, you need some form of ID and a way to communicate with people. I have neither of those two things."

He tilted his head. "Help me out and explain that a little further."

I dropped my shoulders and released my hands. "I lost my phone and my purse in the storm. I'm sort of stuck here until I can get back over there and search my house. Then, maybe I can get with the disaster organization to find some temporary lodging."

Nate was shaking his head. "Yeah, I don't think that's going to happen."

"Why not?"

"I heard today that there are no rooms available anywhere in town. Some folks had to travel two or three towns away to find a room."

I turned to look out the front window, worrying my lip with the fingers that still had his scent on them. This was a big new monkey wrench in the grand scheme I'd cooked up while sitting on my cot. What was I going to do?

He cleared his throat again. "So, I have a spare bedroom. If you need a place to stay..."

I gave him a thorough side-eye. What would he expect for payment if I took him up on his offer?

"I don't do seggs-ual favors, mister." Good grief, could I sound more awkward? No doubt this conversation would replay in my head later when I was trying to sleep. But for now, I needed to keep this in perspective and put some boundaries around this situation. I was not sleeping with him just for a place to lay my head.

His eyes went wide and round. "Oh, no way, I don't expect anything," he backpedaled. "I'm just, you know, offering you a room to stay. Temporarily. Totally as a friend. You know, sort of roommates. Or something."

The way he tripped over his words set me more at ease. He didn't give off a serial-killer vibe. But that was a stupid thought because what serial killer actually acted like a serial killer?

No, Nate gave off a good-guy vibe. The nice-boy-next-door vibe. The hunky hero, drag you out of a collapsing house, and carry you to safety, then save you from a wanking scary-dude vibe.

"Didn't they get you some shoes?" His voice interrupted my internal debate over what kind of vibe he was giving me.

I cleared my throat, wishing I could sink down into the seat and disappear. "The shelter didn't have any. I got this pair of socks off a volunteer that felt sorry for me." I fell silent, and then a different dread filled me. "Nate, are you single?"

Because of course hunky, beautiful hero Nate could not be single. No way he would be.

The question seemed to stop him in his tracks, but he didn't answer. He just sat there, looking all sexy. And heroic. And I had too many troubles to be catching a crush.

Swallowing my pride, and any ounce of cool I ever had, I tried a different approach. "Nate, I don't want to cause trouble. I do need a place to stay, but I don't want it to be an issue," I said quietly but firmly. I'd had enough of cheating from Gerry, and I would absolutely not become that person. Not in any way, shape, or fashion. I knew the cold, hard, hurtful truth of infidelity.

Nate looked at me quietly.

I wiggled my toes in the borrowed socks I wore, relishing the warmth of the heat blowing from the dashboard. If he turned me away and took me back inside, at least I would be warm going back in.

"How many people do you know in this town, Jordan? I figure it's not many since you're at a shelter, instead of staying somewhere safe and warm."

Heat bloomed over my face. This whole situation was humiliating.

He shook his head. "I just can't leave you here. I can't do it. I cannot, will not, send a half-clothed woman, alone, into a room full of horny, strange men. It's too dangerous. But it's up to you. If you aren't comfortable with it, I'll walk you back inside right now."

Tension thick enough to cut filled the cab as I debated my choice.

On the one hand, he was a really attractive temptation. Not that I was ready for any semblance of a relationship, or even a one-night stand, for that matter. But he'd come for me, twice now, and that made my heart swoon.

On the other hand, I really didn't want to go back inside that shelter. It was meant to be a compassionate service to the community, but I didn't feel safe, and the thought of not sleeping for another night was excruciating.

More than anything, I didn't want to be a burden.

Nate sat quietly while I pondered. Finally, I sat up straight in my seat, and swallowed my pride. "I would appreciate, very much, if you wouldn't mind letting me use your spare bedroom."

I couldn't look directly at him, but the warmth of his smile was a brush of sunshine washing over me.

I held up a finger, halting his jubilance. "But only if we agree to some terms."

Silence fell between us, and finally curiosity got the better of me, so I glanced at him.

He was watching with that adorable half grin on his face. "Okay, Skippy, what are your terms?"

"Skippy?"

"Seemed to fit." The corner of his lips tipped up higher.

I rolled my eyes. "Whatever." I flipped a finger out to count my points. "First, this happens for a limited amount of time. Just until I figure out my next steps."

"Sure. I agree to that. What else?"

Second finger. "I'll carry my share of the chores."

"You can gladly have kitchen and bathroom duties."

"Third." I held up three fingers. "This only happens if your girlfriend is okay with it."

A little crease formed between his brows. "I don't have a girlfriend, and I'm not married, but okay, Skippy." He was back to smirking. "If that's what you want, sure. I'm just trying to help you in your time of need. I believe that what comes around goes around. We'll be like roommates or something. What else?"

I swallowed and laid out my last term. "I'm not, under any circumstances, sleeping with you."

The frown was back. "Of course not. I mean yeah, I think you're pretty, but that's not what any of this is about anyway. Why would you even think that? Have I been rude to you or given you that idea at all?"

He sounded way more offended than I thought the situation called for, but it was best to be upfront about all expectations.

But dang, he didn't have to be quite so defensive about it, did he? And how big a fool did it make me, being disappointed he'd friend-zoned me so fast my head was spinning. Especially when I'd friend-zoned him first.

My head swam with confusing thoughts.

What level of crazy was I hitting? I didn't want a man,

and only needed this one because he had a spare room and I needed a full night's rest. I was both relieved and upset that he'd offered me a place to stay and called me beautiful and friend-zoned me in the course of one conversation.

A friend was exactly what I needed. Even if the vain part of me was tickled to know he found me attractive. I was a mess of contradicting emotions.

And now, he was waiting on a response from me. "You've been a perfect gentleman, my own personal hero. I would appreciate it if I could bum your spare room."

"Good, so it's settled." He clapped his hands and rubbed them together. "I accept your terms. Temporary lodging offered to a down-and-out friend."

And with that, he straightened in his seat and slipped the truck into gear, grinning at the front window. "Let's get you home, Skippy."

As I watched the church disappear behind us, I wondered if I had just made a serious mistake. This man was lethal to my resolve to be relationship free, because he was utterly adorable with his nicknames and grins.

I'd just have to remember that we were only roommates, and not read anything more into it.

Chapter 4

Nate

"No, I don't know when we will be able to reschedule the calendar shoot, Mary Catherine." I stood in the bay door of the firehouse, trying to find patience for this ridiculous phone call. "First off, I don't handle that, I just show up when I'm told. Second, we are working around the clock right now with tornado recovery. That's where the priority is."

I slipped off my ballcap and thumped it against my leg in frustration. That anyone could focus on the annual charity calendar during this tragedy was beyond me.

"We were thinking of changing the theme this year to be centered around the tornado damage. Do you think we could do some shots in the areas that were affected the worst?"

Unease rolled through me. "So you're telling me you want to use images of people's destroyed lives as a fundraiser for public safety?"

"Not exactly the way you put it, but I take it you don't like that idea, overall?"

"Fuck no. That's ridiculous and I won't be a part of

anything making a dime off someone else's misfortune. I can't believe you even suggested that."

"Calm down, Nathaniel. It was just a thought."

I slapped my hat back on and ground my teeth at her calling me by my full name. We'd dated a time or two and apparently that gave her permission to condescend.

She continued, "The organizational committee was just tossing ideas out since the photoshoot got canceled."

Captain Collins rounded the front of the fire engine, sticking his ever-present toothpick into his mouth. The guy was never without one since he'd given up smoking. He raised his eyebrows at me, my sign that I needed to get off the phone.

"I gotta go." I clicked off the call, not waiting for her response. Rude, yes. But I was so frustrated that I didn't give a damn.

Captain rolled his toothpick to the corner of his mouth and slipped his hands into his pockets. "I need a team to go set up a first aid station near Lagrange. You mind taking that?"

"I'll be glad to." I paused for a beat, considering the location, then added, "You mind if I run a detail while I'm in that area?"

Maybe me and a couple of the guys could search Jordan's house for some stuff. I'd had every intention of taking her over there, since technically it wasn't my day to be on-shift, but our team had been called in to headquarters to work the field units scattered in the neighborhoods since the big trucks and ambulances couldn't yet navigate the streets.

"Do what you gotta do, just be around if some fool falls off a ladder."

I grabbed Thoren, and we jumped in the UTV and

drove the two miles to Jordan's neighborhood. What used to be idyllic southern homes were now covered by debris. The massive hardwoods that had fallen obscured the homes from view, and many trees lay on top of battered roofs. Large root balls, some twelve feet tall or more, created a dirt wall against the onlookers out trying to assess the damage. Day three and our progress was still impeded by people on foot, looking to find loved ones and help in any way they could.

"We gotta make a quick stop," I told Thoren, pulling up to the pile of debris that used to be Jordan's house. The exterior walls were partially standing, the windows were all blown out, the roof was gone, and a massive tree lay over one end of the house, taking up space all the way to the bathroom where I'd found her. A green couch sat untouched against an interior wall, a rustic table stood alone in the center of a room that had been a kitchen. The two pieces of furniture were a sad contrast to the chaos of the rest of the structure.

"What are we doing here?" Thoren asked, casting a skeptical look at the house. "It's marked as searched."

"I helped the woman who lives here the other night. She was the one I carried to the truck when you asked me about the blood. Ran into her again. She's on her own and doesn't have her cell or her wallet. Thought I might try to see if I could find it for her." I didn't mention that I'd left said woman asleep in my spare bedroom this morning.

"In that mess? Bro, that's like looking for a needle in a haystack." He shook his head but climbed out anyway, and we—carefully—headed into the house.

A bit later, Thoren stood up triumphantly from what remained of the bathroom holding a battered phone in his hand and yelled, "Score!"

I'd already found a purse with her wallet in it, wedged under the couch. It was yet another miracle that the place hadn't been looted. The TV even lay on the floor and looked undamaged. I dug around a little more but didn't see a laptop cord. I'd just have to take her to get another one.

"Should we try to get some of her clothes?" I asked, picking my way back toward Thoren.

"Dude, we're lucky we found this."

I stood on a mound of sheet rock, surveying the room. "I know. I just feel terrible for her. Can you imagine losing everything you own? I just want to do something to try to give her some of her old life back."

Thoren sighed in exasperation but got back to work. "Why's she so important to you?"

I picked my way to a bedroom littered with piles of insulation. "I don't know. I'm just trying to help her out. You do the same thing every day we are on shift."

I turned away from him so he couldn't read what I wasn't saying. That this woman was under my skin.

A picture frame lay face down by the bed. Broken glass fell away as I turned it over. I shook the remains away to find an image of a man and a teenage Jordan standing in front of a waterfall. His arm slung over her shoulders, both of them wearing hiking gear, smiling happily at the camera.

My chest grew tight with emotion. "This is why I'm here, Thoren."

I flipped the photo over to show him.

"Jordan had a life before this storm hit, and now she has nothing. If I can help bring her some measure of peace, just by spending some time picking through debris, it's not going to cost me anything. I'd like to think someone would take care of me if I ever needed it."

Thoren studied the photo, then me. "Okay, I get it."

We dug around a little more until I unearthed a basket of soaked laundry. "Let's take that and those shoes. That should get her by for a bit."

Nodding, he tossed a pair of sneakers into the basket. I slipped the photo and phone into her purse, and we picked our way back to the UTV.

"You got a way to get in touch with her?" he asked as he drove back to our post, whipping around a pile of brush, almost tipping us on two wheels.

"You know, you're a shit driver. And yeah, I'll see her tonight." I grabbed the oh-shit handle as he made a turn and sped into the empty parking spaces around the high school that served as an emergency vehicle lane. "She's staying at my house until a room opens up."

Thoren braked hard enough to pitch me forward.

"Say what?"

"Damn, don't kill me with your fool driving. I said she's staying with me until a room opens up." I tugged off my baseball cap and scrubbed my hand over my hair before resetting my cap. I looked over to find him gaping at me.

"What?" I asked.

Thoren and I had worked together for years, but we were also friends outside of work. We often worked out together, went for beers, took part in the annual calendar fundraiser together.

He turned wide eyes to me. "Nothing, I'm just surprised. This is totally not like you."

I shrugged. "It's not a big deal. She just needs a place to sleep. I have an empty guest room."

His expression changed, turning sly. "Is she pretty?"

"Just stop right there. It's not like that at all. This is just a temporary thing." I said, but from the looks of it, his imagination was running wild. I needed to stop his train of thought.

Tones for our station rang over our portable radios, interrupting us, though the sound was almost muted by the buzz of chainsaws. An elderly man having a possible heart attack. We jumped back into the UTV and Thoren zipped us back through town.

We pulled up to find the patient lying in the bed of his pickup. A young woman sat beside him, clutching his hand, wiping his pale brow.

I grabbed our jump bag from the UTV, knowing my supplies were running low, hoping an ambulance could make it through in time. Climbing up into the bed of the truck with him, I eased her out of the way, and Thoren and I got to work.

After an initial assessment, I looked at Thoren. "How far out is that bus?"

He requested an ETA, and our gazes locked at the delayed response time. Time the man didn't have. He needed immediate care.

"What are you thinking?" Thoren kept his voice low and calm. *We're gonna lose him if we don't act fast*, his gaze seemed to say.

Not today.

I dug through my bag and found two bags of saline. "We're gonna start an IV and bolus fluids until they get here."

We doctored him as best we could on scene until an ambulance could get to him, and hopefully it was enough. By then, thankfully, it was time to head back to the station.

I gathered my things and made sure all my gear was

ready for my next full shift. Fatigue kicked my butt as I headed home, every minute of the last few days weighed on me, but I was oddly excited to not be going home to an empty house.

My ranch-style brick house on the north end of town was far enough out to have to drive to work, but close enough that trips to town didn't take all day. I had a couple of acres of grass that I enjoyed cutting, a large, detached garage where I could do woodworking, and a giant deck that looked out over the woods behind the house. It wasn't fancy, but it was home. Relief settled into my bones as I pushed open the front door.

My entryway was unrecognizable. The pile of boots and shoes by the front door had been tidied, the mat they sat on had been cleared of dirt and grass clippings. The wood floor gleamed. The blinds were all open and the late evening sun cast the room in warm sunlight.

The scent of garlic coming from the kitchen had my stomach growling in an instant.

"Hey!" I called out, propping Jordan's basket on a hip while I dropped my backpack from my shoulder to the bench beside the shoe bin. The hats that hung on the rack had been straightened, the mirror above the rack shone bright and clean.

"Hey yourself! I hope you're hungry," she called back.

I hitched the basket, which was fucking heavy with all the wet clothes, higher and walked to the kitchen. I dropped it in the front room, rounded the corner, and froze.

The oven door was open, and Jordan was bent over pulling out a tray of what looked like garlic bread. Her shorts were impossibly short. The little dip at the top of her thigh, just below her ass-cheeks, winked at me. She straightened and laid the pan on a towel on the counter, then picked up a spoon and stirred something on the stove. Luckily, her back was to me while I figured out how to speak through a confusing mixture of both lust and guilt. I had no business noticing her ass. I was no better than that asshole at the shelter.

"Grab a plate," she called over her shoulder. "I hope you like spaghetti. It's all I could find to throw together." Her voice held the trace of a smile. She sounded...happy. I don't know why the thought struck me, but I was amazed that she seemed chipper, despite all she had been through.

I took a step and found my voice. "It smells great in here. But you didn't have to cook."

She grinned over her shoulder at me. "I don't mind. It's the least I can do. You've probably had a hard day anyway." She turned back to the stove with a little shrug. "Plus, I got a little bored."

My feet were glued to the floor. I should offer to help, do something other than stand frozen, pretending I wasn't checking out her ass and those long legs.

I looked around my kitchen, taking in the clean countertops and the empty sink. "Looks like you did more than cook. This place was a wreck when I left this morning." What she'd accomplished in a day was impressive. And here I stood, nasty from my day.

"Mind if I grab a shower first?"

She shook her head. "Go right ahead, this needs a few more minutes to simmer."

I jumped into a quick, scalding shower. Then my belly led me back to the kitchen.

Jordan was plating food and turned to me with a smile. She had a great smile. I scrubbed a hand over my damp hair as if that could scrub away the disturbing thoughts I kept having about my house guest.

"It's not much, but hopefully it'll fill you up." She said, placing a plate of pasta on the small kitchen table and taking the seat across from me.

I slid into the chair, took a bite. It was all I could do to bite back a moan. "This pasta sauce is so much better than it usually is."

I shoveled food like I hadn't eaten in days and sat back, patting my full belly. "That was amazing. You found that in my cabinets?"

"I may have spiced it up a little. I was going to see if you wanted a refill, but you looked like you were having a moment and I hated to interrupt." She propped her elbows on the table, beer in one hand.

I grinned back at her, shoving my plate away, and getting up for another beer. "You need one?"

"No thanks. So how was your day?"

I turned to toss the beer cap in the trash. "Pretty busy, had one heart attack call. Ambulances are having trouble navigating the streets, so we had to work him until they could get there."

"Oh no, is he going to be okay?" Concern etched her pretty face.

"I hope so. We did everything we could. We had to improvise on scene, but he had a pulse when we sent him off." Often, I wondered how patients did after a call. Sometimes we were able to get updates, but for the most part, once we turned them over to EMS, our job was done. The not-knowing left a hollow space sometimes. At least during the storm recovery, we were able to see the impact we'd made at the end of a long day. Which reminded me—

"I meant to tell you when I got in, but I got distracted by my stomach. I went by your house today."

She gasped and her bottle hit the table with a thunk.

"You did? I didn't know they were letting people go back to their homes already."

I nodded and set my beer down before going to grab the basket I'd left by the door.

"So, I know most of this is wet," I called from the front room, "and I'm not sure we can save it." I plunked the basket on the table. "But we can run it through the washer and see if we can get any of it clean enough to salvage. Your purse and phone are in that trash bag. I'm sorry I couldn't find your laptop charger."

"Oh my God, Nate." Her chin wobbled, and her eyes were glassy as she reached for the trash bag sitting on top. "You went back for this for me?"

I looked down at the pitiful basket, wishing it could be more. Wishing I could do anything to make this situation better for her, embarrassed that I'd only been able to find the bare minimum.

"Well, yeah." I shrugged. "I was working relief in the area, so me and a buddy stopped by."

She nodded as she fingered her meager belongings. "I feel like I could just hug you right now."

She turned those shiny eyes on me and gifted me with a full-on smile. "Thank you so much. I don't know that I can express how much this means. I mean, it's just replaceable stuff, but it was mine."

I studied her for a moment, my heart cracking just a little. I couldn't imagine losing everything I owned, everything I had worked for, everything that defined me.

My own emotions about her situation had me swallowing uncomfortably.

"Um, I also found a photo. The frame is broken, but I tucked it into your purse."

She dug through the bag and lifted the frame. A single tear spilled down her cheek as she stared at the photo.

"Is that you and your dad?" I asked gently, wishing I could reach out and wipe away that tear instead of watching as she brushed it away with the back of her hand.

"Yeah, that was a long time ago." Her voice broke and, in turn, nearly broke me.

Seeing her upset was torture. I'd give anything to make her smile again.

"I have the same phone and an extra charger around here somewhere." I blurted, needing to make her hurt go away. "Let's get it powered up and see if it still works. Tomorrow, we'll try to get back over there and see if we can find anything else."

The next few hours, we washed her clothes, and she went through her purse while I cleaned up from dinner. She was so easy to be with and grateful for every little ounce of kindness. I still felt bad for her, but at least I'd been able to improve her reality a little. I went to bed while she was still sorting her things and lay there tossing and turning.

Coming home to find her taking care of my house had been nice in that moment. But now, the whole situation left me confused.

For as long as I could remember, I'd vowed that I'd never get married, that I'd remain alone, that I didn't need anyone. Growing up in a loveless household had shown me that just because you were married, didn't make everything magically wonderful. You could be a part of a family and still be lonely. And outward appearances were often deceiving.

Still, despite my discomfort at the domesticity, having Jordan here felt... right.

I'd been able to make her situation more bearable, and that was a reward in itself. Yet it bothered me how much I liked her being here—this unusual pull toward her had me unsettled and out of my comfort zone.

Could I stand letting her stay here when every little thing she did affected me? But could I stand it if she left?

Chapter 5

Jordan

The scent of coffee filtered into my sleep-addled brain—the best smell in the entire world. Well. Almost. Actually, the best scent was that of clean laundry.

Rolling over, I buried my face in the pillow next to me, drawing in the scent of clean linen, with a hint of sandalwood to it. I stretched, long and satisfying, then opened my eyes to a room that wasn't mine. The past two days—or was it three at this point? I couldn't recall—came back in a rush. The tornado, the hospital, the shelter, Nate.

I glanced around the cozy room. Even if it was sparsely decorated, I was in a new friend's home, thankful for the roof over my head, the comfy bed, and clean clothes. Laying around moping would not help me move forward, and that was my only option.

I ran a hand over the sheets, such a far cry from the uncomfortable cot at the shelter. Nate was so generous in helping me out. I honestly didn't know where I'd be without him. Sure, I'd tidied and cleaned for him to show my gratitude. The simple act was the least I could do after all he'd done for me.

I climbed out of bed and hit the bathroom before shrugging on a cardigan over my T-shirt and PJ bottoms. Thank goodness I'd been lazy putting away my laundry before the storm and Nate had been so kind to retrieve my things.

I plucked my phone up and checked my messages. I still needed to call my mother, but that would have to wait until I was sufficiently caffeinated.

Her over-the-top reaction would require way more energy than I currently had.

"Jo honey, your father is gone..." was how she'd delivered the news of their divorce. The grief in that moment of thinking my father had died was all-consuming for a twelve-year-old girl. Who did that? Why phrase it that way rather than having a rational conversation?

No, I'd wait until I at least had some answers before I subjected myself to the particular torture of calling my mother. Besides, it wasn't like she'd be of any real support to me anyway. She'd always been judgmental about every little thing I'd done.

I picked up the photo of me and my father, brushing my thumb along the edge. I'd hidden this photo in my dresser because it had been too hard to look at on a daily basis. Memories of that last backpacking trip remained bittersweet.

Time had not healed the hurt. And seeing the photo, now, with older, wiser eyes shifted that hurt to guilt and regret. Being trapped in that house, in that storm, fearing for my life had changed me. Brought into sharp focus all the important things, people, I'd been neglecting.

I should've gone to see my dad.

I should've been there for him.

But seeing him in those first few weeks after his accident had been so hard that I'd taken the easy route and run away.

Pushing those unwanted feelings aside, I set the photo against the lamp on the nightstand and headed to the kitchen, following the seductive smell of fresh coffee.

I made a beeline to the pot and poured a cup, tossed in a splash of cream, and sipped the nectar of the gods. A low moan of approval escaped as I swallowed that delicious first taste. A chuckle behind me brought me back to the present.

"Good morning. I take it you like coffee."

I spun to find a sleepy, shirtless Nate standing with a shoulder propped in the doorway. Adorably tousled in the morning light, with stubble gracing his chin and golden curls flopped down over his forehead. His loose sleep pants teased the sexy V of his hips. He was cover-model perfect. It made sense that he'd be built with the easy way he'd carried me that first night. But having the evidence of that strength displayed before me—my mouth went dry.

He was extremely handsome, and oozed sex-appeal. He was also being extremely nice to me and deserved better than me ogling him.

I swallowed thickly and nodded. "It's heaven."

"Well, after you have your moment with that mug," he waggled his eyebrows, "I thought maybe you'd want to ride out and see if we can find any more of your stuff."

I forced myself to focus on his adorable face and not his muscular chest. "You don't have to work today?"

He pulled a T-shirt off the back of a chair and slipped it on. "It's my shift today, but I took some comp time, because I've been working non-stop for the past three days. So, I'm off, unless I get called in. I thought we could ride over there and go get you a laptop cord."

Embarrassment, humbleness, guilt, and gratitude all swirled in a kaleidoscope of confusing emotions. I wanted to say yes, but facing the wreckage of my house was terrifying. I wanted my things, but I also felt like ditching everything and starting over. And a little piece of me wanted to run away and never look back.

"You don't mind?"

Nate shook his head and opened his arms wide. "Nope, I'm at your disposal today."

"I don't want to put you out. You've done so much for me already."

He made a pshh sound, waving off my gratitude. "Come on, let's get going before they call me in and suck my time away. Besides, if I'm working at your place, I can tell them I'm busy and it won't be a lie."

He glanced out the window and back at me. "It's a little cool out this morning. Do you need a long-sleeve shirt or a jacket?"

I shifted, embarrassed by my current state of full dependence on him. "That would be great."

His expression softened and he gave me a tender smile. "It's going to be okay, Jordan. This situation is just temporary."

Two hours later, I'd shucked the flannel shirt I'd borrowed from Nate and tied it at my waist over my cutoff denim shorts. We were picking things out of the rubble and tossing anything salvageable into large rubber bins that he had unearthed from his garage.

Nate was on the phone, sounding frustrated.

"MC, I can't come to a shoot today. I told you that when

you called the first time. You need to talk to Mike and get the details worked out."

It sounded like he was busy, and I didn't want to pry, so I tiptoed farther into the mess and found the area that had been my bedroom. The walls had caved in, the sheetrock making a sticky mess.

"Hello!" a deep male voice called.

With my feet buried in a pile, I turned my body to see a large man in a police uniform walking up the sidewalk, picking his way around the downed tree. Clearly, I had missed that the men in this town were all romance hero worthy. He was tall, dark, and handsome and filled out his uniform in all the right places.

Nate, phone still at his ear, waved to him, and the guy turned his attention to me.

"You must be Jordan. I'm Mike, Nate's friend."

I gave him my biggest smile and lifted my hand in a dorky wave. "Hi, Mike."

His gaze shifted to my poor house. "I just wanted to stop by and see if I could help."

I shrugged. I'd take all the help I could get at this point but had no idea where to point him. The mess was overwhelming. "Well, if you don't have anything better to do, I'm sure we can find a spot for you to stand in this catastrophe. As it is, I'm kind of stuck."

Mike clambered closer. "Are you trying to get under there?" He pointed at the pile beside me.

"Yes, that's where my dresser is supposed to be."

He leaned down, his uniform shirt stretching dangerously taut over his thick arms, the crackle of his leather belt sounding oddly erotic.

He shifted a couple of things around and stood, turning

to me. "I don't think you're going to want any of this. It's pretty bad under there."

My shoulders slumped. "Crap." I forced a small smile, trying not to let the situation get the best of me. "Well, it's okay. I guess I have enough to get by."

His intense stare made me want to fidget. A bad guy would have a tough time under his inscrutable gaze.

After a moment, a huge smile broke out over his face, and he said, "Nate is so fucked."

"What?" I tilted my head, confused.

His smile lingered as his gaze traveled over me. "Nothing."

Nate joined us and they did some weird, complicated man-handshake in greeting.

"Thanks for coming by. You met Jordan?" Nate tucked his hands into his back pockets.

Mike braced his legs wide, hanging his thumbs on his belt, that big grin back on his face.

Testosterone absolutely swirled around these two.

"Yeah, we met." Mike motioned to the mess around us. "I think y'all have found just about everything worth saving here."

Nate nodded. "Jordan's been getting after it this morning. She's a tyrant."

Hands on hips, I mocked outrage. "I'm no such thing. I just know you're busy and have limited time, and I wanted to make the most of it."

Nate's adorable grin flashed. "It's all good, Skippy, but Mike is right. I think we've done about all we can do."

I scanned the area around me, heartbroken at the thought of all I had lost. A cleaning crew would have to come in and trash the remains.

I sucked in a deep breath, trying to find the positive. At

least I was alive. I could replace things. I'd already done it once before when I'd left Gerry. I could do it again.

Nate's phone pinged again. He'd been a popular guy the whole time we'd been working. He'd stop and answer a text, or take a call, then dive back in. He was the king of multi-tasking.

"Shit, I gotta go in," he grumbled, frowning at his phone.

"More storm relief?" I asked him. He'd been working so hard for the past few days.

He nodded and looked at his friend. "What's Leah doing? Is the studio okay?"

Mike nodded. "The studio is fine. They've canceled classes for the week. She's just out volunteering, helping where she can. What do you need?"

"We've been trying to find Jordan's laptop cord, but I think it's gone forever. If Leah could pick up a new one, I'd appreciate it. I know Jordan needs it for her work."

My face burned with a blush. I hated the thought of putting someone else out. My words stumbled over each other as I rushed to correct him. "It's seriously not a life-or-death thing. There are other, more important things happening right now. Honestly, I'm okay."

Nate looked at me and narrowed his eyes like he could read my mind. "Stop. It's not a problem, and you aren't putting anyone out. These people want to help you. Plus, you need it for your business, right?" He turned to Mike, who was already texting.

"Leah says she'll meet you at your house in fifteen."

Nate held out a hand and helped me climb out of the rubble. "Let's roll then."

. . .

When we returned to the house, Nate ran in and changed and was back out the door in a flash. He'd been working so much, he had to be running on fumes.

Was he eating while he was out working?

I knew he wasn't sleeping much.

He'd been so tired when he'd gotten home the previous night. He'd passed out early, but he had been bright and chipper this morning.

I putzed around the house, worried about Nate's well-being while I tidied things up. I'd just begun sorting through the bins we'd brought back, making a pile of things to wash and sanitize, when a knock sounded at the front door, followed by a soft voice.

"Knock, knock. Jordan? It's Leah." A small woman stuck her head through the doorway. She beamed at me and entered. With her boho style and serene expression, I had her pegged for a yoga teacher in a heartbeat.

She smiled. "Hi. Mike called and said you needed to make a run to town. Is now a good time?"

The people in this community, Nate's friend group, were amazing. "That'd be great, if you're sure you don't mind? I hate feeling like such a burden."

Leah's face melted with compassion. "Not at all, I've been wringing my hands at how I can be productive. I'd love to help you."

Leah hooked her arm through mine. "Don't beat yourself up over being in a situation that you have no control over. Come on, let's go do some shopping."

A couple of hours later, I had some new clothes, new underwear, a new power cord, and enough groceries to feed Nate and myself for a week. Throughout the course of the day Leah had spilled her and Mike's story. Their instant connection had my romantic heart swooning.

I'd gotten over my self-consciousness about halfway through the trip through the women's section, when Leah kept making suggestions, and I finally gave in to her demands. Her best friend, Kylie, had met up with us and between the two of them, all I'd had to do was stand there and say yes or no to things. They were laser focused on shopping and made it easy on me.

Neither had asked me any hard, probing questions—they kept the trip light and teasing and fun.

Kylie had insisted on paying for everything, whipping out her credit card before I even knew what was happening.

When I got back to Nate's, I put on a roast for dinner and plugged in my laptop. I sorted through dozens of emails, letting my clients know what had happened and that I was okay, but I was a couple of days behind on work. For those on deadline, I shifted them to another editor who'd offered to help me.

I'd already contacted my insurance agent and gotten the ball rolling on a claim. I touched base with my landlord to let him know the status of the house, and that I'd retrieved all I could.

Overall, it was a successful day, a good day. I felt accomplished for the first time since the storm. Marking things off my to-do list, getting essentials, being able to do some work. I finally felt like I had some control of my life. I was regaining my independence.

Nate came in from work late and shoveled his dinner like a robot. He looked so tired that I told him to go on to bed and I cleaned up the dinner remains, trying to do my part as a good roommate.

Dreading the last task on my to-do list, I checked the time. Arizona was two hours behind me, so it wasn't too late. I grabbed a glass of wine and dialed my mother.

"Well, hello, daughter. It's about time I heard from you." She threw the gauntlet right out of the gate.

"Hi, Mom. Sorry, things have been a little crazy around here." I hedged, not even wanting to go through with this conversation, but knowing I had too sooner or later. "We had a little weather incident here. Maybe you saw it on social media?"

"What do you mean? What kind of weather incident?"

Of course, this little town hadn't made national news, so I'd have to break the news to her myself.

"We had an EF-4 tornado here. It kind of wrecked everything and I've just gotten my phone back." I braced for her reaction.

Three.

Two.

One.

"Oh my God, Jordan! Are you all right? Why didn't you call me?" Her squeal blasted through the connection.

I closed my eyes as she yelled in my ear.

"I'm okay, Mom. My house got hit pretty hard. And I'm calling you now."

"Oh my God, this is terrible! Were you hurt? How bad is your house? Oh my God, why did you have to move so far away. This never would've happened if you'd not moved so far away."

Just like always, she over-reacted.

"Mom, I hardly think that my living arrangements have any effect on the weather."

"Jordan don't be so droll. I'm just saying..." Her exasperation at me not engaging and promoting her drama often felt like disappointment. I wouldn't go down this path. Wouldn't indulge her hysterics.

Dead air lay between us.

"What, Mom? What are you saying?" I clenched my teeth, forcing myself to be patient.

"Honey," her voice wavered, "I'm just a little freaked out right now. Be nice to me." She muffled the phone and yelled at someone on her end, rehashing what I'd just told her.

She came back on the line, her voice more animated than before. "Jordan, what are you going to do?"

I don't know why she acted like it was the end of the world every time something bad happened. But she did, and it became my job to calm her down.

Keeping my voice even, I said, "I'm not going to do anything right now. I'm staying with a friend until things get sorted at my place. I'm working, I'm moving forward."

"Well, you know Sonny knows people. He can help you." Ah, yes. Sonny. My mom's latest boyfriend apparently had connections to everything and everyone.

"I've got things under control, but thanks." I didn't have anything under control, but I wasn't telling her that. And I definitely wasn't accepting her offer of Sonny's help. That assistance came with too many strings attached.

"Jordan, why do you have to be so stubborn?"

Oh, good, it was time for my mother's second favorite activity—telling me all the ways I needed to improve.

"I'm not being stubborn, Mom."

"You can't do this alone, Jordan. You need help."

I swallowed a knot of frustration. This had always been her fallback. She didn't think I could handle anything. But I was not like her. I'd proven that by starting a business. Living on my own. I'd been on my way prior to this setback, and her opinion wouldn't stop me from achieving my goals.

"I have help, Mom. I'm going to be fine." Keeping the

details of my situation to a minimum was for the best. The less she knew, the less she could criticize.

"I wish you'd just—"

"I've got to go, Mom." I cut in, wanting to stop this before she got on a rant. "I just wanted to check in. I'll call you later. Love you, bye," I blurted and ended the call.

Her hysteria stressed me out. I didn't know what my plans were, but I couldn't deal with my own emotions about this situation, much less hers. Why couldn't she be normal and supportive for once?

With a deep breath, I thumbed through the apps on my phone, searching for mindless entertainment. Something to pull my attention away from all the things still on my to-do list and the unanswered questions rolling around in my brain.

I was scrolling through Instagram, checking the progress my favorite van-lifer was making on a conversion, when an idea hatched. Once it did, I couldn't shake it.

What if I did that? What if I refurbished an old van and took my life on the road? Or what if I could afford a nice, fancy one?

When I'd left Gerry and moved to Georgia to start over, I'd wanted to re-establish my independence. I hadn't imagined making it a long-term thing. This was meant to be a transitional place. And here I was, starting over again, just two months later.

But this time, maybe I could do something different.

I got lost in the videos of the different types of RVs, a thrill spreading through me.

Though we both loved to travel, Gerry hadn't shared my love for outdoorsy things. In fact, after the first time we'd gone camping, he'd proclaimed, loudly, that he made enough money to afford the swankiest of hotels and he was never sleeping on an air mattress again. His idea of travel centered on staying in resorts and being waited on hand and foot.

My idea of travel was more organic. I wanted to see everything, and most of the good stuff had to be searched out and worked for.

I hadn't been camping since that first epic failure with Gerry. I missed it. And I realized now that I'd compromised a lot of my own desires in that relationship.

It'd never occurred to me to go alone, but there was no reason I couldn't travel solo.

As I scrolled and scrolled, I got more and more excited. There was no reason I couldn't have this kind of lifestyle. I had nothing to lose by taking off, no ties to this community.

I could do my job from anywhere. I didn't need a ton of material things to make me happy, which was good considering all that I owned fit into three plastic bins.

Maybe, just maybe, if things worked out with my insurance, I could take the plunge and start a new life adventure. I could be independent and explore the world. See all the places I'd dreamed of.

I knew I couldn't do it alone. I'd either have to buy a new van, which I couldn't afford, or go with the better option of buying a used one and setting it up. And to do that, I'd need to do a ton of research. But considering I'd parceled out most of my deadlines, I suddenly had available time.

And with any luck, maybe my roommate would be up for the challenge of helping me build it out.

A sliver of trepidation tamped down my excitement. Leaving on this adventure would be a risk, one that would also mean leaving Nate, and my new town and the tiny amount of security I'd been feeling, even if it wasn't meant to be long term. This whole arrangement with Nate was temporary, and it was time to move forward.

Two days later, I waited for Nate in the kitchen with a fresh cup of coffee. I liked that I'd woken early and could do something as simple as have his coffee waiting when he finally made his way home after his shift.

We hadn't seen much of each other, mainly because Nate was still working storm relief. While he was working, I'd spent endless hours watching YouTube video tutorials and reading blog posts and articles about camper vans. Now I needed to check in with Nate and see if he was game to help me.

I handed him his mug and we went out to the back porch—a habit that seemed to be forming for us—and spent a few moments just sitting in quiet peacefulness.

"How was your shift? Run any cool calls?" I broke the silence.

"It was pretty quiet. Couple of medical calls, but we didn't have to turn a tire after about nine p.m." A loaded silence fell between us. Gone was my normally cheerful roommate. He was acting weird, staring off into the distance, as if he were thinking hard, taking a breath as if to speak, but then not saying anything. "We had one call that was pretty bad. Teenager in a car wreck."

He frowned down at his coffee cup, avoiding my gaze. I hated to ask but felt like maybe he needed a nudge to open up.

"What happened?" I prodded as gently as I could.

"Kid over-corrected trying to avoid a deer or something, flipped his car into a ditch, hit a tree." His voice was flat, emotionless, but his knuckles were white on the handle of his coffee cup. His throat bobbed on a swallow.

"Did he make it?" I asked as gently as possible. What this man must see on a regular basis in his line of work. How did he not crack under the pressure of all the trauma he faced?

After a long moment, Nate took a sip of his coffee and looked out over the yard with glassy eyes. "He's pretty messed up, but he's alive."

"That's rough. I know you did everything you could to help him." I took his hand in mine. "Please don't take this as me being uncaring...I know what you face every shift is hard. But you are not the cause of the accident, you are the solution to that young man continuing to live his life."

He squeezed my hand and released me, clearing his throat. "Thanks for saying that." Man-speak for he didn't want to talk about it anymore.

We sipped our coffee in the quiet morning until I couldn't stand his brooding anymore.

"Nate, I want to talk to you about something." Butterflies blossomed in my belly. This was it. Time to voice my plan.

His attention shifted to me, his gaze drifting up my bare legs, before meeting mine.

For a brief second, I caught a flash of heat in his eyes. What did he see when he looked at me like that? Was he thinking about me? Or was he still in the memory of that call? If things were different between us, if we were something... more, that look would have me crawling into his lap offering a different type of comfort.

"What's that?" he said, snapping me back to present.

"I was thinking the other night, and I got an idea I want to run by you."

He set his cup down on the armrest. "Okay, I'm all ears." The weight of his full attention sent a thrill through me.

"I was scrolling social media after you passed out. Have you ever seen those vans they convert into an RV? And people doing the 'van-life' thing, where you live in an RV and travel?"

His expression was unreadable, prompting me to continue, "I thought that maybe, instead of finding another house to rent, that I might look into that as an alternative." Hope laced my words, and I lifted my eyebrows, trying to appear positive, instead of nervous.

Nate studied me intently for a moment, his dark blue eyes searching mine.

"That's an idea. I'll think about it."

"You'll think about it?"

He raised his eyebrows. "Well, I mean, are you asking my permission or something?"

I frowned. "No. No, I am not." In the back of my mind, I started forming plan B. If he refused, I'd just have to save a little more and hire out the jobs I couldn't do. And that meant more time that I'd have to put Nate out. It'd only been a week, but what if he was tired of me living here already?

He lifted his brows higher, and I caught a hint of teasing grin. "You're awful defensive there."

I relaxed and swatted at him. "I'm asking if you'll help me find one, and maybe help me fix it up."

Somewhere in the house, his cell phone rang, and he left to go get it. His voice grew agitated, so I turned my attention away to give him some privacy.

I'd been nervous about voicing my ideas. But now that I'd spoken it out loud, excitement crept in.

All I had to do was figure out my funds, find the right van, and then I could take off.

Nate returned and plopped down in his chair. "Sorry, that was one of the guys calling about this photo shoot thing we have to do."

"You don't want to do it?"

"It's not that. It's just not the right theme. I'm holding out until they change the direction of the project."

I patted his arm. "Good for you for standing up for your values."

He blushed and avoided my gaze. He was so freaking cute. He could be the hero, saving the day, and also blush at the slightest compliment.

I had to be careful, because Nate was quickly becoming more than a roommate, and I couldn't afford to let feelings get involved.

"So, would you help me find a van? And would you help me convert it?"

He pondered my question for so long I grew uncomfortable, wondering if my timing had been super crappy with all the emotions he'd been dealing with. Finally, he said, "What makes you think I have the skill to do that?"

That made me pause. Could he? Assuming he'd have the experience, time, and inclination to do this with me when he already had a more than full-time job made me the worst kind of friend.

"I'm sorry. I guess I just assumed that you'd have the skills. And I know I shouldn't ask you to do anything more. You've already done so much for me. It's just that..." I gathered my nerve, "I feel like you are my only friend right now, and I need your help."

Nate looked back out over the yard while he finished his coffee, expression unreadable. "Give me an idea of what you're looking for and I'll see what I can do to help." I laid it all out, all that we'd need to do, every step feeling harder than the next.

I beamed and jumped up, leaning over to plop a kiss on his cheek. "Thanks, Nate!"

I grabbed my empty cup and practically skipped to the kitchen to grab my laptop and start my search. Now I had a mission. And the sooner I could get that mission accomplished and put a little distance between me and this place, all the better. And maybe my enthusiasm would help break the spell his tough shift had cast over him and give him a distraction.

Chapter 6

Nate

"How about this one?" Jordan turned her laptop toward me a week after that terrible call with the teenager. A rusty old conversion van filled the screen.

She was busy online van shopping while I grilled dinner. It'd been a nice day. I'd done all the yard work while Jordan had done some work online. She'd worked to clear her schedule, concentrating on her next plans and getting herself sorted.

I enjoyed having someone around to spend time with, even if we hadn't seen much of each other. It'd caught me off guard when she'd first mentioned her plans, and over the course of the week I'd decided I really didn't like the thought of her moving out.

"I know you want a fixer-upper, but that's more than we can handle." I faced the grill to hide my frown and slid my spatula under a burger, flipping it. Then, I glanced back at her over my shoulder. It was increasingly hard to keep my eyes off her.

She'd spun the laptop back around and slumped with

an adorable pout. "But it's the only one in my price range that I've found." She snapped the lid of the computer closed. "It's Saturday. I figured you'd be going out with the guys or something tonight. Don't let me being here cramp your plans."

If she only knew. I'd rather be here with her, grilling burgers, than hanging out with them.

I flipped the other burgers and took a swig of my beer. "No, you're stuck with me tonight." I gave her a jaunty wink, and she rolled her eyes. "Plus, after the week I've had, it's just nice to be home."

I'd been running for days on end. Being able to be home and relax was a nice change of pace.

"So, what did the insurance guy tell you?" I asked, dropping into the chair beside hers.

Jordan turned in her chair and kicked her feet up on the rail. It was warm enough that she was back in those distractingly short shorts and a t-shirt. "He told me they'd be sending me a check for my car since it was obviously totaled. And they'd send me a check for my renters' insurance once I send an itemized list in."

"And you're going to take all of that and invest it in a van?" I asked, trying to avoid staring at her long legs.

"Well, yeah."

"What about having a car to get around in?"

"I'm not going to get some huge thing, Nate. I want a reasonable-sized one, something that I can go anywhere, live anywhere, and be comfortable."

Unease rolled through me. I didn't like this one bit. What if the van broke down somewhere? What if some crazy person followed her and attacked her? It wasn't safe for her to be solo on the road like that.

"I don't like it."

"Why?"

"I just don't. It's too dangerous."

She gave me a saucy grin, dropping her feet to the ground, sitting straighter in her chair. "Well, it's happening whether you help me or not." She tossed a wadded-up napkin at me. "Lighten up. It's going to be fine."

That didn't do a damn thing to make my insides unclench. "Jordan. You are an attractive woman."

"Thank you." She preened, placing her hands on her knees, arching her back.

"I'm not done," I continued, and she dropped the pose, slumping back in the chair. "You are an attractive woman. It's not safe for you to be traveling alone." I needed her to take this seriously.

Jordan stared at me for a moment like I was crazy before her brows knit together. "Are you serious right now?"

"Hell yes, I'm serious." How did she not realize she was putting herself in danger? She'd already come close to dying once in that damn tornado.

"That is the most offensive thing I've ever heard." Her eyes flashed, but her voice was cool and controlled.

"I called you attractive. How is that offensive?" Was she mad at me? Her calm and collected demeanor was in direct contrast to her icy tone. But it didn't matter if I'd pissed her off, her safety was my priority. Nothing could happen to her.

"You're assuming that just because I am a woman, that I can't take care of myself. That I shouldn't travel alone."

That icy tone could've frozen anyone, but the idea of something happening to her made my guts churn. "Because it's not safe."

"Is it any different for a man?" Her blue eyes flashed.

"Yes, a man isn't going to mess around with me like he

would you." I pushed away from my chair and stood, gripping the deck rail. Was she so naive that she didn't realize that being alone made her a target for sick fucks? A long tense moment passed between us while all manner of bad things flashed through my mind.

"Nate, look at me."

I couldn't refuse her anything, but it didn't mean I had to like it. I swiveled my head and pinned her with narrowed eyes.

"Nate, I am a grown woman, capable of making my own decisions. I can travel by myself like a big girl. I will take precautions and be aware of my surroundings. It may surprise you, but I've been on my own for a while. And while I've had men in my life, I did travel, often solo, until I settled down with Gerry."

She'd mentioned Gerry before, but not in much detail.

"Gerry had the same outdated viewpoint that you do. And I let him convince me I was weak and that I couldn't do the things I wanted to do unless he was with me. I refuse to live like that again."

I studied her for a moment. Golden curls caught back in a ponytail, wearing her favorite shorts and tank top, showcasing all her curves.

"Besides," she went on, "you're one to judge. You run into burning buildings for a living. What's safe about that? Traveling is not nearly as risky as what you do every day."

She was right, of course, and I was being an idiot.

There was no real reason for her not to do this project and set out on her own. Hell, what was I going to do? Ask her to stay here? She'd been looking for a place to rent, but with space at a premium, property owners had jacked the prices sky high.

I swallowed thickly, realizing that I was being unreasonable. It wasn't that I didn't want her to travel solo, so much as I just didn't want her to leave, period.

"You're right. Just…"

She waited patiently. It was one of the things I liked best about her. She just listened and was patient and calm about so many things. Losing her house and all her belongings hadn't destroyed her or sent her into a tailspin. She was the most resilient woman I'd ever met.

"Just be careful about it." I took a swig of beer to buy myself a moment. "Don't put yourself in harm's way, okay? You survived a tornado, for Christ's sake. Don't get crazy and get offed by some serial killer because your wanderlust over-powered you." I tried to make it sound like a joke, even though my gut churned at the thought of her leaving.

She watched me for a minute, her steady gaze cutting through my bullshit like a knife. Then she hit me with a grin.

"I promise, I'll be careful."

How could I refuse her anything when she sat there looking at me with all her hopes and dreams written across her face? I wanted her to be happy.

This woman was dangerous for me.

"She just needs a battery and she'll run like a top." The scruffy old guy pulled the hood open, clipping a metal rod in place to hold it up.

I looked over the engine of the commercial van I'd noticed while running a call. It was clean, the hoses looked to be in good shape, no dry rot. I backed my head out from under the hood and perused the rest of the vehicle. It wasn't too old, no body damage. Needed new tires, but that was a given.

"What did you use this for?" I asked.

"My wife used to have a mobile dog grooming business. When my son didn't want to take it over, the wife and I decided to sell the business and retire. Guy who bought it already had a set-up nicer than this one. He just wanted some of the equipment and the client list."

The van was the perfect size. Not too big for Jordan to handle on the road, but bigger than the conversion van we'd looked at a couple of days before.

"I saw this in your yard when I was running a call, but I'm just helping a friend shop. You mind if I bring a battery and see how it runs?"

"No problem. We aren't in a hurry. Haven't advertised it anywhere or anything."

If this thing ran, it would be perfect for her. "Okay, I'll stop by later with my friend."

I fired off a text to Jordan before hitting the road.

Nate: Hey, You busy?

Jordan: Just reading through a project. What's up?

Nate: Can you take a break? Got something you need to see

Jordan: Sure

Nate: Be there in 10

Jordan was standing on the porch waiting on me when I pulled up, bouncing on her toes with excitement. Dashing down the steps, she had the truck door open before I got the thing put in park.

"What is it? Did you find one?" she cried as she flung herself into the seat.

Her enthusiasm was contagious. I flashed her a playful grin. "You'll see."

I tortured her by making her close her eyes while I went to the barn and grabbed a spare battery I used for fishing and tossed it into the bed of the truck.

She bounced in her seat the entire ride. Her exuberance was fucking delightful.

When we got close to the address, I looked over at her and said, "Okay, close your eyes one more time."

"Ugh," she huffed, but closed her eyes.

"Now, keep them closed for a minute," I warned and got out to get the battery. I went around to her side of the truck and opened the door.

"Okay, Skippy. Open your eyes."

She did, they flew wide, and her mouth dropped open. Her stunned expression morphed to giddy excitement.

"Oh my God, Nate! Is that what I think it is?"

I chuckled, offering her a hand down. "Come on, let's go see if it runs."

The old man met us back at the van with the keys and helped me get the battery connected. I climbed in the seat, Jordan crowding close to me. "Let's see what we've got."

The engine turned over after the second try. I left it running and got out to listen to it. Inspection done, I looked at Jordan and said, "You want to take her for a spin?"

She bounced on her toes, blonde curls bobbing, eyes sparkling like a little kid at Christmas. Adorable. Her reaction to knowing she had a surprise was almost better than the surprise itself.

We took the van for a short drive and negotiated the price a bit, finally coming to terms, planning to come back the next day and pick it up.

"We need to stop by the hardware store on the way home," she declared as we pulled out of the drive.

"What for?"

"I need to price materials. And tools."

She danced in the passenger seat, typing into her phone, a huge smile on her face. Pride bloomed in my chest. I'd done that. I'd put that smile on her face. And I found myself wanting to keep it there. If a surprise and a stop by the hardware store was all it took, I was game.

"I've got the tools, but we can stop and look."

Half an hour later, we had a bag full of nails and incidentals and hit a drive through for dinner. Jordan beamed the entire time, bobbing her head to the radio, loudly singing off-key. Her happiness fused into my bones.

"This has been a good day, Nate. The best day in a long time. Thank you so much."

It had been a good day, and for the life of me, I didn't want it to end.

"It was fun, wasn't it?" I said with a nod. "How about we grab some beer and go watch a game? The Braves are playing today."

"Yeah, that sounds great."

When we got home, Jordan pulled on a sweatshirt and curled up on one end of the couch, feet tucked under her, legs bent against the armrest. I grabbed us each a cold one and sat at the other end of the couch.

MC texted me about halfway into the game, confirming that she'd rescheduled the photo shoot. Why she felt the need to keep me apprised of the schedule, instead of letting Mike handle it, I didn't know.

"What's wrong?" Jordan asked. "You're frowning."

I schooled my features. "Nothing. Just... Mary Catherine keeps texting me about this photo shoot thing."

Jordan tipped her head to the side. "You don't want to do it?"

On the television screen, the Braves had the bases loaded and the winning run at the plate. I paused, watching a few pitches.

"It's not that I don't want to, but I think there are other more important things to worry about right now."

"Well, can't you just tell her that?"

I laughed a little. "No, there is no just telling MC anything. She's part of the organizing committee and she takes it very seriously."

The Braves hitter struck out and the next guy came up to bat. Jordan was silent, watching the screen, picking at the paper on her bottle.

"What?"

She lifted a shoulder, eyes to the screen.

"I know you have something to say. Just say it."

"It's just... You shouldn't do this if you don't want to. And she shouldn't hound you about it. You need to talk to her."

The announcers on TV went wild as the Braves hit a walk off grand slam. Jordan and I sat in silence, watching the runners round the bases, while I stewed on her advice and tried to ignore my body's reaction to the close proximity. I was uncomfortably aware of how she curled into a ball on the couch. All I had to do was pull her legs over my lap...

Eventually, she stood and stretched, the hem of her shorts riding high. Jesus, her legs were gorgeous. And I had no business thinking that, especially when I'd promised we'd only be roommates.

Gathering up her empties and mine, she said, "I'm headed to do a little more work and turn in." She fiddled with the bottles and continued. "If doing this calendar is important to you, you need to do it. Good for you for sticking to your beliefs."

I waited until she passed back through the room on her way to bed and called, "Hey, Skippy, are we good?"

She offered me a thin smile as she paused on her way to her room. "Yeah, we are." She looked as if she wanted to say more, but finally, she just thumped the back of the couch with a fist. "Thanks for a great day."

The game wrapped up quickly, then I did my normal check on the house, making sure it was all locked up. The bedrooms in my house sat almost across from each other at the end of a hall, the doors slightly offset, with Jordan's door being before mine. Hers was closed as I passed by.

Sometimes I could hear her working late into the night, talking to herself while she edited. I'd bet she wasn't even aware that she was doing it. I didn't mind. I was getting used to the noises of someone else living in my house. Truth be told, I liked having her here. We shared the cooking and cleaning, and we got along great.

Plus, every third day I lived with a crew of men, so I was used to being with people all hours of the day.

In an effort to be modest around my roommate, I put on pajama pants then lay down on the bed and flipped the TV on to watch the post-game show. I reached for my phone on the nightstand, but it wasn't there. Shit. I'd left it by the couch.

I tiptoed into the hallway on the off chance that Jordan was asleep.

The bathroom door sat slightly ajar, letting light shine through. As I drew closer, I realized that Jordan was changing, the creamy expanse of her back to me as she slipped off her shirt.

I stood frozen. There was something so freaking sexy

about the curve of a woman's back. Her skin was smooth and pale, begging me to trace my mouth along the curve of her spine.

My dick swelled, and my heart stopped.

What the fuck was I doing?

She was my friend.

I had no business lusting after her.

Hustling to the couch and back to my room, then closing the door as quietly as possible, I crawled into my bed. Images of silky, creamy skin flashed through my mind, making my dick ache. But I would not jerk off to the thoughts of my innocent friend. Even if she did have gorgeous hair and soulful eyes. Even if she did get me.

God, I was an asshole. Thinking about a woman I had no business thinking about. She was my roommate, for Christ's sake.

But if I drifted off to sleep with the memory of light-hearted laughter, and shining blue eyes... Well, it was just because I'd had fun making someone's day brighter.

Chapter 7

Jordan

I connected my phone to the Bluetooth speaker, blasting some T-Swizzle as I opened the back door to my new adventure van. I'd been spending a couple of hours a day working on her. We had stripped the inside of leftovers from the dog grooming business. In the week or so that I'd had the van, Nate and I had planned out schematics for how to finish the inside. I'd put in the insulation and measured out where I wanted everything to go. Now it was time to lay the flooring.

We'd grown into a routine that started each morning with coffee together on the back porch discussing our plan for the day. On the days he was off and available to help, we'd spend the day working together. Then, at night, one of us would cook while the other cleaned. And we'd find a ball game or something on TV and just chill. The loneliest nights were those when he was on duty. I still felt weird about being in his home when he wasn't there, but I was getting used to it.

"Skippy, did you remember to charge the drill batteries?" Nate called from inside the garage.

"Yes!" I called back. I went to the bed of his truck and carted the boxes of flooring to our work area. I'd gone with a pale wood laminate. The cabinets would be white, and the upholstery would be neutrals. If I went with a soft palette, I could add pops of color here and there. Plus, the brightness would be really refreshing.

He came out of the garage, faded jeans hanging low on his lean hips, dirty T-shirt tucked into his back pocket. He was lean and muscular. A tattoo running along his ribs. My mouth went dry at the sight of him shirtless.

I quickly looked away, bending to study the boxes I'd dropped by the back of the van door. His dusty boots stopped in my line of vision.

"Do we need a drill to install these?" I knew full well we didn't, I just enjoyed teasing him. And I needed a moment to gather my composure.

"No, but we might need this."

I looked up to see him swing a mallet up to prop on his shoulder.

It was quick work to get the floor laid. Nate patiently taught me how to score the pieces that needed cutting. Then he took the pressure off me using power tools, and just did it. I was sitting cross-legged on my new flooring, grinning like a fool when he stretched his long body across the floor, leaning on one hip, his head propped on a hand. If he were anyone else, if he were mine, I'd slide across the floor and climb on top of him, forcing him to his back.

"You alright there, Skip? You looked kind of flushed. Did I work you too hard?"

I'd like to see just how hard you could work me.

The thought had me flushing harder.

And Nate, that asshole, just grinned like he knew exactly what I was thinking.

"I'm fine. Just admiring this new wood flooring."

"Oh, you're admiring something. But it's not the floor," he teased, a haughty little glint in his eye.

Cheeky bastard.

I scowled, flipping a rag at him. "Don't you have somewhere to go, someone else you can bother?"

He caught the rag before it hit him in the face. He rose, a devilish smile playing about his lips, pulling the rag through his hand. He stalked toward me, and I was fully caught in his predatory gaze. In another life, he'd be bearing down on me, and he'd trap me up against the counter, leaning his weight on his hands, crowding me with the heat of him. But we weren't like that and too late I realized he'd played me. Caught up in his sex appeal, I'd let him get the upper hand. I spun as he flipped the rag back at me, except he held an end of it, so it popped me right on the butt cheek.

"I like bothering you." Wasn't that the truth. He seemed to love pestering me. The truth was... I liked that about him. If I were staying, I wouldn't hesitate to take our teasing to the next level. Naked teasing with Nate sounded amazing.

But I wasn't staying. I was leaving, and he'd move on, probably with that Mary Catherine chick who seemed to find reasons to text him all the time.

I made a grab for the rag, which he deftly dodged and bolted through the door. I ended up chasing him through the yard, eventually giving up when he cleared a fence in one single athletically graceful move. He stood at the wood fence—the rolling pasture making the perfect backdrop—with his bare chest heaving, glistening with a fine sheen of sweat, laughing his deep rumbly chuckle.

"Truce," I called, bent over with my hands on my knees.

Nate climbed the wooden fence, swinging one long leg over and then the other, before perching on the top board and hooking his boots on the middle rung. I wanted to press myself between those widespread legs. My gaze traveled over his torso to find his heated eyes on me.

He probably wasn't trying to deliberately be so tempting. Probably. But damn if he wasn't a tasty looking man. Any fool could see that.

And I needed to get this van completed because Nate and I were becoming fast friends. Deliciously tempting friends. The kind of friends who blistered each other with long looks. The kind of friends who wanted benefits.

Somewhere in the distance a cell phone rang, breaking the spell.

Nate jumped down and took me in a headlock as we headed back to the van.

"Ew, sweaty armpits! Gross!" I playfully pushed him away, my hands pressing against those ripped abs. That forbidden touch reminding me how easily it would be to let down my guard, change my plans and just let myself have this time with this man.

He grabbed his phone, and I walked to the van to give him some privacy, and to gather my wits. I'd never been able to do casual sex, and I didn't want to ruin this new friendship by dragging sex into the mix, so I needed to get my newly rekindled libido in check.

I busied myself inside, cleaning up from our workday, when his head appeared in the doorway. "You wanna have a cookout tonight? I was thinking of inviting everyone over."

"Sure, that sounds like fun."

"Good deal." He heaved a huge breath in and let it out. "Come on, help me drag out the corn hole boards from the shed."

. . .

A couple of hours later, the sun painted the sky in vibrant orange and pink. Soft music played on a speaker, accompanied by the early spring nighttime sounds. Nate had invited Mike and Leah, Thoren and his girlfriend Bunny.

I'd given everyone a tour of the van project, and the boys were fascinated. Mike braced a palm on the doorway and dipped his head inside, talking to Thoren, who was sitting in the front seat but angled to see the back.

Nate was at the back of the van, discussing the options for power with the other two men.

I felt a brush at my elbow and turned as Leah slipped her hand through my arm.

"I'm really proud of you," she said. Her sweet husky voice held a smile.

I grinned at her. "That's a nice thing to say."

"It's true. You've been through so much, but I can tell your energy is positive. It's catching. Most people would still be trying to sort through their drama, but you are moving forward and making some bold steps."

A hand slipped through my other arm, and I turned to see Kylie. She'd come with Mike and Leah, a situation that Thoren's lady-friend had not been thrilled about.

Kylie leaned close. "Honey, bold would be slipping in and grabbing Nate's fine ass while he was showering."

"Not everyone can just walk up to a man and mess with his crotch." Leah's sweet voice was stern as she sent a playful glare at Kylie.

Kylie rolled her eyes in response. "It was one time."

I stared wide eyed at Kylie. No way. "You grabbed a guy's junk? Like a random stranger? Like, 'He's cute—I'm checking out his package'?"

Kylie flipped her hand at me as if the thought were silly.

"Oh no, girl. It wasn't like that at all. It was just Thoren, and I noticed his zipper was down. I was helping the guy out."

I cracked up laughing. "Y'all are so great. I'm so glad that we met."

"You think I'm joking. Girl, Nate is hot. I'd be all over him in a minute." Kylie eyed Nate's ass.

Jealousy bubbled up, hot and bright within me. Kylie ogling him rubbed me all kinds of wrong. Which was stupid. Because though Nate was undoubtedly hot, he wasn't mine.

So, I swallowed that little bubble of jealousy and smiled at her. "He does have a great ass, doesn't he?"

"Who's up for another round of corn hole?" Nate and the guys had finished their discussion, and he now stood at one board, tossing a bag up and catching it. "And this time, Jordan and Kylie are not allowed to be on the same team."

"I'm telling you that was beginners' luck," I yelled across the yard.

"I'm in." Mike stepped up and grabbed a set of bags. "Me and Kylie, against Jordan and Nate. Y'all stand back and prepare for a lesson."

And that settled it. "Oh, it's on now! Come on, slick. Let's show them how it's done." I high-fived Nate on my way to my spot next to Kylie at the other set of boards.

"You're such a sandbagger," Kylie griped after I sunk the first bag into the hole. Nate cheered for me, and I beamed at them both. The game was tight for a while, swapping leaders back and forth until Nate knocked Mike's bag off the board and then sunk his next toss. I threw my arms up in victory and ran across to double high-five Nate. "Good job, partner!"

No, a game of corn hole didn't normally warrant a level

five celebration, but I was having so much fun with my new friends, it just spilled over.

We filed back to the house, got a refresh on drinks, and joked and laughed over perfectly grilled steaks. In time, the sun went down, and I turned on the porch lights that I'd strung around the railing. The guys told stories on each other, Leah and Kylie talked about the new yoga class they were offering. Bunny had extracted herself from our conversation to perch in Thoren's lap. I didn't like the way she openly flirted with all the men, and it seemed to bother Thoren too.

I was watching Thoren when he called, "Hey Nate, did I tell you I talked to the medic about the guy we ran after the storm?"

"The heart attack guy?"

A hush fell over the group.

"Yeah," Thoren continued. "Saw the medics on another call. That guy lived."

"Really? That's surprising."

"Yeah, they said he coded about the time they went en route, but they were able to get him back. Turns out he had a hundred percent blockage in one artery and ninety-nine percent in another. You don't do that bolus, the guy dies. Chief is probably going to put you in for a commendation."

Kylie flipped a beer cap at Thoren. "What's a bolus, T-bird?"

Thoren snagged the cap and tossed it into the trash. Those two seemed to enjoy picking on each other, regardless of whether Bunny was around or not.

"Bolus is basically flushing the system via IV. In this case, Nate squeezed an entire bag of fluids into the guy before the ambulance ever got there."

I shifted my gaze to Nate, astonished. "Wait. Is that the call you told me about? You legit saved that guy's life!"

He looked down, muttering under his breath. I couldn't be sure, but it looked like he flushed a little, even as he said, "It's part of the job."

"Nate, that's incredible!"

He tipped his beer, looking away as if I were making him uncomfortable. I dialed it back a notch, but inside I was still in awe.

"So, Jordan..." Kylie's voice was loud, pulling my gaze from Nate, "How'd you end up in Newman? What's your story?"

I shrugged. "It's not all that special. I was a Navy brat growing up. We moved around a lot, but my grandma lived here when I was a kid. I'd come spend my summers with her. She died when I was a teenager, and I didn't come back after that. But I remembered how special it was, so when I left my former fiancé, it seemed the natural place to start over."

"And then the tornado hit, and you're starting over again." Leah said quietly. "Poor thing. At least you are doing it on your own terms."

"Where'd you live before you moved here?" Kylie pressed.

"I was living in Washington, D.C., working in marketing as a copywriter for a Senator's office. I'd already started my business because I'd wanted to make the transition out of that rat-race."

"Starting your own business takes some balls. Good for you." Kylie tipped her beer to me, and conversation shifted again.

The evening grew later still, and I was feeling mellow when the song changed to something soft and romantic.

Mike pulled Leah into his embrace, slipping an arm around her waist as he led her in a slow, sexy dance.

"Those two are enough to give me cavities," Kylie griped, flopping into the chair next to me.

Mike gazed down at Leah like he couldn't believe she was real. Leah ran her hands up the contours of his chest, leaning in closer as he tightened his hold on her.

I sighed against the knot forming in my chest, a hollow ache where the remnants of being a couple once lived. "I think it's sweet how in love they are."

Kylie snorted.

"What? You don't want that someday?" I arched a brow at her.

She watched them for a moment. "What they have is rare and special, and I'm happy that she found a good man. But no, I don't think I'll ever find what they have." Her despondent tone had me looking at her more closely. Her gaze traveled to Thoren and Bunny, who were also dancing, and then off into the distance. "It's hard to find a good man who will take you as you are."

She was right, of course. I turned back to watch the couple, my gaze passing over Nate to find him staring at them as well. He shifted and our eyes met and held. An explosion of butterflies erupted in my belly under the weight of his gaze.

There was just something about the man that drew me in. He was kind and funny. He was a good friend. And on top of all that, he was delicious to look at.

"I don't know about that. There are still a few good ones out there," I mumbled under my breath, looking away from Nate.

"I hear you, sister," Kylie murmured.

What would it be like to walk over to Nate and ask him

to dance with me? Would he trail his fingers across my shoulder like Mike was doing to Leah? Goosebumps pebbled my arms, imagining what that small caress would feel like. Would he use those long fingers in a whisper of a caress, or was a solid stroke more his speed? Probably a combination of both.

An involuntary shudder had me shifting my focus away from his hands. "I'm going to clean up," I announced uselessly.

Kylie smirked at me. "Yeah, you do that."

I stood and gathered empties, taking them inside to the trash, eager to put some distance between me and the romantic vibes. Nate was my friend. A sweet guy who let me stay with him after a devastating event. My stupid heart didn't need to turn this into something it wasn't. I was wrong for thinking about how he might use his hands, even if the mental image was a total turn on.

We were Just. Friends.

Besides, his career wasn't something I could overlook. The man ran into burning buildings for a living. Literally chose to put himself in life-or-death situations every day. After everything I'd been through with my dad, after all the drama with the Gerry, and the tornado...I needed safety and security. I couldn't take the risk.

Nate was a broken heart waiting to happen.

I unloaded the trash bag and took it out to the larger bin by the garage to get some space from the dancing lovebirds. As I passed my newly-acquired van, I studied her. I needed to focus on moving forward, moving on. Starting a fresh new life.

I'd let a man derail me once before.

It was time to put myself first...despite the *what ifs* that niggled at the back of my mind.

Chapter 8

Nate

"**S**kippy! Let's go! If you don't get a move on, we're gonna miss the start of the show." I stood on the back deck and yelled across the yard, scrubbing my hair with my towel.

"Hold your horses," she yelled from inside the van. "I'm almost done."

I checked the time. Damn, we were pushing it. I'd wanted to get to the fundraiser concert early enough to get a lawn seat. And Jordan was still working.

We'd spent every available moment working on the van, and we'd made good progress. I was proud of what we'd been able to accomplish so far. Knowing that the work I was doing was making a real difference in her life was satisfying. Even if it meant she'd be leaving.

"We've got all day tomorrow. Hurry up." She was so stubborn and cute when she got all focused on a task.

Her mass of blonde curls peeked out of the side door before she climbed out of the van, closing the doors behind her. I let my gaze travel over her body, enjoying this forbidden pleasure. She had on her work clothes again—an old T-shirt of mine, with the sleeves ripped off, and a worn pair of sweatpants that she'd cut off into shorts. Both were splattered with paint and grease spots and who knew what else. She reached up to flick a leaf off the window, and with a last admiring glance, turned and headed toward me.

I shouldn't watch her, study her so closely. Or feel that little prickle of pride at seeing her in my shirt. But she was just so fucking beautiful. And fun. And hardworking. And sweet. And dedicated. If it weren't for the fact that she was leaving, she'd be perfect.

And I was an asshole for having these thoughts about a woman who trusted and depended on me.

She glanced up at the house and scowled when she saw me. Busted.

"You're a jerk, you know that?"

Yes. Yes, I did know. I offered a cheesy grin in apology.

"I thought you were, like, waiting at the truck for me, and here you are, not even dressed yet."

I ran the towel over my chest, her gaze blistering me as she climbed the stairs. I liked the feel of her eyes on me, the way they drifted over my torso, lingering as if she liked what she saw when she let her guard down and her feelings showed through. So what if I flexed just to watch those eyes flare.

"I've got jeans on. I'm dressed."

She rolled her eyes and flipped me a bird as she passed. "I'll be ready in twenty."

"I'll believe it when I see it." I mumbled but headed back in to put on a shirt just in case she kept to that timing.

Fifteen minutes later, I walked into the kitchen to find her propped at the counter with a smirk on her face.

"Challenge accepted, and I won," she bragged.

"That you did. You gonna get cold later?" I nodded to

her cutoff denim shorts and white tank. Fuck me, it was my favorite outfit of hers, not that she had many. She was putting every dollar into her van and had refused to go buy more clothes. When I'd offered to take her shopping, she'd asked me why she needed more, when she was going to have limited storage space anyway and didn't need an entire wardrobe. She had a point, but it was just another reminder that she was leaving.

"I'll be fine. I borrowed a flannel if that's okay."

"The same one you borrow every time it's cool out?"

"Yeah, sorry about that." A rosy flush tinted her cheeks. Gorgeous.

"It's fine, I'm just teasing. Why don't you just keep it." I liked the idea of her taking something of mine with her when she left. "It'll remind you of your awesome roommate when you are out there on the road. Come on, let's roll, we've got a concert to get to."

Mike called while we were en route to let me know they'd saved some space for us. It seemed that everyone was excited to get out and do their part if the stop-and-go traffic was any indication. The bright sunny day didn't hurt either.

Thankfully, the light changed, and traffic moved again. The intoxicating smell of her shampoo filled the cab of the truck, wrapping around me. An image of her naked, fresh out of the shower, flashed in my mind. Those droplets of water trailing down her back, begging to be licked.

I cracked a window and shifted uncomfortably in my seat. Changed the radio station. Adjusted the air. Anything to force that image of naked Jordan from my mind.

"Are you okay?" Jordan's voice cut through the chaos in my head. Shit, could she read my mind? Were my pervy thoughts bleeding over where she could read them?

I slung my wrist over the steering wheel and braced

myself against the door. "Yeah, I'm fine." Out of the corner of my eye, I could see her rubbing her hands down her smooth legs. I bet it'd be just like silk to touch her there.

She settled an arm on the console between us, leaning closer to me. "So, who all is going to be there today?"

I couldn't ignore her, didn't want to. I shifted in my seat again, trying to ease the tightness of my jeans, and propped my elbow next to hers on the console. The heat of her arm next to mine was electric.

"Should be the regular gang."

"So, a bunch of fire department guys? Any of the girls going to be there?"

"Yeah, should be."

"So, how's it going there, anyway? Are things settling down at the station any?"

"Yeah, mostly it's back to normal. We've had a bunch of politicians coming through doing PR stuff." I frowned at the reminder of the latest bunch, who'd shown up in their fresh jeans and clean dress shoes and stood in front of the decimated high school.

"You sound a little miffed about that."

She knew me well.

I parallel parked by the station and turned to her. "Maybe? It's weird right now. Like the higher-ups are all politicking for attention, but not really caring about the work that needs to be done. And I just want to do my job to the best of my ability and help people. It matters to me that what I do makes a difference to the citizens. I'm not one for the dog-and-pony show."

She eyed me, her lips pursed. I fought the urge to lean over and have a taste.

"No, I don't imagine you are. Did you grow up wanting

to be a fireman? Run around with a cute little helmet, putting out make believe fires?"

I chuckled. "Not so much. We lived next door to this old man when I was growing up. I was about seventeen, I guess, and his house caught on fire. I was home, outside doing something, smelled the smoke. I ran over to check on him. Ended up going in after him, helping him out. The crew that pulled up read me the riot act for being a stupid kid, not waiting on them. But after, they hooked me up with a youth program and basically recruited me. Being in the fire service is a calling. It's either in your blood or it's not."

"Well, from what I know, you're good at your job." The corner of her mouth lifted in a teasing half grin. "I mean, I appreciate you." The grin spread to a smile and her eyes sparkled with the mischief I was beginning to adore. "I'd still be pinned to my bathtub if it weren't for you."

I swallowed thickly, needing to get her and her smooth skin, kissable lips, and sparkling eyes out of my head.

"Nah, but lucky for me, I got to carry your sorry, no-shoe-wearing ass out of there. Though my back will never be the same." I winked at her and climbed out of the truck, smiling as I opened the back door and grabbed a blanket from the seat.

She met me at the front of the truck and punched me in the arm. "You are such a jerk."

Happy that we were back on safe, solid ground, I grabbed her in a headlock, tugging her to the sidewalk.

The park where the concert was taking place was a couple of blocks from the fire station. The entire town had come together to make this event happen. Store fronts were decorated with the NewmanStrong hashtag and people were sporting custom t-shirts that had been designed for relief money. The mood was festive and friendly.

Four weeks had gone by in a heartbeat, and recovery was well underway. Some people still lacked internet, but power had been restored everywhere. Clean-up continued as well, and tarps covered most of the buildings.

"Wow, so much has been cleared since I was last through here," Jordan said.

We ambled our way up the sidewalk, dodging foot traffic. "Yeah, the state sent in their transportation crews. They did a good bit of the debris hauling. The different municipalities came together and worked to get the biggest messes taken care of. I mean, there's still a bunch left to do, but everyone has been working hard to get life back to normal."

"I've been so focused on my work and updating the van, but maybe I should've been doing more to help others. I feel a little guilty."

I stopped walking, grabbing her wrist and turning her to face me.

"Jordan, stop," I said, looking deep into her blue eyes. She needed to understand this. "No one expects you to do anything other than what you are doing." I slid my fingers down and laced them with hers. "And what you are doing is the same thing that all these other people are doing. Putting your life back together."

With pooling eyes, she nodded at me. I squeezed her hand and held it as we made our way around the corner to Main Street.

The crowd in town was huge. Blockades allowed pedestrian traffic on the roads around the courthouse.

"I thought this was at the park." Jordan said, releasing my hand. I missed it instantly.

"It is, this is just the art walk section. Each store is staying open late, and a part of their sales is going to the relief fund. There's also a silent auction happening some-where, but I'm not sure where it is."

We passed a food truck, and my stomach growled at the smell of tacos wafting from it.

"Can we get some food while we're here?" Jordan eyed the taco truck like a starving woman.

With a bag full of tacos and soft drinks in hand, we entered the park. "Oh man, the statues are gone." Jordan pointed to an empty pedestal. "The dancing girl was one of my favorites. Seeing her always made me smile, she looked so real and carefree with her skirts flowing in the breeze." She tucked a strand of hair behind her ear, sad eyes glued to where the iron piece had been. "Seeing her made me want to kick off my shoes and twirl like her."

Emotion clogged my throat as I studied the empty pedestal. I'd been so focused on people and their homes that I hadn't truly catalogued all the little things that had been lost in the storm. "You remember the horse sculptures?" When she nodded, I continued, "I remember when they introduced those. Different groups would paint them, each one had a theme. So many people thought they were ridicu-lous." I paused, smiling at the memory. "But then everyone came downtown to see them, admiring the uniqueness of each one. And those led to the trains, and trucks, and some-where along the way a pig showed up." A grin tugged my lips at the memory of that brightly-painted pig.

Jordan bumped my shoulder with hers. "There's been so much lost, it's good to see all these people here. It's... healing."

Without thinking, I slipped my arm around her shoul-ders and drew her close, "You're so right, Skippy." In that moment, with the sun on her face, and her heart in her eyes, it would be nothing to lean in and kiss her forehead.

A shout from the park interrupted the moment. I looked up to find Mike waving us over to an outer corner of the park. Leah was with him sitting on a blanket, picnic-style.

"You're a good woman," Mike said, reaching to take the bag of tacos from Jordan.

"Touch them and die," she warned, and Leah burst out laughing as Mike backed away, hands raised in surrender.

Passing my drink to Jordan to hold, I spread out the old quilt I'd brought with me. Jordan passed out tacos to everyone—giving Mike his last with a teasing glare—then plunked herself down on the blanket.

With a groan, I lowered myself next to her.

"What's wrong?" she asked around a mouthful.

"My back is just tight from hose testing last shift." I stretched out a leg and bent the other, leaning back on an elbow, just trying to get comfortable.

"Like, literally hooking up each hose and checking it?"

"Yeah, but we did the big five-inch ones. They weigh about a hundred pounds each. We hook them up, roll them out and make sure they all function properly. Inspect for holes and stuff. Then we roll them back up and put them away."

She stared at me for a beat. "Wow, that's impressive. All I did yesterday was prime the walls of the camper."

I reached up and tugged a curl. "Yeah, but you did the whole van in a day. It's looking good, by the way."

"How is the van coming, Jordan?" Leah asked.

"It's coming along great." Her face lit up. "I should be able to paint tomorrow. After that, it's building the platform for a bed, and putting in appliances and doing finishing work."

"Wow, and you're doing it all yourself?"

Jordan glanced quickly at me, then back to Leah. "Well,

I can't say that. Nate's been a super big help. I'd never used a power tool before this project, so it's good that he's teaching me all this stuff."

"What are your plans when you get it finished?" Leah asked.

I perked up at this, because suddenly I realized I didn't know what her plans were beyond "go somewhere else." A curl of unease rolled through my gut. I'd gotten so used to having her around. The thoughts of her leaving, and going back to my life-before-Jordan, were unsettling.

"I don't know exactly, but I'm thinking about traveling around to some national parks out west. Or maybe I'll head north. I'm not sure. It'll have to be somewhere that has some kind of Wi-Fi, so I can stay in touch with my clients. But otherwise, my plan is pretty much wide open." Jordan fiddled with the hem of her shorts.

"Out west?" My words came out strangled. She'd be so far away.

"It's somewhere I've always wanted to explore." Jordan was matter of fact.

And how did I not know this? I knew she planned to travel. How did I not know that she'd be on the other side of the country?

"Why now?" I croaked.

"Because she can?" Mike piped in. "Hell, it sounds pretty fucking awesome."

"Hey, guys." Thoren's voice interrupted the conversation. "Is there room for us?"

Thoren and Bunny stood at the edge of our blankets, and he was already laying theirs down.

"Why'd you ask if you were going to put your stuff here anyway?" Mike argued.

"Oh, don't complain, you know you love me." Thoren

mock flipped his hair at Mike, who sent him a chilling scowl.

Mike kept it up for a moment before he grinned and flipped a piece of ice at him. "Yeah, but sometimes I wonder why."

The ladies greeted Thoren and Bunny, and with Bunny's forced smile, I got the impression that she didn't care for them. The whole exchange was uncomfortable.

Leah turned to Jordan. "So how long until you get it finished?"

Jordan shrugged and looked at me. "I don't know. What do you think, Nate? Another week or so until it's livable?"

Caught off-guard, I cleared my throat. "Uh, yeah, I think that's a possibility."

A week or two? I didn't know how I felt about that. On the one hand, it was a good thing that her life was getting back on track, and she could move forward. On the other, I enjoyed having her around, having the sounds of someone else in the house. I liked that we watched ball games together and had our morning coffee together on the porch.

Thoren stood and offered to get a round of beer. Bunny was busy on her phone, Leah and Jordan were heavy into a discussion about the van. Mike leaned behind Leah and caught my eye. I braced on an arm behind Jordan to see what he needed.

"What's up at the FD?" Mike asked. "I heard a rumor that the chief is leaving?"

"I don't know. I try to keep my head down and stay out of the drama."

Jordan broke into laughter, leaning back, her back bumping into my chest.

A blast of awareness shot through me. Just like in the truck, and every other time I'd been around her lately—

when she brushed past me in the hall or we slid by each other in kitchen while cooking—every part of my body recognized her, responded to her.

She sat forward quickly, whipping her head around, catching me off guard. The beachy scent of her shampoo, my laundry detergent on her clothes, something...a little more Jordan, surrounded me.

"Sorry, I didn't know you were there," she mumbled.

The impulse to slide my hand around her waist and keep her close beat through me. I'd slide a hand into her silky curls and taste her lips.

Her tongue peeped out, wetting her bottom lip before it disappeared behind her teeth.

For a moment, it looked like our thoughts mirrored each other's. Her hand landed on mine, our pinkies entwined. Something about that simple touch had my blood pumping through my veins like a freight train. I wanted to turn her hand over and trace the lines of her palm. Run my fingertips over the smooth skin of her wrist.

Withdrawing her hand, she popped up from the blanket and announced to the group at large, "Y'all devoured those tacos, and I'm still hungry. I'm going to grab something else from the food truck. Anyone else want anything?"

Leah stood and took Jordan's arm. "I'll go with you." And with that, the two women set off, leaving me in a mess of conflicting emotions. Despite the way she'd jumped up nervously, I was almost certain I'd seen a flash of something in her eyes at the not-so-innocent touch of our hands.

I needed to get my head on straight, stop thinking about how good she smelled. Stop imagining what she'd taste like. But as I watched Jordan walk away with Leah, I knew I was lying to myself. Everything about Jordan called to me.

It was time to tamp down these feelings for Jordan.

Keep my distance. There was no point in starting something beyond friendship. Because in the end, she was leaving.

A shout erupted across the lawn snapping me out of my Jordan-induced haze. Mike and I sat up. Thoren returned with a round of beer and set the cups to the side, watching the disturbance nearby. In direct contrast to the overall peacefulness of the concert, a group of young men were arguing, pushing, and shoving. A wall of onlookers encircled the fray.

The three of us hurried over. Mike motioned for me to take the left side and Thoren to take the right.

The crowd split and people started running away. One guy had pulled a knife on the other. Mike stepped out cautiously. "Hey, man, let's settle down. There's no need to draw a weapon on anyone. Put it away and we can go somewhere to talk."

A quick glance around didn't show any uniformed officers in sight. We'd have to de-escalate this scene before someone got hurt.

As Mike talked to the guy holding the knife, Thoren flanked his rear, keeping watch that no one got the jump on him. I sidled up behind the guy, taking my cues from Mike, hyper-aware of every detail of the moment. One look and I'd be ready to subdue the guy.

Uniformed officers came running, taking over the scene, talking the knife-wielder down, and we made our way back to our friends. I flopped down next to Jordan, noting her concerned expression. "Are you okay? What happened?"

I reached for a bottle of water and slugged it back. "Yeah, sure. That guy was just drunk, belligerent. Thought a concert surrounded by public safety officers was the place to confront his buddy about sleeping with his wife or something."

"Does that happen often?" Jordan's voice held a tinge of worry.

"What?"

"You, stepping in for police officers."

"If you mean do I have their backs in altercations? The answer is yes. We look out for each other. I don't go looking for trouble, but I'm for damn sure not going to stand by and just let a bad thing happen if I can help defuse the situation."

She swallowed thickly and looked to the stage where the next artist was getting set up. I studied the set of her jaw, the straightness of her spine. For whatever reason, she was upset that I'd been involved.

"Hey." I nudged her with an elbow. "Are you okay?"

She offered me a tight smile. "It was just a little scary watching you walk into that situation is all. But it sounds like you have experience and know what you are doing."

I nodded. "You can bet we would've kept the situation contained. Besides, we had plenty of backup. You weren't in any danger."

Jordan's gaze searched mine for a moment, then she looked away. Were she any other woman, I'd have wrapped my arms around her, because even though she'd said she was fine, she looked rattled. But she wasn't any other woman. She was Jordan, my Skippy, and I was afraid that if I wrapped my arms around her, I'd not want to let go.

I was frustrated, or maybe bitter, that we'd clicked so quickly on so many levels, and yet nothing could come of the obvious attraction between us. Because she was leaving. I wouldn't be a good friend if I held her back. But that didn't mean I had to like it. Best to stop the hurt before it had a chance to start.

Chapter 9

Jordan

I stood in the doorway and admired my newly-finished van. It wasn't totally complete. I still had a few minor things to finish up. But as she stood, I could move in and hit the road.

The thought of leaving sent a pang of confusion through me.

Part of me was ready to get the hell out of dodge and start this new adventure. Once I'd decided on my plan, the wanderlust burned brighter than ever. More even than before I'd allowed Gerry to extinguish my spirit.

Everything I'd been through—moving away, the tornado, relying on Nate—had all strengthened my resolve that my independence was key.

But another part of me was riddled with insecurity. I'd laid down more roots in this town in the last month than I had in the two-ish months before the storm. Leaving my new friends would be hard, and that wasn't usually an issue considering how often I'd moved as a kid. Although, with the new age of technology, I could video call and text and chat with everyone on a regular basis.

Plus, I could always come back.

Hell. I could go anywhere I wanted.

Making this new lifestyle a success had to be my priority.

I finished making up my new bed and surveyed my work. I still needed to test my setup and make sure I was comfortable, but mostly, I was ready.

Maybe I'd try sleeping out here tonight.

Some space between me and Nate would be good anyway.

In the week since the concert, he'd been testy. At first, I'd tried to find out what was upsetting him, but after a day of his attitude and non-responses, I'd decided I had better things to do than tiptoe around him. And his waltzing into that fight had left me unsettled, more than I wanted to admit. So when he was off duty, I worked in the van, and the days that he was on duty, I worked in the house.

I'd thrown myself into finishing this vehicle. Now, all that was left to do was to move my clothes in, gas her up, and I was ready to roll. I ran back to the house to grab my workbag and a couple of personal things and moved them to the camper.

I'd finished up a critique letter when I heard a tap at the door. Nate's head appeared in the doorway. His gaze traveled over the van, lingering first on the bed, then on my workstation.

Bags sat heavy under his eyes, his expression was drawn, and he avoided looking directly at me.

"Have I been such a sorry roommate that you decided to move out?" he asked, his voice low in the quiet van.

My heart fluttered. This was a new side of him I hadn't seen before. Remorseful.

I'd been so intent on avoiding him because I didn't want

to deal with his attitude. Now that he was here in front of me, I realized it had been a good thing to put some distance between us, because I was struggling to stay in the friend-zone.

The easy way out would be to assure him that everything was fine. To smile and let it go.

But we'd been honest with each other from the get-go, and I didn't feel the need to sugarcoat anything anymore. Not after the hell I'd been through. If he couldn't take me being honest with him, so be it.

"You've been a jerk this week."

His head snapped back at my sharp tone. He held my gaze, then propped a hand on the doorway and leaned on his outstretched arm.

"Probably." He eyed the van, displeasure written all over his face. "You've been busy out here while you were avoiding me."

I didn't like his tone, and I was over his attitude. I sighed in defeat and plopped into a chair. "Look Nate, I'm tired of playing games. You seem like you're ready for me to go, and I realized that it's time. You've been more than generous, allowing me to stay here, helping me out so much. But I think I've overstayed my welcome. So, yes, I've been working hard to get it ready to go."

A muscle in his jaw ticked. I guess he was still pissy, despite my heartfelt confession. "Who helped you with the stove install?"

Why did it matter who helped me? Why was he being so moody and weird?

"Mike called a buddy of his. The guy stopped by in between jobs to get it done the other day when you were at work."

Another moment passed in silence. This whole Broody Nate was a real pain in my ass.

"So, it's all done and ready?"

At my nod, his lips firmed.

"Where are you going?" Again, with the tight voice and blank expression.

I couldn't tell if he was pissed off or sad or happy that I was ready to move out. This was a far cry from the Nate that I'd enjoyed hanging out with. The carefree, fun-loving, playful Nate. I missed that guy.

I stood and resumed unloading a basket I'd brought out, an effort to quell both my discomfort in the situation, and my nerves at the thought of doing this solo. I was determined and excited about my adventure, but that didn't mean I wasn't also feeling some apprehension about it.

"I booked a spot up in the mountains to do a trial run."

"For when?"

"Tomorrow," I said quietly.

Something thumped and I turned to catch him bumping the side of his fist against the door. He looked away, bumped the door again. When he looked back, his expression had changed once again, morphing from stoic to troubled. He opened his mouth, stopped, cleared his throat and started over. With a visible effort, he gentled his features, hiding behind this mask, this rip-off version of the Nate I'd come to know. Half of me wanted him to ask me to stay. The other half was ready to leave already.

"Well. If that's the case, we need to grab some pizza and beer and catch a game before you head out. Invite the crew over for a farewell party."

It was an olive branch. I'd take it.

I let out a soft breath of tension. I didn't want to leave

feeling like I'd lost my friend. "Sounds great, but don't you normally do something with the guys on the weekend?"

"Not tonight. Tonight, we're going to hang out and watch the game."

Ah damn, he was killing me. Sweet Nate making a surprise appearance.

I cleared my tight throat. "I'll finish up in here and head inside. You go order the pizza and send an invite to everyone."

By the time I strolled in, Nate had the game on and was kicked back on the couch. I grabbed a slice of pizza and curled up in my normal spot.

"I hate it that Mike, Leah, and Thoren couldn't make it. I wanted to see them before I hit the road," I said around a bite. It had been a last-minute deal, but it would've been nice to see them all once more before heading out of town.

Nate lifted a shoulder, eyes on the game.

The tension between us was unusual and uncomfortable and I didn't know what to do. So, I addressed the elephant.

"Nate, we need to talk."

"What is there to talk about?" he replied, not taking his eyes off the game.

I picked up the remote and hit pause on the game. He looked over to me. This was it. I had his attention, but what should I say? Did I tell him how amazing I thought he was? That I'd missed spending time with him during the week? That I'd had vivid dreams that he starred in? How much I was going to miss his smiles?

No.

There was no point in revealing any of that. No point in us becoming more than friends when we had no future.

"What did you want to say, Jordan?"

I swallowed my confession and tried for a smile. "Nothing. Just...thanks so much for everything."

"You make it sound like you're never coming back." His voice was low and soft in the room.

Was I? The thought of hitting the road and being free was compelling. But not seeing him again left a hollow, empty ache around my heart. "Well, if things go well, I might not be back. I just want you to know, I appreciate all you've done for me."

Nate reached over and grabbed my foot, giving it a squeeze. "I'm sorry I've been a jerk. My head got all confused, and I didn't handle it well. But I'm proud of you, and what you've accomplished. And I'm going to miss you being here."

I swallowed hard against the lump in my throat. The confusing mix of pride and sadness caused my eyes to well up, making it hard to draw a full breath.

He gave my foot another squeeze, then turned back to the game. "Now, can we continue with the game, or am I going to have to tickle you until you pee?"

I smirked and started the game. Things felt a little more normal as we cheered and analyzed plays. Almost like before whatever chasm had split us.

At the end of the game, I stood and said, "So, I think I'm going to give the new bed a try tonight."

"Tonight?" Nate turned his blue gaze to me, brow raised. I'd surprised him.

"Well, yeah, I didn't make it up for nothing." Plus, putting some distance between us might be a good thing. It'd been too tempting to snuggle up next to him during the game. To rest my head on his chest, and maybe he'd slide his arm around me and hold me.

He gave me a single nod, his expression unreadable.

"Okay, make sure to lock up. But take the house key with you, in case you chicken out in the night, and decide to come home. I mean, back inside."

I didn't miss his slip, but I let it go.

"I'll be fine."

A low rumble of thunder woke me with a start. Then the lightning started in earnest, the flashes illuminating the interior of the van. The similarity between this storm and the night of the tornado had my breath hitching. Rolling over, I grabbed my phone to check the weather app. As I unplugged the phone from the wall, rain began pouring down. Harder and harder, until it changed to a more distinct sound, and I knew it was hail. It had to be.

Dear God, there was no protection in this van. Any minute a tree could fall, or the roof could cave in, and I'd be pinned inside. I rolled out of the bed, dragging the pillows and blanket with me to the floor, and curled into the smallest ball I could.

My heart pounded. Tears welled in my eyes as every memory of that terrible night of the tornado flashed through my mind. I waited, listening for the sound of cracking trees over the howl of the wind.

A powerful gust shook the van, and something slapped against the front window.

OhGodOhGodOhGod. Here we go again.

The wind grew louder, as if the doors and windows were open, as if the roof had been torn away.

I burrowed under the blanket, curling to make myself as small as possible.

"Jordan! Jordan! Hold on, I'm coming." Nate's voice

sounded far away. In my mind, I saw him as I did that first night, my savior. Just a voice in the dark.

The sound of rushing wind died quickly and then the blanket was peeled back from my head, as Nate's warm voice crooned, "Oh, sweetheart."

The blanket lifted, and I was tugged into his warm embrace. My face was pressed against damp fabric as strong arms cradled me, and his hand smoothed over my hair.

He was here.

He'd known I'd be scared, and he'd braved the storm to come to me.

"Breathe with me, Skippy. Inhale, now exhale. Good, keep doing that. Everything is okay. It's just a little storm. It's ok, I've got you."

I gripped the fabric of his shirt and held him close to me, letting his soothing words wash over me, matching my breath to his, until the worst of the terror subsided.

Finally, the storm passed, I unclenched my grip on him, and relaxed a little. He kept stroking my hair.

When I could finally speak, I whispered, "You're here."

For a long time, I sat there clutching him to me, sharing his warmth. Just as I was drifting off, he shifted, his voice a low whisper in my ear. "Come on, let's get you back into bed now. The storm is over."

I nodded but didn't let go. He unclenched my fingers and rose, picking me up off the floor and laying me gently on my brand-new bed. He drew back as if to leave, and panic raced through me.

"Please, don't leave me. Please, stay with me," I whispered, reaching for him.

I searched the dark for any sign of him, then heard his soft sigh. "Scoot over."

I slid over, making room for him. He settled next to me,

slipping an arm around my shoulders. I turned to him and buried my face in his neck.

Breathing in the safe scent of Nate, I drifted to sleep.

I woke to the delicious warmth of another person in my bed. I was snug and cozy, and I didn't want to move, but unfortunately, now that I was awake, I needed to pee.

Nate shifted next to me, rolling to his back with a full body stretch, arms bunched up by his head, back bowed, belly hollowing out under the snug t-shirt. What a shame he was wearing a shirt, depriving me the chance to see those muscles flex and stretch.

He dropped his chin, facing me with a soft smile. "Morning, Skippy."

I returned his smile sheepishly, feeling foolish for being afraid of some wind and rain. "Morning slick. Thanks for coming last night. And staying." I studied his face, looking for any remains of the aloof jerk that my friend had become in the last week. At least he was back to calling me by that stupid nickname.

His warm eyes traveled my face. "You're welcome. But I have a question. What are you going to do when you are on the road and a storm comes?"

I rolled to my back. We slipped so easily into comfortable companionship. My foot brushed his, and I played footsie with him while I considered his question. "I don't know. Freak out?"

He shifted to his side, bracing on his elbow, head propped in his hand. "Seriously, Jordan. What are you going to do? You had a full-on panic attack."

I sighed. "I don't know. I'll figure it out as I go. But for now, I need you to move your big ass. I need to pee."

He rolled to the edge and sat up so I could get by him. I did my business, not even caring that the attractive man just outside the door could hear me.

When I came out, he had the bed made and was standing by the door.

"So. I guess this is it." I checked my watch. He was scheduled to be on duty in an hour. "I guess I won't be here when you get home tomorrow morning."

"This was a trial run, right?"

I took in his pained expression. We'd lost so much by not communicating over the week. I hated myself as I admitted, "I had planned on it at first. But now it seems like I should just go."

He nodded, looking everywhere around the van but at me. And we were right back to awkward again.

"Will you be back?" he asked the floor.

"Sure. At some point," I said lightly. Trying not to dwell on the fact that this was goodbye.

He nodded again and swallowed. "Fuck," he muttered, then stepped to me, wrapping his arms tightly around my shoulders and burying his face in my neck. I slipped my hands around his waist and held tight. For a long minute, I basked in the feel of him. Memorizing how his arms felt wrapped around me, basking in safety and security. How his smell calmed me. Tears pricked my eyes. This was so hard. But I had to do it. I had to say goodbye.

With a kiss to my cheek, he released me and cupped my face with his hand. "Look after yourself, Skippy. And don't be a stranger." After a lingering kiss to my forehead, he walked out the door.

· · ·

That afternoon, with a semi-broken heart and filled with anticipation, I pulled out of his drive. After gassing up, I plugged in the coordinates of my campsite and hit the road. I got to camp and got set up, spending some time chilling by a gently flowing creek. I worked, I read. I made myself a campfire.

I decided my van needed a name and came up with Pearl.

I shot Leah and Nate a text, letting them know I'd made it and was fine. The service indicator on my phone showed that I had one bar, but my messages weren't going through. Not having cell service was unsettling.

I glanced at the approaching night sky. No clouds were present, and the weather app had shown no rain for a couple of days. No threat of a panic attack.

Nate would've been proud of how I'd stayed close to camp and been hyper-aware of my surroundings.

By nightfall, I was curled up with a good book, refusing to let myself be intimidated by the solitude. And if I was a touch bored, lonely even, I chose to ignore it.

I stayed at the first site for two nights and after talking to the people camping next to me, I decided to move. I found a new spot about an hour away, one they promised had cell coverage.

Everything was fine and dandy, until I was traveling a two-lane road, out in the middle of nowhere, and a rusted-out pickup truck dropped a couple of two-by-fours on the road in front of me. I tried to avoid the debris but clipped a piece. Praying that I didn't do damage to Pearl, I forged on, but soon the *thump-thump* of a flat tire had me banging the steering wheel out of frustration.

I limped Pearl to an abandoned gas station, scared to death and wondering if I could handle this alone.

One hour—filled with some pretty inventive cussing—later, I pulled Pearl back out onto the road and was on my way.

After checking in and setting up camp, I set my chair out on the bank of the creek with my Kindle and a cold beer. Though I was in the mountains, the campground itself was flat, with spacious campsites, a nice parking pad, and plenty of lawn space. Bonus, it had electric hookup and excellent cell coverage.

I looked around, reveling in the knowledge that I'd just handled a major problem on my own. Pride welled up within me.

I was doing it. My dreams were coming true.

The perfect afternoon settled around me, and I sank into my chair to begin work, but reading the disaster of a manuscript was beyond me when I was so pumped. I needed to share this moment with someone.

Picking up the phone, I dialed Nate's number.

Chapter 10

Nate

My phone vibrated while I was standing at the checkout counter at the sporting goods store, buying fishing lures and a rod-reel combo I didn't need. I had no idea why I'd driven nearly two hours north to buy fishing stuff I already owned. But the days since Jordan had left had been long, and with nothing else to do, it felt like a good time to spend a day out of town.

Pulling my phone from my pocket, I swiped without looking to see who it was.

"Go for Nate."

The guy in front of me finished up his transaction and I stepped up to pay.

"Nate! Oh my God! You'll never guess what I just did." Jordan's voice teemed with excitement and put an instant smile on my face. I'd be willing to bet if she were standing in front of me, she'd be bouncing on her toes.

"Hey Skippy, what'd you do?" Her enthusiasm was contagious.

"I changed a flat tire on Pearl. All by myself!"

I turned my goofy grin on the cashier and handed her

my card, not caring even a little bit about what my total came to.

"Wait. What did you say?" My brows furrowed as her words registered. "You had a flat? What happened? Where are you?"

The cashier handed me my card and bag with a look of apprehension, like maybe I was flying off the handle and about to unload my crazy on her.

I hightailed it to my truck, slinging my bag into the passenger seat as I hopped in. I still had enough time to get to her if she needed me. Good thing I'd headed north.

On the other end of the line, Jordan laughed. "I moved to a different campground, and as I was on my way over, I ran over a board with a nail in it. But Nate! I changed the tire all by myself."

What she was saying sank in then.

She didn't need me to come rescue her.

She had rescued herself. The tension whooshed out of me, leaving a strange hollowness in its wake. I sat back, draping an arm over the steering wheel. I missed her. The realization slammed into me.

"Well, that's great then. Go you!" I gave a fist pump like she could see it, swallowing my pride that she didn't need me at all. Didn't sound like she missed me at all.

"You just did a fist pump didn't you?" I closed my eyes against the teasing sound of her voice. "You goober."

I opened my eyes again on this new world where Jordan was gone, but still in my life. I'd take what I could get. "Yeah, well. No one saw me."

She turned serious. "Thanks, Nate. I couldn't have done it without you though." She sounded appreciative. And I knew that if I could see her, her eyes would be gleaming, and she'd be giving me that beautiful smile. "I kept hearing your voice in my ear, teasing me that I was doing it wrong, and I just had to prove that I could do it the way we practiced."

The memory of the afternoon we'd spent going over the technical aspects and maintenance that she'd need to know while she was on the road fell into that hollow space in my chest.

"So other than the flat, how's the rest of the trip going?" I tried to make my voice sound casual.

"It's great so far. No storms, Pearl handles like a dream. Oh, that's right, my text where I named the van didn't go through. So yeah, I named her Pearl and she's great. I'm not sleeping all that well. I'm a little restless, but not because I'm uncomfortable. Mostly, because everything is new."

I looked around the parking lot as she rambled, feeling a little lost without my friend, without the project to work on. Before Jordan, I hadn't thought twice about how I spent my days. Now, her absence amplified the realization that, unless I was at work, I spent my time in solitude.

"That's great, Skippy. I'm proud of you."

"So, now that I have cell coverage, I just wanted to call and share a celebratory beer," she said, and I heard a can popping open.

I smiled. Her joy was contagious. She'd been through so much. From surviving the storm, to building out that van, she'd proven her resilience.

"You deserve all the good things, Jordan. You've been through a lot in a short period of time. I'm glad you are enjoying yourself," I said, truly happy for her.

We chatted for a while, and she filled me in on some of the cool things she'd seen. I hated myself for wasting the last week we had together by getting all up in my feels. Jordan was my friend, and I'd missed time with her because I was a fucking idiot. My issues weren't her fault.

I was the one in the wrong. I'd pushed her away because I didn't want to get any closer to her, knowing she was leaving.

But I was a fool. Because in the short time that she'd been gone, I'd learned that I'd rather have Jordan in my life as a friend than not have her at all.

She wrapped up a story about the neighbor's dog that had been hanging out with her at the water. "So anyway. Now that I've bored you to death, how are you?"

How was I?

"I'm doing okay. The house is weirdly quiet without a certain blonde making a bunch of noise."

She laughed. "Aww, you miss me."

The truth lingered in those words. "Maybe. It's just quiet. I guess I got used to having someone around all the time."

"Well, enjoy the silence. Besides, me being gone will give you plenty of time to do all the things you didn't get done while we worked on Pearl. That's part of the reason I decided to go ahead and leave. It was time. I'd worn out my welcome." Her voice was quiet, intimate on the line. She might as well have been sitting next to me. I felt closer to her than I ever had.

I pinched the bridge of my nose, ashamed that she'd felt like she wasn't welcome anymore.

"Jordan, you did nothing wrong. I'm sorry you felt like you had to leave."

Silence descended between us, as I sat just listening to her breathe with the distant trickle of the stream in the background. My gut churned because it was time to let her go. Part of me wanted to cut the ties—maybe that would make this feeling go away—and another, bigger, part of me wanted to tell her to come home, that I missed her.

"So listen," I started, my voice low and rough. "I'm feeling weird about you being on the road alone with no one knowing where you are."

She huffed a small laugh. "I'm a big girl, Nate. I changed my own tire after all. I can do anything now."

I chuckled. "I know. You're a real badass. But would you do me a favor?"

"Well, that depends on what it is."

I gripped the steering wheel. I was stupid for even asking. I had zero business intruding on her privacy. "Would you mind sharing your location with me on your phone? I'd just feel better knowing where you are."

"No way. You'll come stalk me and pull a prank in the middle of the night," she replied with mock outrage.

I swallowed, nervous because I suddenly needed to know that I could find her if she needed me. "I'm serious, Jordan." What could I say that wouldn't be overstepping the lines of friendship? "I don't like the thought of you being out there all alone."

She grew quiet.

The sun blazed through the windshield, heating the interior of the truck. In front of me, a family was heading to their RV, kids dragging little miniature fishing poles on the ground, no doubt something they'd begged for that they'd forget in a heartbeat. Still, it was nice seeing a family do something together, though it left me with a tinge of longing.

When I was growing up, I'd been a latchkey kid. My parents worked all the time. We never took family vacations or spent any time together. It wasn't a surprise when my folks split up when I was thirteen. When they were together, the underlying tension, the arguments, the cold way they treated each other, the way they complained about each other... My family dynamic was different than the way my friends' families operated.

I'd gotten used to being alone at the house for long periods of time. I'd learned to rely on myself. Learning how to cook my own meals and do laundry when most of my other friends were out goofing off. Hell, it'd been the perfect opportunity to raid my dad's stash of porn magazines. My parents eventually reconciled, but we were never a loving family.

When Jordan moved in, it was the first time that I'd shared my personal space with anyone since the fire academy a decade ago. The short time she'd spent with me had made a difference, and I was feeling the loss. Missing having someone to share meals with. Missing working on the van. Missing having her close to talk about my day, and to hear her stories.

"Nate, are you there?" Her soft voice interrupted my thoughts.

"Yeah, I'm still here." My throat felt tight.

"Why do you care so much about my safety?" She sounded...unsure? Hopeful?

That one was easy. "Because we're friends? Or at least, I thought we were friends."

Hell, she was probably my best friend.

"We are. We are friends. Good friends." She had a smile in her voice, and what I wouldn't give to see that smile in person.

"Okay then, Skippy. Wouldn't you hate for your friend, your best friend, to worry?"

"Oh, we're best friends now? What are we, twelve?"

Something about her stripped away the facade I'd been

hiding behind and I found myself admitting, "I've never had a best friend, so maybe?"

She grew quiet, and in those moments, regret took hold. Too much, too soon, too...honest. Fear bubbled while I waited for her response.

"Really? Not even when you were a kid?" she said gently.

I cleared my throat and wiped my palms on my jeans before answering. "Nope. Parents were gone all the time. I was pretty much alone except for a few kids at school. There weren't many kids in my neighborhood growing up, and those that were there were little assholes." I kept my tone light, even though being this open was ripping a hole in the wall I'd built around my heart.

"What, they didn't want to hang with you?"

"More like they'd rather do drugs and get into trouble." It was easier to talk about the hard stuff when I didn't have to look her in the eye. "My folks forced me to stay home, and not have anyone over until they got home. But they worked so late, usually it was bedtime before they got in. They'd let me hang out with the old man that lived next door, but that was it."

Silence followed my admission, and I immediately regretted saying anything.

"Wow," she said softly. "I thought you were kidding. You've never had a best friend?"

Shame shut down my vocal cords, so I just grunted. I knew I'd missed out as a kid, but it felt all kinds of pathetic when she said it out loud.

"Well, in that case, I'm honored to be considered your best friend. And I'll share my location and make sure I check in on the reg and keep you in the loop."

Her voice might as well have been a hug as relief shot

through me. Having her friendship meant so much to me. More than I cared to admit, even to myself.

I talked her through how to set up the location share on her phone and then she said she was running out of battery. I let her go, making her promise, again, to keep me in the loop of her plans.

I drove home thinking of how much fun it would be to take this new fishing pole and surprise Jordan. Did she like fishing? I bet she would. She'd be the one to push me into the water. The thought had a grin stretching over my face.

When had she become so important? And why had I let myself get so deep? And what was I going to do about it?

Chapter 11

Jordan

"So, you see, you take this little thing here, and slip it down into that hole. Then you are ready to dump your grey water."

Roger, the nice older gentleman showing me how to use the dump station, bent over and flipped a lever, and the water started flowing through the line.

"What kind of toilet system you got in this thing? Betsy said it looks kinda fancy," he said around the toothpick hanging from his meaty lips.

His wife, Betsy, and their little dachshund were checking out the flowers lining the dump station.

"You want to take a look inside?" I offered.

"I sure would," he said, shooting me a toothy grin. I marveled at his ability to not lose the toothpick. "Betsy's been talking about how nice it is inside. You fixed her up yourself, didn't you?"

I beamed. "I sure did. Well, I had some help from a friend, but we did most of the work ourselves. Pearl already had a subfloor system when we got her, so we just laid the flooring and finished her."

Roger ran his hands over the wood countertop with a whistle. "This is some quality work."

"Thanks. My friend Nate did that."

Roger nodded, white hair flopping adorably over his brow. "Yes sir-ree, he sure did a good job."

I opened a cabinet, revealing my hidden composting toilet. "This is what Betsy was gushing over. It tucks away. It's biodegradable. I just replace the liner and the composting system regularly."

"Isn't that something. Goll-dern. I don't even smell it at all." Roger's eyebrows shot up on his wrinkly forehead. He stared at the hideaway toilet, then turned back to me, astonished.

"Well, it wouldn't be that way in our camper." Betsy said from the doorway. Her short grey hair, about an inch long, stood straight up from her head. Little Wilson, the wonder pup, wriggled in her arms.

A smile crept up my face as I reached for Wilson. Any minute now, Betsy and Roger would start their lovable bickering.

I'd camped by them for a week and had come to adore the way they badgered each other. Poking and prodding until they got a rise out of the other. Cut-downs were their favorite and they had me in stitches multiple times as they called each other out. Their relationship reminded me of the fun times with Nate.

When I'd asked Betsy about it, she'd told me that their playfulness kept the spark alive. Then she'd winked, and I'd gone beet red, which had made her hoot with laughter.

"Where are you headed, darlin'?" Betsy climbed into Pearl and lovingly rubbed the leaves of a plant she'd given me.

"I'm headed to North Carolina, maybe on into Virginia.

Maybe toward the beach. But then again, Charleston also sounds lovely. So, I'm not really sure. I'll go where the moods strikes when I hit the road, I guess."

Betsy nodded, planting her hands on her hips. "Well, this is goodbye for real then. We're headed down to Florida to see the grandkids. It's spring break and they think they need to go to the Gulf, so that's where we're headed."

I smiled sadly at her. "I wish I'd gotten the courage to chat with you sooner. I feel like I missed out."

Betsy patted my arm. "That's all right, sweetheart. Don't you worry. You were just keeping yourself safe. We understand. We've run across solo women camping before, not all have been open to conversations with random strangers. I'm always impressed by their gumption. I could never do it."

I tilted my head at her. "What makes you say that? I think you'd be fine at it." Wilson wiggled in my arms, so I let him down to run around the van.

"Well, for one, Roger makes the best pot of coffee. If he's not with me, I have to make my own. Plus, this old coot can't survive without me. He'd never know where anything is. Lord knows he doesn't know how to look for anything on his own. I'd rather be with him, so he doesn't ransack the camper. Besides, beautiful places are best when shared with someone you love."

I laughed, even though her words left a tinge of sadness behind. I pushed it away and focused on my new friends.

Roger finished his perusal of my toilet and stood with his hands on his hips.

"If you get close and are up for a short hike, you should check out Hawksbill Mountain. And there are some great hikes out on the Blue Ridge Parkway, if you get over that way."

"Thanks, I'll do some research on that," I said, nodding once at him.

Betsy put a hand on my shoulder, turning me to her. "I really am proud of you. I know we just met, but I think you are a strong woman."

Tears welled at her sweet words. I wasn't used to having such kind, open-ended support, especially from a stranger. "Thank you. That's an awfully sweet thing to say."

She pulled me into a hug. "I'd like to keep in touch with you and hear about your journey."

I backed away, smiling. "I'd like that."

Roger tugged me into his embrace. "You be careful out on your own, missy. It's okay to take risks. Just make sure the risks you take are worth it."

I patted his back then moved to find a piece of paper to scribble my email for them.

We finished at the dump station and said our goodbyes.

I'd only just met them, but they'd been so sweet and made such an impact on me. I watched them drive away, feeling a little morose.

I left the campground and gassed up, then found a coffee shop. I found a table while I waited for my chai latte. It still felt awkward to eat alone sometimes, but thankfully my phone pinged with a message.

Leah: Hey girl, just checking in on you. Hope you are having fun.

Me: Hi! Just waiting on chai and then headed out to the next spot.

Leah: Where's that?

Me: I'm not sure. I know that sounds crazy.

Leah: Having a plan would be a good thing.

Me: I know. It's not like me at all. But I'm going with it.

How are things there? Everyone doing okay? I feel like I'm missing so much.

An image from the cookout, all my new friends laughing and having a good time, flashed in my memory. Even though I hadn't known them very long, I was missing them. A pang of loneliness pierced my heart. This friend group thing was new and foreign to me. Moving around, never settling in a space long enough to form real attachments, had never bothered me until now.

Leah: Things are good. Recovery is still ongoing. Mike has threatened getting me a dog. Kylie and I added another class. Nate's been keeping to himself some since you left.

The server called my name. I grabbed my coffee and Danish and went back to my table to wrap up my chat with Leah.

Me: I'm glad things are going well. Tell everyone I said hello. I miss you guys.

Leah: Have fun adventuring and let me know where you end up, please. I'll keep a candle burning for you.

I enjoyed my Danish and pondered texting Nate. He had wanted me to stay in touch. And friends kept in touch, right? It shouldn't be an issue, but then again. I'd started feeling *more-than-friends* feelings for him before I left. I didn't necessarily want to feel those feelings, but I was missing him. As I sipped my coffee, debating if I should reach out to him, my phone pinged with another text. Probably Leah again, wishing me love and light.

I flipped my phone over to see Nate's name.

Nate: Why are you stopped at a parts store? Is everything okay?

What? I looked out the window toward Pearl to see that I'd parked her at the far corner of the lot. The lot shared by an auto shop. So, he'd been stalking me after all. A thrill ran through me.

Me: Stalking much?

Nate: Yes. What's going on? Do you need help?

Me: Actually, stalker, I'm enjoying coffee and a Danish in the coffee shop *next* to the auto shop.

Nate: Thank God. I was worried for a moment that I'd have to take valuable vacation time and come rescue you.

Me: Aww, you'd use a vacation day for me?

Nate: Maybe, but it would cost you.

An inappropriate image of how I could repay him flashed in my mind. Me with my hands bound in his, pressed up against a wall. I couldn't stop the shudder that passed through me at the image.

Me: I don't need anything that bad.

Nate: You aren't even going to ask what it would cost?

Me: No, I'm sure it would be something ridiculous.

Nate: Fair enough.

Nate: So how are things? You OK?

The phone in my hand grew blurry. I missed him. Missed our time fixing up Pearl. Missed watching ball games with him. Missed the towel popping fights, sharing dinner, hearing about his shift over coffee. He'd been so reluctant to tell me at first, then the longer I lived with him, it became so natural for him to just start telling me about the calls he ran. I liked to think it was his way of decompressing from particularly rough calls. Was he talking to anyone now about the things he saw on his job? A wave of jealousy washed over me. I wanted to be the one he shared his day with.

Nate: Hello?

Nate: Answer me

Nate: DON'T MAKE ME COME FOR YOU

And he would. I had no doubt.

Me: I'm here, crazy pants. Settle down and quit shouting at me. I'm fine. Sitting here pondering where to go next.

Nate: What are your options?

Me: Options are endless. I was just going to hit the road and see where it leads.

Nate: I recommend having a plan doofus.

Me: LOL, I'm kidding. I'm leaning toward North Carolina and doing this hike that my camp neighbor was telling me about. Sounds like it might be fun. He said it was a good workout, but the view was worth it.

Nate: Camp Neighbor? Who is this guy? You didn't give him personal info, did you? Are you traveling together now? Dammit, Skippy! I told you to look out for yourself.

Nate: Skippy. You are not going on a trip with some rando.

Nate: Dammit. I never should have let you leave.

Nate: I'm coming to get you. Taking up with a stranger. SMH

Nate: ARE YOU CRAZY??!!

I cracked up, laughing at him blowing up my phone, and patrons at the next table turned to stare at me. I offered them a smile and waggled my phone at them.

Me: Cool your jets, you psycho. Roger is 70, married to Betsy, has a cute dog that loves to snuggle.

Me: I'm fine.

Me: Besides, you were a stranger when you moved me into your house. That turned out ok.

Nate: That's different.

Me: Ok, whatever.

A bubble with three dots popped up and then disappeared. I waited for a few moments.

Nate: I'm worried about you Jordan. Be careful.

This was serious Nate. Serious Nate was sweet and kind and caring. And I missed him even more than I missed Fun Nate.

Me: I'm fine. Really. How about you? Are you doing okay? Enjoying the quiet with me gone?

I was fishing, I knew it. But something in me needed to know that our friendship mattered to him.

Nate: It's too quiet sometimes. Which is weird to admit.

Me: I get it. It's too quiet in Pearl sometimes, too.

Nate: No problems?

Me: Dude. Seriously. Quit worrying. You are giving me a complex.

Nate: Ok then. Are you having fun?

Me: Yes, it's been amazing.

Nate: Good. That's good.

I finished my Danish and gathered my trash. I forced myself to get moving and went out to Pearl. That hike sounded more and more appealing. I punched in the address on the GPS, then texted Nate a last message.

Me: I'm rolling out. Thanks for checking in on me.

Nate: Have fun. Send pictures. I miss your face you goober.

Nate: PS This would've been easier as a phone call.

I smiled as I typed out my response.

Me: So, call next time.

I left the shop, grinning from ear to ear and feeling much lighter. Because maybe next time, he would call.

. . .

The hike up Hawksbill wasn't as terrible as Roger had made it out to be. Overall, it was only a little over a mile to the top, but the views were breathtaking. I sat on a slab, taking in the 360-degree view. The rock outcropping jutted out at angles. I inched my way to the edge on my rear, too chicken to stand and walk right up to the edge. The valley below me was tucked in between rolling green hills.

It wasn't an enormous mountain like out west. But the Appalachian chain was old and historied. Beautiful.

I hadn't passed a single person while I made the climb and had my choice of flat surface to rest upon.

All around me, nature happened. A falcon hunted from a nearby tree. Squirrels scampered at the tree line below.

Closing my eyes, I lay back on the warm surface, soaking up the sun, listening to the wildlife around me while I caught my breath.

This was what I'd been looking for. This peacefulness. This sense of accomplishment. Being afraid and pushing through that fear. Being tired and still working my way, step by step, inch by inch, toward my goal.

Even with all the drama that my life had become, I was in control of how I handled it. I was making my life happen on my terms.

All the swirling emotions gathered and brought tears to my eyes.

After Gerry's betrayal, I'd been floundering, trying to find my place in the world again.

Then the tornado happened.

Then leaving Newman.

What did it all mean?

Every risk I'd ever taken had hurt me. Just like it had eventually hurt my dad.

I tossed my arm over my closed eyes. That wasn't true. I took a risk in quitting my job. It was paying off.

Though leaving Gerry had hurt, in the long run, I'd come out stronger. I'd not let him break me. I was happier now than I had been while we'd been together. I didn't even realize what I was giving up when I just stopped doing the things that I loved and sacrificed them for time with him.

I'd taken a risk on staying with Nate, that had turned out okay. I'd taken a risk with Pearl, and so far, it was going well.

I was resilient. I was strong. I was motivated. I'd done all these things. Yes, Nate had helped me with Pearl. But I was out here doing it on my own, crushing my goals.

And yet, while I was feeling so empowered and accomplished, I was also...empty inside.

I climbed down the mountain and went to a nearby town to fuel up. At the roadside bistro, a table of women sat chatting, their laughter ringing over the din of customers waiting in line.

I thought about Leah and Mike, Kylie, Nate, and Thoren. Was it normal to be this homesick when I'd only been gone for two weeks? Our friendship had cemented from the start, so maybe it made sense that I missed them at random times. Like now, when I spied a random group of women enjoying themselves.

I grabbed a sandwich and found some shade at a nearby picnic table, pulling out my laptop to do a little work. This was a definite perk to my job, being able to work anywhere. I was just finishing invoicing a client when the tinkle of laughter caught my attention.

I looked up to see a small child—a little girl in a yellow sundress—being tossed into the air by her father. They were both laughing, the little girl squealing in delight. An older girl stood nearby. She couldn't have been over ten years old, holding an ice cream cone in each hand. Their dad, a young, handsome man, secured the little girl on his hip and took the cone the older girl offered. He passed the cone to the girl in his arms, then reached back to clasp the older girl's hand. All three connected, smiling, enjoying a sunny summer day in June.

Memories flooded me of another time, and another little girl. Me.

Homesickness washed over me again, this time going beyond the friends I'd left behind. I had once been that blonde, curly-headed child with one man in her world. The most fun-loving man that had ever lived. He pulled her close and spun her around, shared his ice cream, held her hand, and made her feel like a princess.

My dad had been my world as a young girl.

Then came the divorce.

Then the accident that changed everything.

The day my dad had his crash, I'd been waiting on him to pick me up to go on an adventure. He never came. In my misguided young mind, I felt abandoned, like he chose his travel and adventure over me.

Years of anger and resentment had fooled me into thinking that it was his fault. That his own decisions took him away from me. That he chose to leave Mom and me behind. That he chose to replace us with a new wife. That his adventures eventually led to him taking a risk that changed all our lives.

Despite being a child at the time, I'd not been innocent. I had chosen to stay away, deciding that it was too hard to see him after his accident. I couldn't bear to be reminded of all that he was and would never be again. And I'd stayed away. For far too long.

I was a selfish, misguided asshole.

And I was missing the relationship, both with him and my stepmom. It'd taken me losing everything to realize that the most important things in life weren't really things.

The most important things in life were the people in it.

Suddenly, I knew what I needed to do. I needed to see him and make right all the ways I'd abandoned him.

Chapter 12

Jordan

I white-knuckled the steering wheel as I pulled Pearl into the convalescent center parking lot. I was up near Martha's Vineyard, and the travel to get there had been a slog. But the places to stop and explore along the way had been amazing.

I sat staring at the building, gathering my courage to go inside. From the outside, you'd never know what went on behind those walls. Hell, I wasn't even sure what went on inside. Not like I had ever set foot in there. And he'd been at this center for several years.

It had always been easier to just avoid the situation. To stay away and pretend like my life hadn't ended the day my stepmom called me to tell me that Dad had been in a plane crash that killed the pilot and had left my dad with a brain injury.

Seeing my beloved daddy in a coma was the hardest thing I'd ever been through, and my teenage brain couldn't comprehend the emotions I was feeling, so I'd pushed them down. Ten years later and I was still disassociating, still ignoring the hard emotions as a twenty-six-year-old.

Keeping in touch with my stepmom, Sandi, via email had been easier than actually talking to her on the phone. Using my mom and grandma as a buffer for information became the norm, until I just stopped reading and responding. Eventually, Sandi quit including me.

I hated that I'd missed so much. Just willfully ignored it for years.

I had no idea what I would find when I went in the building. No idea if they'd even let me see him. No idea where Sandi was, or if she would even want to hear from me or let me see my dad.

The words "brain injury," "induced coma," and "paralyzed" all rambled around in the recesses of my mind as I walked to the front doors of the convalescent and rehabilitation center. Wiping my palms on my jeans before opening the door, I entered a brightly lit lobby. Green plants lined the full wall of windows, light brown loveseats sat in clusters around small magazine-filled tables.

Gathering my courage, I made my way to the reception desk, where a young woman greeted me with a smile.

"Hello, how can I help you today?"

I clutched my purse to my stomach. "I'm not sure if I'm on his visitor list, but I'm hoping to visit Waylon Ashley."

"Oh, Mr. Waylon is such a sweetie. He's in room 202." She clicked around on her computer and beamed at me. "But right now, he should be in the gardens for some outdoor time. Do you need directions on how to find him?"

Armed with a highlighted map, I set off to find the man I hadn't seen in years.

The gardens, as she had called them, were in a courtyard of sorts. I pushed open the door and followed a paved path along a row of rose bushes to an area that opened to a small pond amidst a green patch of grass.

A man sat in a wheelchair, his head resting on the padded headrest, arms crossed awkwardly in his lap, legs bent with his feet braced in the footrest of the chair. His thinning hair was brushed in a combover, and his light grey sweats were loose and baggy over his frail frame. A seatbelt held him secure.

His eyes were closed, mouth slack.

I approached silently in case he was sleeping. As I drew closer and sat on the bench near him, he roused a little.

"Daddy?" I whispered, my voice catching.

His eyes opened, and his head tilted up at an angle as he looked my way.

The eyes of my childhood hero landed on me, but this broken stranger looked nothing like the strong man I remembered. My heart cracked and I swallowed back a gasp.

"Are you an angel?" His halting voice was familiar, his words a blast from my past.

"I'm not an angel, Daddy." I responded with the words of my youth, emotion making my voice tremble.

A misshapen grin transformed his face. "Oh, yes, you are. You're my angel."

His speech was slow and measured, as if he had to concentrate on pronouncing each word, but I understood him. I'd thought I'd never hear him call me his angel again. Tears spilled down my cheeks as I launched from my seat and hugged the first man I ever loved.

"Hey, kiddo," he whispered to my hair. And just like that, I was a teenager again.

I pulled back and swiped my tears away. "Hey, Daddy."

"Pull me closer and sit with me a while."

I did as he asked and pulled his chair closer to the

bench. He reached a hand toward me, and I clasped it like the lifeline I didn't know I needed.

His gaze roamed my face. "You sure turned out beautiful." His halting speech pattern quickly became normal to me. "Tell me about yourself. Tell me everything. I've missed my sweet girl."

Tears filled my eyes again.

"I'm sorry, Daddy. I'm so sorry for not being here." I choked on the words but needed to say them.

His gnarled hand squeezed mine.

"Shh, baby. It's all right. If I'm honest, I didn't want you to see me like this." His words broke me.

"I love you anyway, and I'm just so sorry that I've missed all this time." The full weight of all that I had neglected squeezed my heart, and I struggled to say what needed to be said. "I'm so ashamed that I didn't come sooner." I pulled his hand up and pressed my lips to his fingers. "Please forgive me."

He pulled his fingers free and cupped my cheek. "Nothing to forgive. You're here now."

I pushed Dad's wheelchair down the long hallway back to his room, laughing at his silly dad jokes, marveling that he still remembered them to tell them even after all this time.

He made a motion to stop with his hand—I was quickly learning his communication methods—right in front of the nurse's station.

The two women looked up at him, smiling. "Hi Waylon, who is this?" The one closest to us asked.

"My daughter. Isn't she beautiful?"

"She sure is. Looks like you are a lucky fella today. You've got a visitor waiting in your room."

My eyebrows crept up my forehead.

Dad clapped his hands together, so I rolled him to his room for his next surprise. I pushed us through the doorway to see my stepmom, fluffing the pillows on his bed.

His room was a standard hospital room, with a large mechanical bed along one wall. The windowsills were filled with potted plants and picture frames. There was a dark brown wooden armoire in a corner. The wall beside it held a bulletin and white board combo that had photos and card mementos. A colorful fleecy blanket covered the foot of the bed, giving a splash of color against the white linens.

My stepmom straightened as we passed through the door, a wide smile aimed at my dad. "There's my handsome fella."

"Jo, honey." Mom wrapped me in a fierce hug, tears streaming down her face.

"Mom, what's wrong?"

"It's your dad."

I froze, paralyzed with fear that something had happened to Dad.

"What happened, Mom?"

"Oh, Jo, he's getting married."

I pushed away from her. She was crying just like she had when she'd told me they were getting a divorce. She scared me to death that time, and my dad had walked through the door an hour later and we'd talked everything out. Now she was doing the same thing. Honestly, I'd known this was bound to happen. Dad was too full of life, and he and Sandi had been dating for a while.

And yet my mom was acting devastated. Again.

I pushed him farther into the room and stood awkwardly to the side, shrugging off the bad memories as

Sandi came to him, giving him a hug and a peck on the cheek.

"You look great today, sweetheart. And I see you've brought a straggler with you?"

Her gaze shifted to me.

For a moment, my heart sputtered. The last time I spoke to this woman, I hadn't been nice. And though she'd still sent me updates on my dad's health status for a while, I'd been a brat and hadn't responded to her. I'd been no better than my mom, overreacting about the news of their divorce, closing myself off from them, long before his accident.

Shame and remorse were such a bitch combo to deal with.

I squared my shoulders, knowing I deserved any kind of crappy comment she made. I looked her in the eye and offered a reconciliatory smile. "Hi, Sandi. It's been a while."

She reached for me, pulling me into a hug. Her soft hair brushed my cheek as she whispered to me, "Thank you for coming. This means everything to him."

I swallowed against the emotion clogging my throat and blinked the moisture from my eyes as she pulled away. I had been such a shit daughter to them, essentially cutting them off. And here they were, offering me unconditional love, open acceptance. Like I deserved it.

We got Dad settled into the bed and I finally got the balls to address the elephant in the room. I owed them an explanation and an apology.

"You guys, I know it's weird me showing up here. And it feels weird to me that you've both just welcomed me so much. I guess I expected anger and resentment."

Dad looked at my stepmom, their eyes lingering as though they were having an entire conversation without saying a word. Had I ever had a connection with someone like that? Where an entire conversation could pass between two people with a gaze?

Sandi cleared her throat and grabbed Dad's hand.

"Well, Jordan. I will confess that I've been frustrated with your lack of effort at different times over the years. Your dad and I eventually decided you'd come when you felt ready. And if you didn't, then we'd have to accept it. I'm not going to lie and say I was happy about it. But Waylon didn't want me to give you a piece of my mind, and so I focused my energy in a positive way. I just hoped and prayed that you'd come to realize what you'd been missing."

Her words stung that tender place in my heart and I had to look away. I knew I deserved the harsh words, and their disappointment, but it still stung.

"I know I was wrong, and I don't have any excuses. But I'll be better about making the effort moving forward. I guess I grieved losing the dad I had and didn't appreciate the dad I still have." I looked up at them both, forcing myself to face them. "I love you, both of you. I'm sorry for not being here. But I am now. And will be from now on."

Dad shifted and reached his hand to me. I clasped it, feeling a tear trickle down my cheek. "I love you, too, kiddo."

After an emotion-filled moment of Dad and I staring at each other, Sandi clapped her hands and said, "Okay, we're done with the hard stuff. Tell us all about what you've been doing."

I launched into my life story, covering college, through my relationship with Gerry, and ending with my move to Newman, the tornado, and Nate's rescue. I finished by describing Pearl to them and my adventures since taking her on the road. By the time I was done talking, we'd shared laughs and more hugs and that little empty place inside of me had started to fill.

Chapter 13

Nate

I finished my outdoor chores, checking my little vegetable garden that was coming along nicely, and flipped on the lights on the deck. The sun had set but it was not yet dark. The last orange rays of the sunset set my hard work on display like a painting. It reminded me of the evening Jordan had first put up the lights.

Smiling at the reminder of her, I sent her a quick picture of the backyard overlooking my new garden.

My phone rang instantly.

I answered after the first ring. "That was quick."

"Please tell me that's a garden I see in the background," she said excitedly.

Of course she noticed that first. I grinned, because I'd known as soon as I sent the photo that she'd pick up on it.

"Yes, ma'am, it is. Tomatoes and cucumbers are in the ground," I boasted, my mood lightening by the second.

"You must really be bored now that I'm gone if you're resorting to growing a vegetable garden."

I grinned. "Hey, now. You drove off in my hobby and I had to have something to do."

"Okay, whatever. You aren't allowed to guilt-trip me when you agreed to help." If she'd been here, she would've thrown something at me, teasing me.

"And you aren't allowed to make fun of my gardening skills."

Her laugh made me smile in earnest. "Okay, slick. Truce. I think it's cool you planted a garden. I hope it does well."

I leaned back in my chair and shifted to get more comfortable. "So, where have you and Pearl gone lately? See anything cool?" I asked, like I hadn't been checking her location every single day. Like right now, I didn't know she was up north near Cape Cod.

"I came to see my dad."

"Oh, wow. That's cool, I guess? I mean, is that a good thing?" She'd not mentioned her family. And I felt like a shitty friend for not asking before.

"Yeah, it's been really good, actually. I've had a chance to reconnect with him and my stepmom. I've been visiting him every day. Pearl is parked at a nearby campground and the owners have let me borrow a bicycle. Oh my gosh, you would've cracked up laughing at me on that thing the first time I tried to ride it."

I kicked up my feet on the railing and listened to her laughing about falling over on the bike, forgetting to put her feet down. She was so animated and full of life. A far cry from the injured quiet woman I'd carried out of that house that first night that we'd met.

I laughed with her about her dad's corny jokes.

She told me all about how she handled a small leak in the sink on Pearl.

And I couldn't get rid of this stupid grin on my face.

I'd missed talking to her every day. I hadn't even realized how much I'd cared about her, until she was gone.

But I was also happy for her. She was in the middle of a story about a puppy when I interrupted her. "I'm proud of you, Skippy. You're doing great out there on your own."

She grew quiet. "Thanks, Nate. I appreciate you saying that."

I cleared my throat, uncomfortable with the emotion clogging it.

"So, you went to see your dad, huh? How was that?"

"Hang on, let me plug my phone in." Something rustled, and she sounded closer, like she'd shifted and pulled the phone closer to her mouth. I imagined her laying in the fluffy bed in Pearl, with the blankets wrapped over her legs, maybe her tank top glued to her ribs, outlining her breasts.

She'd have an arm up, using it as a pillow, her long hair cascading behind her on the mattress.

"It was good to see him. I guess I've never told you about what happened with him. He was a pilot and flight instructor. One day he was helping a student get certified. It was him, the student-pilot, and a guy from the FAA. The student made an error landing the plane, I don't know if it was windy or what happened, but she clipped the wing, and it sent the plane spiraling and flipping down the runway. Dad was thrown through the windshield, the pilot died, and the FAA guy walked away."

"My God. That's horrible."

"Yeah, after that I couldn't face seeing him. I couldn't bear the thought of him being anything less than the man he'd been. So I was an asshole and stayed away." She paused, and finished quietly, "So yeah, this time with him has been good. Healing." I grabbed a second beer, because this was some heavy shit she'd dealt with.

"Sounds like it. I'm happy for you, babe. So, what's next? Are you going to stay there for a while?" The darkness of the evening lent an intimacy to our conversation. It felt like she was here with me, though she was miles away.

I waited for her to reply.

"Hello, Skippy, did you fall asleep on me?"

"No," she blurted. "I'm still here. Uh, I'm not sure what is next. I'll probably stay here a little longer, and then I don't know. Maybe I'll head back south. Maybe I'll head west."

"Well, I'm having a Fourth of July party if you head south around that time. You can park Pearl in the yard. It'll be like old times."

Suddenly, I wanted that. Wanted her here. Jordan had been under my skin since day one, despite the lies I told myself.

"We'll see," she said on a yawn. I looked at my watch—we'd been talking for hours.

"Damn, I guess I better let you go. It's late and I'm on shift tomorrow."

"Oh, okay. Wow, I didn't realize the time." She laughed softly. "I guess I better finish this edit so I can go play tomorrow."

"This has been fun, Skippy. It was good to hear your voice."

"Yeah, it's been good to catch up, much better than through text. I guess I've been a little homesick for everyone there. I didn't mean to talk your ear off."

"You didn't. I enjoyed it. I'm here if you ever, you know, feel like you're getting too homesick." And now I sounded like a fucking teenager. I needed to shut the hell up before I said too much.

But talking to her felt so right.

"Don't be a stranger, okay?" I said.

"Okay. Have a good shift tomorrow. Maybe you'll call me and tell me about your day? I miss hearing your stories."

And just like that, I knew I was fucked. Everything Jordan did called to me and made me want to spend more and more time talking with her.

The three weeks that Jordan had been gone had been long and lonely. If she'd been homesick on the road, then I was homesick for her. Maybe not her, but the company she provided.

Nothing had been the same after Jordan. Life went back to normal, but suddenly everything seemed lackluster. Ball games were boring to watch. The house was too quiet. Coffee on the back deck didn't hit the same.

One evening I'd noticed the scuffs on my kitchen table, so I drug it out to the shed to sand it down and re-stain it. That project led to me redoing the tops of my coffee table and end tables as well. From there I made a list. The kitchen counters needed to be refinished. The walls needed a fresh coat of paint. The bathroom needed updating. The deck needed to be pressure washed and resealed. Even the floors needed to be redone.

I had plenty of stuff to do to keep me busy, each project I ticked off the list more satisfying than the last. I left Jordan's room alone, not wanting to disturb the lingering memory of her. As if I redid that room, I'd be erasing the last of her being here.

I'd get to it eventually, just not yet.

And if I paused at the doorway of her bathroom, where I'd gotten that glimpse of her naked back, it didn't mean anything.

If I remembered her standing at my stove cooking or

sitting with her feet propped on the deck railing, or dancing in the kitchen, it was just a fond memory of the fun times we'd shared.

If I found a pair of her lacy underwear stuck inside a t-shirt, it didn't mean anything that I put it in the drawer where I'd see it every day.

But after hearing her voice, and the resulting ache that settled in my chest after we said goodbye, the truth was hard to ignore. I missed her, and it was way more than just me missing her as a friend. This longing in my soul had to mean something.

Chapter 14

Nate

"Pull that line and let's run some tests on the six-inch LDH," Collins growled around his toothpick.

We were three hours into hose testing, and everyone was over it. I was hungry and tired and hot. The sweltering humidity made breathing a chore. Sweat ran down my face and my shirt clung to me as we pulled down the large diameter hose. Each hose weighed about seventy pounds rolled up, even more with water in it.

And we still had five hoses to test.

Collins slipped his toothpick out, flipping it to the trashcan and grabbed a water, dousing his head with the remains. "I don't know what Chief's problem was, but he crawled up my ass this morning, and made sure to point out that every hose in this station was to be tested today. After that, I want you to make sure all those radios and extra batteries are charged."

We finished hose testing and got everything cleaned up and put away. I had enough time to grab a cold shower and some food before tones started dropping. We were on a medical call for difficulty breathing in a house that looked like it should have been condemned.

Thoren met me at the back of the ambulance, looking back at the house. "I can't believe anyone was even living in this house."

"I hate to see it. I wish there was something we could do." I peeled off my gloves and tossed them into the trash at the back of the bus.

"I know. That one civic group did that silent auction fundraiser. Wonder what they are doing with that money."

I scoffed. "That fundraiser was a joke. It was just a way for people who didn't want to get their hands dirty to feel like they were doing something."

"You sound a little bitter about it."

I sighed. "I'm not bitter. Well, maybe a little. That whole situation was a fucking joke. I wanted to join a group to do some real hands-on work."

"So, what I'm hearing you say is that you are going to do something about it instead of waiting on someone else?" Thoren raised a brow at me, calling me on my bullshit.

I squared my shoulders. He was right. If I wanted to see a change, I needed to be the one to make it happen.

We loaded the patient and climbed back into the truck. I took one last look at the house before pulling away.

I had the tools and the skills. Maybe I could do some good and help some of these people out.

That idea rattled around in my head the entire way back to the station.

Later that night at the station, I was getting my bed made when Jordan called. We'd gotten into the habit of checking in nearly every night.

"Hey Skippy, what's happening?"

"Nothing much, just sitting here finishing a project. How's your day?"

"Pretty good."

We chatted about regular stuff for a bit, teasing and playful, until she paused and said, "So, I was thinking about heading down to your party."

"Really?" I couldn't stop the smile that spread across my face.

"Yeah, you mind if I park Pearl at your place? I mean, if it's a problem, I can park somewhere else. Leah says Thoren has lots of property and he probably wouldn't mind."

"You aren't parking Pearl at Thoren's," I demanded.

"Who's parking what at my house?" Thoren stuck his head in my room.

"No one," I said to him at the same time Jordan asked, "Is he there? Maybe I should ask him."

I pulled my phone away and put it on speaker. "Jordan, you're on speaker, so that you and Thoren can both hear this at the same time. Thoren, if Jordan asks to park her van at your place, you tell her no. She's coming to my house."

"But what if I want her to park at my house?" Thoren shot me a smirk.

"That doesn't matter. She's parking at mine."

"But what about what I want? Doesn't that factor in?" Jordan's soft voice cut through my bullshit. And damn. Look at me being an overbearing asshole. Forcing what I wanted, instead of considering her wants.

Thoren raised his brows at me, as if to say, this one's on you, and gave me a finger wave as he walked out of the bunk room.

I clicked the phone off speaker and put it back to my ear, feeling all sorts of confused. Why was I acting like this?

"Damn, Skippy. You know how to cut a guy." I pinched the bridge of my nose, feeling like a total shit.

"I'm not trying to make you feel a certain way. I'm just asking. Does it matter to you what I want? And why?"

I swallowed thickly. "Of course it matters. How about this? You just tell me what your plan was, and I'll shut up and color."

She laughed a little. "Honestly, I don't have a problem staying at your place. I don't want to be a problem for you and get in your way."

Gripping the back of my neck, I studied my shoes. I needed to come clean with Jordan and tell her how much I missed her and wanted her around. I wasn't sure why I hadn't told her yet. Maybe because it was safer for me if she kept things platonic. Which was such a pussy thing to think, especially when I was the one rubbing one out every night to the memory of her.

"So, uh. That's not really an issue that you need to worry about."

"Of course it is, Nate." Her voice was low and concerned and struck a nerve somewhere deep within me.

"No, it's not. I don't think I'd ever get tired of you being around," I admitted.

I heard a rustle through the phone and her voice went soft. "Did I ever tell you about Gerry?"

I stretched out on my bed, bracing my head on my arm. Did I want to hear about her ex? Not really. But then again, I wanted to know everything about her. "No, we never talked about him."

"I guess we never talked about relationships. But anyway. Gerry and I had been together for a couple of years. We were living the dream, planning on getting married. Then one day, I came home from work unexpectedly and found him in bed with another woman."

"Damn." What kind of fool would cheat on Jordan? "What'd you do?"

"Oh, what any irrational woman does. But that isn't the important part. I've been thinking while I've been on this trip. About *why* he felt like he needed to do that."

"And?"

"And I thought about calling him to get some closure on it."

"That sounds like a very mature thing to do," I said, unable to bite back the snark.

"I can't move forward until I sort this out."

"See, this is the difference between men and women. You guys need to process and have closure. I'd have made a decision and moved on. You don't need him, even the memory of him. He was a fool, and you should just let it go."

Jordan sighed in frustration. "Okay, you go on doing your manly man thing and bury everything. Meanwhile, the rest of us will continue to emotionally evolve. But whatever. You do you."

Her frustration with me didn't settle well. I cleared my throat and dropped my hand to make sure my nuts were still intact.

"Are you pissed at me?"

Laughter filled my ear. "No, Nate. You just keep on living your life the way you want and continue ignoring everything."

"I'm sensing some sarcasm here."

"Look at you, being all smart. Picking up on clues and stuff. Listen. I'm tired and this conversation is just going to lead nowhere. I'll let you go, talk to you tomorrow." And with that, she hung up on me.

As I pulled my phone away to confirm that she really did hang up on me, Thoren popped his head around the corner.

"Everything okay?" His brows lifted at my expression.

"No. She hung up on me."

"What did you do?" He braced a shoulder on the doorframe.

"We were talking about her ex, and then she essentially told me off, and hung up on me."

Thoren's brow creased. "Well? Were you rude?"

I sat up, bracing my elbows on my knees, and hung my head. "Not really. I think I got a little pissed off when she mentioned talking to her ex."

"Are you jealous?"

Was I?

Why should it matter if she got some closure on a relationship? It wasn't like we were dating. I had no claim on her at all, other than us being friends. And I obviously needed to remember that. I pushed off and stood, taking a step toward Thoren.

"Nah, man. I'm not jealous. Jordan and I are just friends."

I brushed past him on my way out to the bay. I didn't have a lot to offer Jordan. She had these dreams of traveling, and I loved my job and couldn't go with her. Even if I felt like she understood me better than anyone and she'd been the only person to show me they cared in forever.

Jordan and I were just friends, and I needed to remember that.

Chapter 15

Jordan

Sandi was waiting for me when I strolled into the bustling coffee shop near Dad's center. I'd already said my tearful goodbyes with Dad before his rehab session. My visit with them had healed a piece of my soul, but it was already late June and although I'd loved my time with them, it was time to move along and see something new.

She greeted me with a hug, and then pushed a paper bag into my hand.

"I figured you didn't eat breakfast yet, so I grabbed you something for the road."

"Thanks, I'm sure I'll dig into it about a hundred miles or so from now."

"Which way are you headed this time, or have you even decided yet?"

I grinned. Of course, she would know I didn't have an actual plan.

She shook her head at me, a wry grin playing at her lips. "You are so much like Waylon, it's not even funny. That wanderlust is just as alive in you as it was him back in the day."

"Thanks, I guess?" I said, oddly complimented by her statement.

"Well, you are different in a couple of ways. You need more structure, and he was always flying by the seat of his pants."

I chuckled at her massive eyeroll, and the memory of my dad in his earlier years.

"But," she continued, reaching a hand up to tuck a lock of hair behind my ear, "I think you need more roots than he did. You need that soft place to land, people you love around you regularly."

I nodded. "Dad said the same thing. And it makes sense."

"I think it's a part of the reason he and your mom split up. She hated traveling, and he loved it. It's part of why we worked so well. But the other part of that is that we have always been friends."

I considered her words for a moment. Sandi had been so good for my dad. "I think I resented that you two had that shared love."

"I know. I tried to make it better—to build that bridge and encourage you to join us, but a lot of times your mom wouldn't allow it. I bet she never mentioned we wanted you to join us, did she?"

I tried to recall a time that my mom had ever told me they invited me to join them on a trip and couldn't bring anything to mind. Most of my memories were of her talking bad about them, until I finally quit listening to her poisoning. By then, Dad had been in the accident, and I was too ashamed to reach out.

"I think you needed stability. That's why you chose that Gerry fella, though he wasn't right for you."

I tilted my head to the side, interested in her opinion, because it was the exact opposite of what my mother preached. "What makes you say that?"

"He was in an established career and had his own place. He was a safe choice for you. But he wasn't the man for you. I can tell because you aren't destroyed over the loss of him. You don't feel like you left a part of yourself with him."

I traced a trail of condensation trickling down the side of the plastic cup of my iced coffee with my thumb while I pondered what she'd said.

Did she have a point? Was she right?

Leaving Gerry had been liberating, like I'd broken free of a mold not made for me.

I met Sandi's tender gaze. "I've been thinking about what I could have done differently. I think I didn't know my own self. I tried to be what I thought he wanted me to be. So, it was a real slap in the face to be set aside and replaced, to be cheated on and treated like I didn't matter. But now, I think the cheating part hurts more than the actual break up did, if that makes any sense."

She slid her hand over mine. "I get it, honey. You deserve a man and a love that puts you above all else. Don't settle. But to do that, you have to know yourself first."

I nodded.

"And someday, you'll find a man. If you're lucky, he will be your best friend, and you won't have to change or hide a single thing about yourself. He will appreciate you for all of you. Warts and all."

Immediately, my mind jumped to Nate.

From the very start, I'd felt like he'd known me. Could see the real me.

Sandi tightened her hand, drawing my attention. "What was that thought?"

"I'm sorry, what?"

"You just got the dreamiest look on your face." Her kind eyes were glowing, a smile tilting her lips up.

I shrugged. "Do you remember me telling you about the guy who rescued me that night of the storm?"

Her eyes sparkled, her face lit with excitement. "The hot firefighter?"

"I never said he was hot, did I?" My cheeks burned with embarrassment.

"Oh, honey, you didn't have to say the exact words. But your description of him, the way you light up when you speak of him, leads me to believe that there might possibly be something more there?"

I wadded up my napkin, examining the paper like it held all the answers. Suddenly afraid to admit out loud that, yes, maybe there could be something more with Nate. "If I don't say it out loud, that means it's not true, right?"

Sandi's brows knit together. "Don't you want it to be?"

All around the cozy shop, people chatted, the barista called out orders, the door constantly opening and closing with an endless carousel of customers. Those people seemed a world apart from our little wooden table and the suddenly heavy conversation.

"I don't know." I slipped my hand from hers and wiped my sweaty palm on my leg. "He scares me a little. I wouldn't want to lose the friendship. But I also don't want to lose myself and get hurt in the process if things go sideways. Plus, I feel like I need to reach out and talk to Gerry about why he did what he did."

Her expression softened. "Is talking it over with Gerry

really going to help? Because I don't think it will. Or are you just scared and running from Nate?"

I waited, sensing she had more to say.

"I think you should let it go with Gerry. It'll only cause you more hurt. And if you're scared, you just take it slow with Nate. But don't give up on the relationship before you ever give it a chance. You talk a good bit now, don't you? Maybe up your flirting game a little and see how he responds."

I groaned. "Well, I would, but we sort of got into an argument today."

"Oh honey, that will work itself out," she said with an eye roll, leaning back in her chair. "Normal couples argue, it's actually a healthy thing to do. What you do is apologize..." She leaned forward and lowered her voice. "...and then, start sending him some racy pictures."

My jaw dropped. "Sandi, I am not just going to start randomly sending him nudes. That's creepy."

"You could 'accidentally' send him one." She made air quotes around the word, eyes sparkling mischievously.

"No." I fixed her with a stern look.

She chuckled. "I'm teasing. Just, you know, like, include a bare leg in a shot every once in a while. Or some cleavage, or maybe do that Instagram shot where you take off your sports bra and take a picture of your naked back." She waggled her eyebrows at me, cracking me up.

"Maybe I'll do that. Although, I will say, it makes me feel weird that I'm considering propositioning my friend."

Weird and thrilled and scared all at the same time.

Laughing, she reached over and captured my hand again. "Having your best friend become your lover is the best." She grew quiet, her expression turning wistful, her gaze traveling over my face. "It has been so great to spend some time with you. I've missed you, Jordan. You must let me know when you send him pictures and what his reaction is."

I flipped my hand over to hold hers. Had my own mother ever been so supportive of me? Why had I missed out on having a relationship with this sweet woman and my dad? It was time to stop letting the past dictate my future.

"Sandi..." I started, needing to apologize, but not finding words to say all I had on my heart. She squeezed my hand, her eyes swimming with emotion.

"I know, child. But we can move forward from here. No going back."

A little while later, we hugged and said our goodbyes. I'd already seen my dad, and now it was time to go. But this time, I knew where I was headed, and a peacefulness washed over me. I was going home, and I was going home for Nate. I didn't need to talk to Gerry. Sandi had nailed it. I was using that as an excuse to hold Nate away.

And why? I'd been brave enough to set out on my own, to come on this journey. Why not be brave and take a chance with Nate?

Starting today, it was time to seduce my best friend.

"So, do you always hike shirtless? Or was this a special occasion?" Nate's voice was low and intimate in my ear on our nightly phone call.

"What are you talking about?" I hedged, hoping he'd admit that he'd been stalking my Instagram feed.

"Come on, don't play games with me. Why were you naked in a waterfall, Jordan?"

"It was National Hike Naked Day." I kept my voice flippant, though I gripped my phone, scared to play this game with him. A fission of pleasure skittered across my skin that he'd seen those pictures.

"No, you didn't," Nate growled. My unease unfurled like a ribbon, and a tiny ray of hope sprouted at the jealousy in that growl.

"You should've seen the guy's face when I asked him to take my picture topless." I ventured further, reclined on my bed, on top of the covers, because the night was a little warm.

"No, you didn't," he repeated.

I'd been alone at the waterfall and had set up my tripod and taken some video that I later trimmed to photos and posted. I'd felt so free, so empowered standing out there, just me and the wild.

"Well, at least one of us had pants on, for a little while anyway," I teased, taking perverse pleasure in the possessiveness in Nate's voice. I doubt it even meant anything, but I could pretend.

"Fuck."

My breath hitched, and I pressed my legs together against the sudden arousal caused by the intensity of that groaned word.

"Skippy, you can't post things like that." His voice was deep, intimate in my ear, and it was doing all sorts of sexy things to me.

I twirled a lock of hair around my fingers, coyly, as if he might see me, and shifted my legs, enjoying the delicious slide of skin on skin. It had been way too long since I'd had sex, so long since I'd even had the desire to consider it. His voice had me amped up, and I was pretty sure I could come if he'd just talk dirty to me a little bit.

"Why? Didn't you like them? I thought they were rather

attractive." I replied, sounding husky and breathless to my own ears.

"You sound funny. Are you okay?"

I shifted my legs again, stifling a moan. Somehow this had spiraled wildly out of control. "I'm fine, why?"

The next thing I knew, my phone rang with an incoming video call. I swallowed, glancing down at my tank top and pajama shorts. My nipples were hard pebbles standing out under the white tank.

Were we doing this? Was I taking this opportunity to push the boundaries of our friendship, to see if I could tiptoe us over that line? We both had baggage to sort out, but there was no denying the chemistry between us. I swallowed down my nerves at the thought of making this leap and decided now was as good a time as any to test the waters.

I clicked to accept, and Nate's smiling face filled my screen.

"Hi." I returned his wide smile.

"What are you doing, Skippy?" He raised an eyebrow at me, his smile falling away.

I lifted the phone farther away, so he could get a good view, trailing a finger down my chest. "I'm just lying here, talking to you."

Nate's eyes went dark as he followed the path of my finger.

"Damn, Jordan." He swallowed thickly, gaze trailing over me, drinking me in, before settling on my face again. "I thought we were friends. You could've at least given me a sneak peek of those photos first."

Taking that comment as a positive, I pushed a little harder. I drug my finger back up my torso, rimming my nipple as I pretended to ponder his question.

"You gonna show me what you showed a random stranger at that waterfall?" He said darkly as he shifted in the screen, the angle of the phone changing, giving me a view of his pillow.

Oh God, he was lying in his bed, watching me touch myself. I shifted my legs, again, unable to hold still. "Is that okay with you?" I whispered to him, pulling the phone closer to show only my face.

"Am I fine with you showing me what I've been dreaming about? Absolutely."

He'd been dreaming of me? In this way?

His eyes locked on mine and crinkled at the edges when he smiled. Though he was a thousand miles away, it felt like he was in the room with me.

He pulled his phone away from his face, giving me a shot of his bare torso. Tilting his head at me, he asked, "Are we doing this?"

I swallowed thickly. Things wouldn't be the same between us after this, but I was ready, even if I was nervous.

My gaze roamed his chest. I'd seen him shirtless before, but I took the moment to study the curve of his pecs, the light smattering of hair covering his torso. I trailed my fingertips across my own collarbone, imagining the feel of his skin, shifting the phone so he could watch. Wanting him.

"Yes," I whispered. "We're doing this."

"Does that feel good? Running your fingers over your body? Would you like that to be my fingers right now?" His voice was low and guttural, almost whispered.

I nodded, making the strokes over my torso longer, more languid. How many times had I watched him, and imagined what his touch would feel like?

"I like how you do that, but I want you to move your hand down lower, Jordan."

He was wicked, and I was under his spell. My nerve endings flared to life. My entire body at his command, so aware of every tiny brush of the sheet below me, the soft tank glancing across my nipples, the seam of my shorts pressing into me.

"Skim your fingertips down your breasts, but don't touch your nipples. Just run them right along that gorgeous curve. That's where I'd like to run my nose, soft enough to barely blow a breath across your nipples, to see them peak."

My breath was shallow, almost panting, as I followed his direction. And the bliss of not having to think, to just be, and do as he wished heightened my arousal.

"Good, that's perfect. Now trail your fingers across your belly. Imagine that's my mouth you feel. Tracing that smooth skin with my lips, memorizing you."

Goosebumps skittered across my skin. I whimpered at the image his words conjured, glancing at the screen to make sure he could see most of me.

"Keep drifting that hand down. Now, press your palm. Right there. Between your legs. That's where I want to be right now." He whispered, his seductive assault on my senses halting, as if he was as affected as I was. "Use that pretty little hand and press down on your clit."

The shock of Nate dirty talking me skated over my skin, set me on fire, and I gasped at the pleasure that pressure brought, arching my back to get more.

"Damn, look at you. You are gorgeous." I heard a rustle, then his soft moan. Was he touching himself while he coached me through this?

"Have you ever done this before, Jordan? Have you ever touched yourself while someone watched you?"

I shook my head, catching my lip between my teeth to stifle another moan. I loved this unexpected naughtiness in him.

"That's it, sweetheart." The approval in his tone washed over me, and I pressed harder into the bundle of nerves, wishing it were his hands on my body. "Feel how good that is. Imagine I'm there. I'd slide my hand in your panties and see how wet you are. I bet you are soaked."

Helpless to stop myself, I shifted my hand under the waistband of my shorts, gliding a finger through my folds. So wet. I was so wet, and so needy.

"Now, I want you to slide a finger through that wet pussy and then draw up and circle your clit." He continued guiding me on this exploration.

Coating my fingers, I did as he commanded. A gasp escaped my parted lips as my mouth dropped open. "How does it feel?"

"I'm so warm, and wet." I barely recognized the husky voice as my own.

"God damn, you are so sexy. If I was there, I'd drape your legs over my shoulders and run my tongue down your crease and suck your clit. I'd slide my fingers deep inside you and..."

I panted, swept away imagining his head between my legs, the feel of his hands instead of mine, his mouth on me, tongue in me. Mirroring his words with my hands, I dipped a finger inside myself, arching, moaning, needing more.

"Open your eyes and look at me." His demand cut through my passion, and I focused on him, on his arm moving off screen. The shift of his muscles, contracting rhythmically.

"See what you do to me? You've got me imagining it's

your hand clamped around my dick, pumping me hard, while my fingers are buried in you."

Needing more, I dipped my fingers deep again, picturing his fingers spreading my wetness over my clit.

"That's it, sweetheart. Rub harder, a little faster. Now arch your back for me and spread your legs a little wider."

I'd never felt so in tune to a person that the sound of his voice was as erotic as his was in that moment. Every word he said, every demand he made, was connected to the orgasm building in me.

"Now, bury those fingers in that tight pussy, in and out, as deep and hard as you can. Picture my fingers there, I'm the one driving you wild. You're so close. I can feel you tightening around my fingers."

Holy shit.

I arched and pumped, grinding myself on my hand. The thrill of his voice, knowing he was watching me, washed over me.

"That's it, baby. Come for me."

I pulled my fingers out and circled my clit again, igniting the orgasm, gasping his name as it washed over me.

"That's it. Oh, goddamn. You are a treasure." His words wrapped around me, filled with an intensity that heightened everything.

"Eyes on me, sweetheart. It's my turn." I opened my eyes to see his head jacked back into his pillow as he gasped his release. He was so fucking hot—I'd have given anything to be with him at that moment.

We both lay panting, staring at each other through the magic of the cell phone, until a smile crept up my face, matching his.

"I've been thinking about you like this for so long,

Jordan." He broke our afterglow, his voice quiet and intimate.

"Really?" I whispered. My heart slammed in my chest for more reasons than the orgasm alone. Was this real? Were we on the same page and ready to move forward? Was our timing right, now?

"I knew it was wrong to be having these feelings and thoughts when you were living with me. But, Jordan, I like you. I like talking to you and spending time with you. And doing this with you, though I'd like to experience it first-hand someday."

A rush of adrenaline, mixed with an acute homesick-ness, flooded my system at his words, overwhelming me. "I like you, too. I feel like you know me better than anyone," I whispered.

"Are you okay with what just happened?"

I rolled to my side, getting comfortable, propping the phone on the pillow next to me. "Am I okay with having an orgasm? Yes. Do I wish you were here? Also, yes."

What I wouldn't give to be able to lean in close for a kiss or nestle in the warmth of his embrace.

In the little box on the screen, Nate shifted his pillow. "I know. I wish you were here too. But you'll be home soon, right?"

I nodded, smiling at his use of the word. "Yes, I'll be home soon."

Chapter 16

Nate

Nightly video calls with Jordan the next week became my favorite thing. Knowing that I'd get to process my day with her every evening made even the minor frustrations through the day seem more manageable.

She'd surprised the hell out of me that first night, when I called after getting pissed off about her social media pictures. She'd taken them down the next day, and I let her know how much I appreciated that.

We hadn't talked about what would happen when she got back, but I hoped I could convince her to stay with me, preferably in my bed, instead of in Pearl. But it'd be enough to know that she was close by and safe, regardless of where she slept.

I'd never asked someone to live with me, preferring to keep my space my own. But it made sense with Jordan.

She consumed my thoughts. Every day I wondered what she was seeing, experiencing, while she explored. And every night she would give me the rundown. She explored during the day and worked late into the night, sometimes choosing to work while I watched a game, and we were just on the line with each other.

The sound of a hammer banging drew me out of my daydreaming about my favorite distraction. Across the street, a crew ripped up the remains of a rotted deck.

I shook my head to clear it and glanced down at the lumber in the back of my truck.

"You have that stupid grin on your face again," Mike said, rounding the back of my truck. "How's Jordan?"

"Why would you automatically assume I'm thinking about Jordan? I could be measuring this to be cut or taking stock of what we need from the hardware store."

"Because no man ever looked at lumber with that expression," he retorted, slinging a toolbelt on the tailgate before hoisting himself up.

"Right. Okay, lover boy. I forgot you're the king of relationships now that Leah has domesticated you."

His gaze traveled across the yard of the house we were working on, to where Leah was sitting on a swing in the yard with the resident.

"I appreciate you taking the lead on this, man, and including me and Leah on it." Mike's voice was low and gruff. "We'd been feeling pretty helpless, wanting to help, trying to do something, and not really able to find the right way to go about it."

I knew what he meant. We'd all been trying to do something, anything, to help the people that still hadn't had much result in getting repairs made. Most of the people in this neighborhood were lower income, living in shotgun houses, dependent on their property owners. And many of the property owners weren't handling things at all. It'd been nearly two months since the storm. We were stepping in to make sure the tarps on their roofs were still secure. This was our last scheduled stop of the day.

"I get it. It's taken some work to get through to the right people, but finally I was able to make some headway with the leader of that non-profit. I'm hoping I can continue this on a larger scale."

Mike slipped off his work gloves and laid them across his leg. "What do you mean?"

I leaned a hip against the tailgate, anxious about admitting what I'd been doing in the past few weeks. "I filed the paperwork to open a home improvement business. I'm hoping that I can take some side jobs and help some of these people rebuild."

His eyebrows shot up his forehead. "Dude, that's great."

I shrugged. "Maybe? I'm concerned with my timing. That people won't think I'm legit. But I can do small jobs. Mostly, if I take a job, I can subcontract with licensed people, and make sure they are legit for the homeowner."

"Like a project manager, almost?"

"Yeah, a contractor." I was nervous as all hell to step into the role, especially when I knew enough to be dangerous. But I was good at connecting people, and a good judge of character. Mostly though, I had the desire to help, and I figured that had to count for something.

"That's good. You know enough people in this town to know who to ask if someone is legit."

"Yeah, and I'm banking my reputation on it. I live here. These are my people. I'm not going to let someone do shady shit if I can help it. Plus, I can do the small stuff mostly myself."

Mike jumped down from the tailgate. "I think that's great. What made you decide to do this start-up?"

"I don't know. I enjoyed helping Jordan fix up her van. It felt good to do something, to be useful. When she left, I was bored. I started a garden, but it wasn't taking up enough of my spare time. I did some work on my house, fixing it up. And decided that I knew enough to be able to help, and if I don't know how to do something, I know enough people that do."

He clapped a hand to my shoulder. "It's good for you to have something of your own that you love to do."

A knot of tension, worry, released at his approval and support. "I'm hoping it takes off. I like the thought of being my own boss. And I'm not doing it for the money. I just want to help people rebuild."

Mike was nodding and watching me with approval. "I like it, dude. Let me know if you need an extra set of hands. Now, I'm gonna go get my woman." He walked away from me, and I let out a relieved breath.

I hadn't told anyone about my new business venture, just in case it didn't go anywhere, but my pride swelled at the thought of that business certificate I'd gotten in the mail. I was doing this. I was making it happen.

We cleaned up from our workday and spent the evening grilling burgers. When Jordan called, I included the whole group in the video. We didn't talk long though, and I missed our one-on-one time. Most nights, I fell asleep talking to her while she worked. I didn't know what would happen next, but for now, I was enjoying where we were headed.

I was sitting in a recliner at the station when the Chief called my cell phone asking what my location was.

"Nate, I need to see you. Where are you?" his authoritative voice barked in my ear when I answered the call.

"I'm at the station, sir, unless we get a call."

"I'll be there in five."

I walked out to the bay so I'd be waiting when he got

there. If he was going to chew my ass out, I wanted a little bit of privacy while he went about it.

His big shiny SUV pulled around the back of the station, the tinted windows not allowing me to see faces, but I could tell he wasn't alone.

He parked directly behind the engine, and both front doors opened. A tall, dark-haired man climbed out of the passenger side. The rear passenger door popped open, and a child hopped out of the back seat.

The two strangers approached slowly, the little kid taking his father's hand, hiding behind him, as Chief rounded the front of the vehicle.

"Nate, this is Walter Crowley and his son Wesley. Gentlemen, this is Lieutenant Nate Williams. Nate, they have something they'd like to share with you."

The little boy peeked from behind his father. He couldn't have been over eight or ten years old.

Walter stuck his hand out. "Nate, it's a pleasure to meet you."

I stepped forward, taking his hand, giving him a nod. "How can I help you?"

"We don't know each other, but you helped my father."

The little boy poked his head out. "You saved Grandpa."

Walter looked down at Wes, a smile stretched across his face. "Wes, you want to give the firefighter what you brought for him?"

The little boy shifted forward and lifted a picture in his outstretched hand. "This is for you."

I took the photograph and studied it as Walter explained. The photo was of an older man, white hair peeking out from under a fishing hat. A younger version of the little boy, Wes, was at his elbow. They were holding a fish on the line, the grandpa looked to be teaching Wes how to remove the hook. His expression was one of patience as Wes looked not at the fish, but with adoration at his grandfather.

"You were on the call for my father," Walter explained. "He was having a heart attack, and you guys saved him."

I looked back to Walter to see him swallow with effort. His voice trembled on the last few words.

"The day after the tornado?" I asked.

Walter nodded. "We just wanted you to know the difference your effort makes." His words, thick with emotion, slammed into me.

Wesley piped in, "And we wanted to say thank you. Grandpa is almost well enough to go fishing again. He says real soon we can go."

Walter put a hand on his son's head, smiling down at him, the very image of what I thought a proud father looked like. "That's right, kiddo." He looked back at me. "We figured you guys don't get much recognition when things go right. We wanted to let you know how much we appreciate what you do. And to let you know how grateful we are that you were there on the day that my father needed you the most."

It wasn't often that I got to see how I made a difference in someone's life. Too often, calls didn't go well, but every now and then, we were able to get someone back. Emotion and gratitude welled up in my chest.

I studied the photo for another moment, recognizing now that the grandfather was the man we'd helped in the days after the storm. Walter's father had coded in the back of the ambulance on the way to the hospital. But by the time they got him there, he'd had a pulse. Thoren had shared as much, but it was nice to know that he'd survived surgery as well.

I looked back to Walter and Wesley, catching Walter blinking rapidly. His throat bobbed with a swallow.

"Wes and Dad have lots more fishing to do because you were there that day." He looked down at his boy. "Right, son?"

Wes nodded and inched his way toward me, looking back over his shoulder at his dad. I squatted so that I'd be less intimidating as he got close.

"Can I give you a hug?" he asked.

"Sure, buddy."

Wes's little body slammed into mine and I rocked back before wrapping my arm around him.

"Thanks for saving my Gramps."

My heart burst at his sweet little voice. Son of a bitch, these two had me all up in my feels.

I gave Wes a squeeze. "You're welcome, buddy. You enjoy fishing with your grandpa. And stop back by sometime and let me know if you catch a big one."

I slipped my hands in my pockets as they drove away, taking a moment to compose myself. This was why I did my job. I'd entered my profession just wanting to make a difference. Knowing that I had a part in a little kid getting to go fishing again with his grandpa, that a family still had time with their loved one, and it was a direct result of my actions, was humbling. I absorbed their gratitude, thankful for the validation that I was doing exactly what I'd always felt called to do.

Chapter 17

Nate

"We're headed to the Alamo for some pizza and cold beer later, you in?" Mike asked, placing the last of the tools in the back of the truck. We'd finally finished this deck repair project.

It'd been a long week of hard work, first removing the old, damaged deck, and then rebuilding the new one. I had several other remodeling projects lined up as my new business gained traction by word of mouth.

Exhaustion seemed to be my norm. Between the back-breaking jobs, the long shifts at the station where call volume was on the rise, and my late-night talks with Jordan, I was ready for the weekend and some down-time.

"I don't know, man. I need to do some stuff around my house. The July Fourth party is only a week away. Plus, I need to get things picked up before Jordan gets here. I haven't had much time to keep things up, we've been so busy."

"Well, you still gotta eat," he argued.

"I'll let you know," I replied, trying to be noncommittal, hoping he'd let it go.

He bumped a hand against the top of the truck bed and sighed. "All right, but it's Cal's turn for first round, and you know that cheap bastard needs to pay for skipping out last time."

Cal was notorious for leaving the bar tab for someone else. It'd serve him right to get stuck footing the bill for once.

"You're right. I'll be there."

Mike thumped the truck again and turned away. "See you there."

I walked into the Alamo an hour later to see Mike with his arm wrapped over Leah's shoulder. Though I hadn't planned on it, and didn't really feel like being out, spending another evening alone felt sort of pathetic. It'd do me some good to try to be social. Mike smirked as I nodded from the doorway and bent to Leah's ear. I waved as she looked toward me and then stopped by the bar to get a beer before heading to their table.

One thing I loved about this bar was its cool atmosphere. The interior walls of the one-hundred-year-old building were original, exposed brick. Arched windows and antique-looking light fixtures, combined with the vintage beer signs, gave the whole place an eclectic vibe. In a previous era, the place had been a theater—the old red velvet curtain still hung at the stage.

The bar itself was a polished slab of wood, lined by wrought iron and wood chairs. The new owner had done a great job of restoring the building to its former glory, while adding in a few modern touches, like the strand of LED lights that ran under the edge of the bar, and an updated sound system. He'd even hung a vintage disco ball over the lower level that doubled as a dance floor.

Laughter rose from our regular table where my friends gathered. Thoren stood with Cal, scowling at Kylie, who was draped over some guy I didn't know. I grabbed my beer and made my way to them, giving Mike a quick chin lift. Leah was gesturing animatedly to the woman in front of her.

Curious, I made my way closer. The woman wore a red bandana printed dress, held together by a simple knot over her exposed back and tight enough to display her curves. Whoever she was, it was clear she wasn't wearing a bra and had a killer body.

I did a double take at the blonde curls. The woman looked a lot like—

Was Jordan sitting in that chair laughing with Leah? But that didn't make sense, Jordan wasn't due for another week.

Cal and Thoren stood on the other side of the table, and Cal tipped his beer at me, calling, "Nate, it's about fucking time you got here."

The woman turned in her seat, giving me a profile view as she first looked at Cal, then turned my way.

Shining, joyful eyes met mine, and her face split into a wide grin. Jordan jumped down from the seat and ran to me, screaming, "Surprise!" She hit me square in the chest and wrapped her arms around me. Mine closed instinctively around her, my palm landing on her bare back. Sizzles ran up my arm, and my dick jumped to life.

For over three weeks, we'd shared intimate phone calls, and I'd jacked off at least daily, if not twice daily, to thoughts of her. That she was here, when I'd thought she was another week out, was a huge surprise, and I was reeling.

"What are you doing here?" I asked stupidly.

She tried to pull away, and I stopped her by gripping

her waist. She was here. This was real. All I could do was stare down into her beautiful eyes and not let her go.

She looked up at me with an expression that stole my breath. Happy. She was happy to be with me. "I missed you, so I skipped a part of my trip and got here early. Is that okay?" she asked quietly, almost shyly. My heart flipped over in my chest.

Wrapping my arms around her, I buried my face in her neck, breathing in the scent I'd missed so much. I ran my hands up and down the smooth skin of her back, wanting more. Every naughty phone call we'd had, every fantasy I'd jerked off to, none of it compared to having her in my arms. I lifted her feet off the floor, her squeals of delight lighting me up inside.

"It's perfect. You are perfect. I missed you." I pressed my lips to her throat, wanting to take her lips in a kiss—one that would burn us both to the ground—but I was vaguely aware we had an audience. I didn't want our entire friend group to witness our first kiss. That kiss should be special and sweet and just between the two of us.

Crazy to think I'd been sharing orgasms with this woman and hadn't tasted her yet.

She lifted her head, so I set her feet back to the floor, but didn't release her. She pulled away slightly, hands framing my face, then she was pulling me down, and pressing those perfect lips of hers to mine.

And I lost my fucking mind.

The moment her lips hit mine, all thought, all care about who might be watching just...vanished. She tasted cool, refreshing, maybe like the seltzer she preferred. Her lips brushed mine once, twice, then her tongue glided across my lips. I opened to her, shifting a hand to her head, gripping her hair and tilting her head as I dove my tongue into her mouth. I ran my other hand down that glorious expanse of smooth skin on her back, until I had a perfect cheek in my hand.

I turned her head to one side, then the other, tipping her just the way I needed to delve into her hungry mouth. Our tongues collided, thrusting and licking, exploring each other. Each slide more ravenous than the next.

I could spend the rest of my life kissing this woman and die a happy man.

A cat-call whistle broke the spell. "Get a room!"

"Damn, what a kiss!"

Shouts carried over the roar of blood pumping through my veins. I pulled back to look into her eyes. Her lips were plump and wet, her tongue peeped out, licking a spot of moisture. Heavy lidded eyes gazed at me from her dazed expression.

She should always have that look on her face.

I dipped low to whisper in her ear, nipping her lobe with my teeth while I was there. "Best surprise ever."

I stood, grinning at her, sliding my hand to cup her neck so I could swipe my thumb across her jaw.

A seductive smile spread over her face as she backed away from me, clasping my hand and tugging me toward the table. I grabbed my beer and positioned myself directly behind her chair so I could block the view of her back from the rest of the men in the bar. My position did double duty to hide the erection I was sporting.

Dinner talk carried us for a while, then the DJ set up and couples started moving to the dance floor. I dropped my hands to Jordan's shoulders, my thumb caressing a knot at the base of her neck. She moaned and tipped her head to the side, giving me better access.

After a minute, she twisted in her chair, her eyes locking with mine.

"You ready to go?" I asked, ready to get her home and show her all the ways I'd missed her.

She glanced at the dance floor. "I was hoping we might dance before we get out of here."

I needed to get her home and spend all night discovering her body. Instead, I stepped back and offered my hand, wrapping my fingers around her delicate hand when she placed it in mine. We joined the other couples swaying to a slow country song.

I spun Jordan out, then pulled her back to me, using the dance to my advantage, stealing touches every chance I could. Relishing the way she leaned into my chest with her arms looped around my shoulders.

"Pretty sure I haven't stopped smiling all night." I leaned in to press a kiss to her cute nose, happy that she was here, and that I could kiss her all I wanted.

"I'm glad Mike could persuade you to come down here. Otherwise, I was going to just show up at your door and waste my cute outfit." The light from the disco ball overhead bathed her in a warm glow.

"You do look beautiful. I should have told you that the moment I saw you." I was an ass for not complimenting her sooner. She should be reminded every day that she was the most beautiful woman in the world.

I splayed my palm between her shoulder blades, my other, I dug in at her hip, pulling her hips closer to mine. She grinned up at me as I spun us around in a circle, enjoying the way our legs and hips brushed as we moved in time to the song. I glanced down to where the fabric of her dress draped over her breasts, teasing at what lay beneath.

"I do like this dress."

"Thanks, Kylie let me borrow it. I hid at her house today when I got in so I could get ready. I was so nervous until you walked through that door." Her thumb brushed the nape of my neck.

"Why were you nervous, sweetheart? We're on the same page here, aren't we?" I shot her a lascivious grin. "We have been having some rather graphic phone calls lately."

An adorable blush stole over her features. She bit down on her bottom lip, the v between her brows puckering. "I don't know why I was nervous. And maybe nervous isn't the right word. Maybe...excited is a better term." Her eyes glittered, her entire face lit with excitement.

I knew that feeling. I'd been over the moon thinking I would see her in a week. "So, where is Pearl? I didn't see her when I pulled in."

"She's around back. Kylie hadn't planned on coming tonight, so I had to drive on the off chance that you didn't show, and I needed to hunt you down."

"You're telling me there is a bed right outside?" I teased.

She grinned at me. "That's what I'm telling you."

I broke my hold and lunged toward the exit. Jordan laughed and tugged my hand back.

"Not until I finish my dance. I've never danced with you, and I'm kind of liking it. I didn't know you could move so well."

"Sweetheart, there's a lot of things you don't know about me...yet." I drifted a hand up her ribcage to brush my thumb under her breast. "But you'll learn some of those things tonight."

She sucked in a sharp breath, her nipples puckered under the thin material.

I slid my hand down her back pressing her closer. "You'll learn how much those dirty little phone calls have been driving me crazy." I brushed my nose along the curve of her neck, breathing in her sweet scent. "You'll learn what it feels like to have my mouth and my tongue on you." I nipped kisses along her jaw. "I'll learn what it feels like to slide deep inside of you. Fuck, Jordan, I've been waking up hard every day to dreams of you."

I brushed the corner of her lips with a teasing kiss, then hovered there, just out of reach. "I can't wait to learn every inch of you." She groaned, tugging my head down to hers, sliding her tongue into my mouth, licking at me like a starving woman.

"You ready to go now?" I asked against her lips.

She pulled away, her eyebrows high on her forehead. "Are we going to fuck in Pearl?" My dick punched the fly of my jeans in response to her choice of words.

"We are going to fuck on this dance floor if we don't leave right now," I declared.

She led me off the floor, laughing, straight to our table where she grabbed her bag on the fly.

"Bye, guys." She called over her shoulder, laughing as she slid under my arm and wrapped hers around my back. A second later, her hand slipped into the back pocket of my jeans, squeezing my ass.

I leaned close, my lips brushing her ear. "Keep it up, Skippy. You want to make it out of here with all your clothes on?"

Her giggle wrapped around me. Some weight I hadn't known I was carrying just...lifted away. This feeling must be happiness. I grinned the whole way to the front door.

As the cool night air hit my skin, Jordan spun around, grabbing my hand, walking backwards, pulling me along. Her gaze scanned over me, and a devilish grin played about her lips. "Pearl is around back. Also, I'm not wearing any panties."

I groaned. I was so close to being inside her, to having all of her, it was almost unbearable. Closing the distance between us, I dipped low, hugging her hips and lifting her up, bringing her breasts right to my face. "We better find her quick."

Chapter 18

Jordan

Nate pushed me onto the bed inside my van, my decorative pillows cast to the floor with one swipe of his hand, like he couldn't be bothered to stop long enough to care.

I opened my legs and pulled him by the shoulders down on top of me, his weight a delicious pressure. He kissed me like his soul was on fire, and I the only remedy. Hands raced over my body like he couldn't get enough. It was a heady feeling knowing he was so close to losing control. What would push him, make him go wild on me?

We tumbled over each other, a mash of seeking tongues, and impatient fingers. Every drugging kiss deeper than the one before, every touch more sensual, until I was panting and rubbing my bare crotch against his dick, soaking the denim between us. I never wanted this moment to end.

Nate broke the kiss, leaving us both panting, and rolled, pulling me over him.

I sat up, straddling his hips, and immediately my body begged for more, my hips moving, pressing into the seam of his jeans. Just a little more and...his big hands found my hips and stopped my grinding.

"Fuck, Jordan," he growled.

The deep timber of his voice shimmered over me, through me. I reached for the button on his jeans and slid the zipper down, the sound loud in the quiet of the van. I needed him. Now.

As I slid my hand in his jeans, eager to feel him, voices sounded outside the van. The thrill of getting caught ratcheted up my excitement.

His hand fell on mine, stilling me.

"Skippy, I hate myself for saying this, but we need to pump the brakes right now."

I raised a brow at him as anticipation swelled. "Oh, we definitely need to pump something, but I don't know if it's the brakes." I gave him a solid stroke over his underwear. Finally, finally getting my hands on him. How many nights had I imagined this? He was every bit as solid as I'd imagined he'd be.

His eyes glittered with mischief as he thrust into my hand. "You dirty girl. You'd like to get caught right now, wouldn't you?"

I bit my lip as I gave him a squeeze, tightening my thighs at his waist, enjoying the sound of his groan and the way he arched into my touch, shimmying his jeans down his hips, freeing his erection. I braced my arm at his shoulder, so ready for there to be nothing between us. A shift of fabric and I began rubbing my wetness over his hard length, my hair a curtain around us.

"Fucking A, you feel so good," he rasped, as his dick kicked against me. I ground down on him, bending to devour his mouth, riding him, needing him inside me.

The van shook as if someone was rocking it. I sat up. The window curtains were drawn, a hint of light filtering around the edges. Laughter blasted from outside the window, and the van rocked again.

"Son of a—" Nate shifted me off him, and stood, tucking himself back into his jeans, headed for the door.

"What are you doing?" I called.

"I'm going to go bust some faces." He shoved a hand in his hair, paused like he was contemplating busting the door open.

"Just ignore them." I leaned back on my elbows and let my bent legs fall open, hoping like all hell that I looked tempting and sexy, and not totally ridiculous. His hungry gaze stole over me, like he wanted to eat me alive.

"I've got a better idea. Why don't we drive Pearl to my house, and then we can test out multiple surfaces?"

Intrigued, I bit my lip. "Multiple surfaces, huh?"

The residual frustration drained away from his face, and he was back to heated teasing. "I've made some upgrades since you left."

I reached over and nabbed the keys from my bag, flipping them to him. "Well, by all means, let's go check out these surfaces."

Pulling into Nate's drive felt surreal. Hell, riding in the passenger seat of Pearl was weird enough, but knowing that we were headed back to his place to finally do the deed was both heady and nerve wracking.

It'd been a long time since I'd been intimate with a man, much less been naked in front of one. Hell, Gerry and I had pretty much been on a schedule and most of our sexual relationship was spent in the dark. The day I walked in to find him tied to the bed with another woman dripping hot wax on him had opened my eyes to more than the fact that my fiancé was cheating on me. I'd left feeling like I'd never really known him, nor myself.

Nate and I were friends. And if our blazing hot naked phone calls were any sign, he liked what I had. But being on the phone and being naked in person were totally different in my brain, and I suddenly found myself wiping my palms on my skirt and trying to calm my heart rate.

What if he thought I was ugly?

What if he thought I was desperate?

What if I was bad at sex and that's why Gerry strayed?

"I see you thinking over there, Skippy. What gives? You having second thoughts?" Nate's voice was gentle, the darkness lending intimacy to the van. It was like the night he'd come to pick me up from the shelter. Like how we'd started this friendship, sitting in quiet darkness.

His warm hand landed on my bare thigh. I was sure it was meant to be a comforting touch, but the sensation of his thumb, scrapping across the sensitive flesh sent heat straight through me.

Parked in his driveway, there was no outside light to break the dark.

I swallowed heavily. Nate was my friend. He'd always been straight with me. Even now, he was patiently waiting on me. No pressure, just being his normal, steady presence. Still, nerves made my voice tremble when I finally found the courage to answer. "I'm not having second thoughts. But I am having thoughts."

Without a word, he exited the car. I watched as he crossed in front of Pearl, opening my door and offering me a hand and helping me down. The door closed softly behind me as he pulled me close to his side, holding my hand, leading me out to the fence at the edge of the yard.

And something about that simple gesture, just walking in the night air, holding hands, settled my nerves.

"After you left, I'd find myself walking out here late at night." Nate's hushed voice melded with the background of nighttime creature noises, crickets and frogs singing their evening tune. The contrast of this gentle silence versus the bar with the loud music and crowd was deafening.

I nodded, though he couldn't see me.

"Sometimes I thought about work, sorting out problems and to-do lists. Sometimes I thought about projects I need to do around here." We reached the fence and he turned to lean his back against it, tucking me between his legs. "Most times, I thought about you."

"Me?" I studied his eyes in the moonlight.

The corners of his mouth tipped up, and his palm cupped my cheek, his thumb brushing gently across my jawline. His gaze traveled over my face as if he was memorizing me.

"I spent many nights thinking about you. Worried that you were safe. Worried that you were scared. I thought about you constantly. Thinking that maybe if I had been more open, had told you that I wanted you to stay, you never would've left."

"Nate..."

His thumb touched my lips to halt me.

"But I think you needed to leave. And I needed to wake up to see what I had in front of me."

My heart pounded in my chest. He was speaking so softly I had to strain to hear, but every one of his words crossed the chasm in my heart that Gerry had created, filling that part of me that needed to be loved. That needed acceptance and support and understanding. That needed to know I was worth the work, worth the wait.

He pulled my face close to his, barely brushing his lips over the corner of my mouth.

"What do you see?" I whispered, clutching at his shirt for dear life.

"I see a woman who listens to me. Who cares for me and accepts me as I am. A woman who takes the time to appreciate life, all of it, big things and small." He peppered my face with kisses then pulled back, looking me in the eyes. "I see my best friend."

My heart melted to a puddle at his feet. How could I have ever thought he would be anything but wonderful? I knew him. He knew me. "I'm sorry I got nervous."

He kissed me again. "Don't be. Hell, if I'm honest, I'm nervous too." He wrapped his arms around me, snugging me up to his chest, and I felt so cherished with that simple movement.

"Really?" I whispered to his shirt.

"Of course I am. What if you get weird and start making farm animal sounds or something in the middle of it?"

I slapped his chest. "Oh my God, you turd."

"What if you have like some funky body hair, or a third nipple? Not that it would be a problem if you did, just give me a heads up so I'm not surprised."

I laughed at his stupid jokes.

His shoulders shook with mirth. "Seriously, warn a guy, okay?"

"You're a jerk. I'm not talking to you," I said, trying hard to stop laughing.

He clutched my hands, entwining my fingers, leaning back to look at me.

"Seriously, Jordan. I'm just happy you are here. I missed you so much. Whatever happens between us...I'm just glad you're back."

I smiled at him then, all nervousness gone. This was my sweet Nate. I'd lost half my heart to him before, and I was in serious danger of losing it all to him now.

"So, what's really got you nervous?" he asked.

I opened my mouth to tell him I was fine, but instead all my insecurities poured out. "What if you think I'm bad at it? Or you don't like the way I look?"

His hand brushed over my hair, tucking an errant tendril behind my ear. "So, you're saying you really do have a third nipple?"

My forehead hit his chest and I busted out laughing. "No, I'm saying that I'm scared I won't be the perfect woman you have imagined. The last man I was intimate with cheated on me, and now I feel like something is wrong with me, even though he was the one that cheated."

He lifted my chin with a thumb, planting a soft kiss on my nose.

"Sweetheart, you are everything to me. You make every day brighter just by being in it. If we have sex or not, you are still more important to me than you'll ever know. Sex between us will be amazing. And I do want us to take that step. But having you in my life is what matters most," he said intently.

"Being able to hold you." His arms tightened, snuggling me closer. "Being able to kiss you." He kissed my forehead. "Being able to talk to you, and laugh with you, and share an evening with you." He moved his lips to mine, and laid a long, lingering kiss there. "Those are the things that matter most to me right now. The rest can wait."

I cupped his cheek and kissed him back, pressing my body against his, tears gathering in my eyes.

"He was a fool," Nate whispered, "and if I could take away that hurt from you, I would. But you have to know, I think you are beautiful inside. The gorgeous package you are wrapped in is a bonus."

How could I have doubted this connection between us? I'd felt it from the start. Nate saw to the heart of me, taking this next step and opening myself up to losing my heart to him was as natural as breathing. I'd run across the country, and he remained under my skin the whole time. He was my person.

I kissed him again, wrapping my arms around his shoulders and going up on tiptoe to get even closer.

Nate hugged me close as our mouths worked to discover each other.

His arms slid down my back then he bent and lifted me up. I wrapped my legs around his hips, burying my hands in his hair. He tasted so good, the feel of his mouth, the glide of his tongue, making me want more. His body was hard against mine, and yet, he was so soft and gentle with me.

With my dress hitched up, the cool night air hit my naked bits, setting me on fire. I needed more. I needed him to make love to me.

I broke the kiss and panted, "Nate, I want you."

He pushed away from the fence and carried me back to the house, pausing at the door to let me slide down the length of his body. He was all hard muscle and strength, and he was mine.

Once inside, he crowded in, forcing my back to the door. I practically purred as he bent his head, hot breath skimming from my shoulder to my ear, rekindling my desire. He reached behind me and clicked the lock on the door.

Something about that simple act of him making sure we were tucked in safe demolished any reservations I still held.

Fisting his shirt, I pulled him to me, sliding my other hand up under his shirt, finally touching his skin the way I'd been dreaming of for so long.

Nate dipped low, dragging the hem of my skirt up my legs, his fingers sliding up my skin in a long slow tantalizing caress, while his mouth left a trail of kisses across my shoulder.

"Fuck, Jordan. You are perfect." He slanted his mouth over mine, his tongue diving in to tangle with mine.

I made a useless needy noise and shifted, raising a leg to wrap around his hips. Now that I'd decided to move forward with sleeping with Nate, my body was ready. Throbbing in heady anticipation. Being pressed to every hard line of his body wasn't enough.

Reaching between us, I unbuttoned his jeans and slid the zipper down, shoving my hands inside and taking his hard length in my hands. I'd been waiting for this, fantasizing over being with him, for so long, that now that it was happening, I wanted to both savor every second of it, and jump him immediately.

He groaned, his hips thrusting sharply against me, his hands diving into my hair where he gripped and tugged my head back.

"I had plans for doing this right the first time," he growled. I kind of loved that I was making him lose control.

"This isn't right?" I ran my thumb over the tip of him, and then pressed him down, sliding his rock-solid heat through my wet folds. "Feels right to me," I gasped. Just a little more and he'd be inside of me.

"Hold on," he gasped, letting go of me and dropping his forehead to mine.

I groaned my disagreement. "What now?" I all but whined. If he didn't hurry up and drive into me, I was going to have to tackle him to the floor.

He lifted his head, his chest heaving with every breath. "Condom, greedy girl. That's all."

"Hurry."

Nate picked me up, strode into his bedroom and tossed me on the bed. Just like he'd dropped me in Pearl. I smiled in anticipation because there would be no interruption this time. But maybe, I could have some fun with him.

I scooted up the bed, reclining on his stacked pillows as he opened the drawer on the bedside table. Catching my lower lip with my teeth, I made sure his eyes were on me, then trailed my skirt up my leg to my hip, before letting my legs fall open. His muscles flexed as he peeled his jeans off, gripping himself as his blistering gaze roamed my body. He was so beautiful standing there, hair mussed, chest heaving. Reaching for me, he spun me by the hips, so that he could kneel between my thighs.

The open mouth kisses he trailed from my knee up my inner thigh, nipping and biting, teasing left me a writhing whimpering mess. He blew softly across the quivering bundle of nerves at my core, and my hands flew to grip his hair, trying to pull him to where I needed him most. I was so close. So ready to feel him inside me.

My hips rose off the bed, seeking his mouth. "Nate, please."

"What do you need, baby?"

"You."

His tongue brushed over my folds, working my clit, then he latched on, sucking hard. My hips shot off the bed, chasing the perfect angle. One long finger slid over my crease, then he eased it inside me in one slow, controlled movement that drove me wild. My orgasm blasted over me, as he added a second finger, continuing to work my body, wringing every last ounce of pleasure from me.

"Fuck, look at you." He growled from between my legs. "You are so beautiful. Is this what you imagined I was doing all those nights we spent together on the phone?"

He pushed the dress up higher, exposing my bare breasts. Leaning up, he sucked a nipple into his mouth, while his fingers pressed deep within me.

"Oh my God, Nate, I need— "

When he pulled away, I popped my eyes open to see him dragging his shirt over his head. "I know what you need."

I sat up, running my hands over his solid chest, down the ribbed muscles of his abs, to grip him, guiding him to my mouth.

Holding him at the base I licked up his length, dragging my tongue around the head, before sinking my mouth onto him.

"Oh Jesus, that feels good," he rasped.

I sucked hard as I withdrew, pushing his jeans down at the same time.

His hand cupped the back of my neck, twisting and tugging at the tie of my dress. Giving up, he reached down and just pulled the whole thing off over my head, dislodging my mouth. I grabbed him and lay back, pulling him on top of me.

"Quit messing around, Nate. I want you. Inside me. Now."

He raised an eyebrow at me. "My, my, so bossy. Who knew you had a little mini-domme side."

I smirked and flipped us over so I was on top.

"Let's try this my way again." I slid over him, coating him, rubbing my clit, drawing a moan from us both.

Nate blindly reached for the condom, ripping the package open with his teeth and holding it to me. I raised a brow at him, taking it from his fingers and rolling it over his hard length.

Then I shifted and slowly sank onto him.

"You feel so good."

"You are perfect."

Our words mingled on breathless sighs. Bracing my hands on his shoulders, I began to move.

His hands splayed wide on my hips, then shifted to grip my ass, holding me still as he pumped inside of me.

"Jordan, I want this to last, but I don't know if I can. You feel too perfect." He was so right, this moment, us, was perfect. I was in awe as I rode him. Not wanting to end this perfect moment, and at the same time wanting to drive us both crazy so we could do it again.

I dropped down hard on him, causing us both to groan, and shifted a hand to rub my clit. His drifted up to play with my breasts, then he sat up and his mouth was on me, lavishing one nipple at a time. One palm splayed up my side as he took my mouth in a searing kiss.

Done with my playing, he turned us over, taking control. His arms braced on either side of my head, he began pumping inside of me with hard strokes, taking us both to the edge.

Wrapping my legs around his waist, I met him thrust for thrust. And then, he shifted the angle and hit a new spot, causing me to clench around him. "There. Again," I gasped.

Nate repeated the movement with a roll of his hips and my core went tight as my orgasm shimmered. "I'm so close, Nate."

Two more pumps and my second orgasm claimed me, my body tightening on his as we both groaned our release.

We lay spent for a moment, the warm weight of his body anchoring me to the bed. Eventually, he rolled off, pulling me into his arms. Being with him had been worth the wait, and better than I'd ever imagined. And now that we'd taken this step, I knew beyond a shadow of a doubt, that I was ruined for anyone else.

Chapter 19

Nate

Morning birdsong woke me, and two things immediately registered. Jordan's lush body was pressed to mine. And this was real.

I'd missed everything about her while she was on her trip. Our morning coffee on the porch, our evenings with a beer and a game, her scent and voice always floating through my house. That she was here, now, in my bed, was perfection.

She lay with her back pressed against me, so I shifted, rolling to my side, sliding my arms around her, spooning her.

I tucked my hand against her stomach, letting my thumb drift over her soft skin, and buried my face in her neck. This spot just below her ear was my favorite. Every time I touched it, or brushed my lips over it, her body shivered. I didn't know if she even realized it.

I nibbled across her shoulder, getting the delightful reaction of her shifting her ass back to press against my crotch. My dick grew rock hard.

Leaning into her, I inhaled deeply, shifting my legs to

cradle her body with mine. I drifted my hand over her body, cupping her soft breast, my thumb grazing her nipple in a leisurely back and forth.

Her head turned slightly, so I moved my head, and was rewarded with a soft kiss pressed to my jaw.

"Morning, big spoon," she whispered.

I chuckled. "Morning, little spoon." My voice was low and raspy with sleep.

I lay my head next to hers on her pillow, closing my eyes and relishing this closeness. She slid her arm over mine, entwining our fingers, and her legs parted, weaving between mine. We were completely wrapped around each other.

Had I ever been this content in my life?

Had I ever felt this close to anyone?

Could I trust that she wouldn't leave me behind?

I continued brushing her nipple with my thumb, focusing on the feel of her to chase away my insecurities. With a gentle pressure, she placed her thumb on mine, guiding me.

Then she moved our hands to her other breast, before drifting them down together to the warm space between her legs. She parted her legs, draping her top leg over mine, our fingers sliding together through her wet folds. My dick pulsed against her ass with her sharp inhale.

Our hands slid together, with her guiding us, drawing her wetness around her sweet cunt until she slid one finger inside of her, drawing out and guiding me back to join her.

"Oh, that feels so good," she crooned. This woman undid me, showing me what she liked, guiding me on how to pleasure her, opening up to let me see how she'd done this to herself while we'd been apart.

"That's it, baby, show me what you like," I rasped in her ear, finding that favorite spot again with my mouth.

Together we fingered her, her hips flexing to meet each dive in.

I pulled back and shifted so that my dick was sliding against our hands. She pulled her hand away from mine, her fingers brushing my length while I dove mine back into her. I groaned at the exquisite torture of being so close to her heat and not being inside of her.

"Oh fuck, Nate, I need you inside me," she pleaded.

I shifted and slid into her, her tight heat clamping around me, feeling so damn good I nearly came with the first thrust.

"Oh shit, Jordan, we forgot a condom." I jerked twice, unable to stop moving within her.

"It's okay, I'm on the pill. Don't you dare stop now." She gasped.

I rose on an elbow to see her face. "Are you sure? Because if we don't stop now, I don't know that I can. You feel too good."

I'd never gone bareback with anyone, and it felt so fucking good I was sure I'd be a two-pump chump and be making up for it the rest of the day. This woman was destroying me, taking me to new places, opening me up, diving deep into my heart with her sweetness. I could fall so hard for her.

Jordan grabbed my hand and slid my fingers to her clit as she arched back into me.

Fuck.

"Fuck me, Nate," she demanded.

I lost myself to her, to our bodies moving together in a slow grind. Our hands working together, I rubbed her clit and she split her fingers over where we joined so that every time I withdrew, I felt the slide of her fingers over my dick.

"God damn, Jordan. That feels amazing."

Our hips pumped together, and it was too much. My balls drew up and I fought for control until she cried out, clamping down around me. She arched back and I gave a hard thrust, burying myself in her, and let go, coming so hard little stars glittered behind my eyes. Jesus, she was going to be the death of me.

Never had sex been so good. Maybe it was our connection. Maybe it was that she knew me, that she saw me. Whatever the reason, this woman, this sweet, kind, caring woman turned me inside out, and made me want things I'd never wanted before.

I snuggled her close to me, kissing along her perfect jaw.

"Best way to wake up in the history of ever," she said with a sigh.

We lay for a few minutes, letting our breathing return to normal and then she squirmed. I pulled out and rolled out of bed, she climbed out and met me at the end of the bed, hustling to get to the bathroom.

I trapped her in a hug, and she giggled, "Move, you big lug, before I make a mess all over myself."

"I'll clean you up." I vowed, dragging her into the bathroom and pushing her into the shower.

Chapter 20

Jordan

The view out the window over Nate's kitchen sink was a glorious one. Not only was the grass vibrant and green, but his little garden was thriving, despite the late June heat. Washing dishes, with a view of shirtless Nate tending his vegetables, had quickly become my favorite part of the morning in the few days I'd been back. There was something so domesticated about watching him do his chores. On his shift day, I'd volunteered to take care of nurturing his plants for him. His answering grin and giant bear hug had been worth the few minutes of work added to my own daily routine.

The days we spent together, we worked around his house, or I'd go help him with his side business during the day and work on my edits in the evening, and then get caught up or ahead on the nights he was on duty. But every night that he was home was filled with consuming passion.

Nate was the sun, and I was firmly in his orbit.

My cell phone pinged with an incoming message. I snagged a towel, not taking my eyes off Nate, and dried my hands before grabbing the phone from the counter.

Leah: Wanna meet for coffee this morning? I have a few minutes between classes if you are free.

Leah and Kylie had texted me every day. I was enjoying having girlfriends, that my roots were growing here, and Nate wasn't all that existed for me.

I hadn't had a friend group, or much of a life really, when I'd lived with Gerry. We'd moved together to D.C., and then we'd both been so wrapped up in growing our careers, somewhere along the way, we forgot about life outside of work. We'd lost each other, and I'd lost myself.

Determined not to fall back into those old habits, I made time for my new friends when they texted me, fostering those relationships. My friendship with Leah and Kylie was as important to me as my new relationship with Nate.

Were we starting a relationship? We hadn't had The Talk yet, and I didn't want to bring it up, but I could possibly see a future with him, aside from the whole danger thing. Maybe some girl-time would help me sort that question.

Me: Sure, I'll see you in 10

Leah: *smiling emoji*

I shoved my phone in my back pocket and pushed out the back door, meeting Nate in the yard.

"Hey, handsome, I'm going to go meet up with Leah. You want anything while I'm out?"

"I'll take a shot of leggy blonde when you get back," he said with a lascivious grin.

I pecked him on the nose, then the lips. "Deal."

The coffee shop that Leah loved was right off the court square, with a view of the historic courthouse. The majestic old brick building, with its copper dome, was a centerpiece of the town. It was a marvel that the tornado stayed two blocks to the south, leaving the landmark untouched.

Being on part of the block that the bar sat on, the coffee shop shared the same rustic interior brick walls. Exposed pipes, local art, and old wood floors gave the shop a cozy, welcoming feel.

Leah sat at a small table at the front window, waving to me through the glass as I passed by.

I pushed open the front door and heard a familiar voice call, "Welcome to Daily Brew!"

Behind the counter, a woman with familiar short curls stood with her back to me as she prepared an order.

From behind she reminded me of..."Jules?"

She turned, her face lighting with a smile.

"Jordan, hi! How are you?"

"I'm doing well, thank you. How are things with you? How is Nelson?" I hadn't seen her or her puppy since the night of the tornado. Running into her now tugged at my heartstrings.

"He's doing great! The repairs at the house are moving along, finally. I'm tired of seeing that tarp on my roof, but otherwise, we are back to normal. Your old house is still a mess though—that property owner hasn't done a thing. Where are you staying?"

"I'm staying with a friend. After I got my insurance settlement, I bought a camper van and I've been traveling."

"That's wonderful." She held my smile for a moment then her expression dropped and she looked down at the counter. When she looked back, her eyes held remorse. "I'm sorry I didn't reach out. Things got a little crazy for a bit."

"I understand. It's not like I called you, either. I was crazy focused on just getting by."

"Well, now that you are back, don't be a stranger." She said with a small smile.

I grabbed a coffee and bagel, and took the seat across from Leah, pausing to receive her hug.

"I'm so glad you made it," she said with a smile, reaching over to clasp my hand.

Leah was one of those women who could wear anything. Mostly she rocked a boho yoga style. I checked my ripped shorts and t-shirt, lamenting not taking a moment to change into something more presentable.

"Thanks for the invite," I replied, taking a sip of my latte.

"So, I had an ulterior motive. I hope you don't mind." Her eyes searched mine. She seemed...nervous almost.

"Well, that depends." I cocked my head to the side. I was pretty sure that Leah was the kind of person who didn't ask things lightly. If you were in her life, she wanted you there.

"I enjoyed keeping up with you on your trip. But I found myself wishing that we could meet and just have girl time."

I found myself grinning at her, loving the idea of having girlfriends to hang with and maybe talk over all these feelings I'd been ignoring about Nate. Plus, maybe she could help me understand how she dealt with Mike's job. "Aw, well, I'm glad you invited me. I need some girlfriends."

"So, the ulterior motive was, I wanted to ask how things are going with Nate. Y'all seemed pretty hot and heavy when he dragged you out of the bar the other night."

A cup of iced coffee dropped onto the table. The chair to my left clattered across the wood floor, and Kylie plunked herself down. Her wild red and blonde streaked hair stood out from her head in charming disarray, and matched her equally funky outfit of red tank top and flowing yellow skirt.

"Yes, girl. We really just wanted to make him let you up for air." She gave me a wink, then leaned over to peck Leah on the cheek.

My cheeks burned at the thought that all our friends witnessed Nate and I having our reunion.

"Don't worry, we didn't let anyone follow you out." Leah graced me with one of her beautiful smiles.

"So...spill." Kylie demanded, eyes gleaming. "That Nate is a mystery. But damn girl. He is so hot. Did y'all get it on in Pearl?"

I laughed nervously. Was I about to spill my guts to these two? This was a new thing for me, having friends to share everything with. Moving around so much as a child had meant that relationships never really stuck. By the time I got to high school and college I was so focused on just getting out and getting done, I never stopped to make lasting friendships. I'd missed out on a lot by not making the effort. I'd not make that mistake again.

"We ended up going back to his place, it was a little crowded in the parking lot. We were...interrupted." My blush extended from my throat to my hairline. I ducked my head, avoiding their gazes as I studied the bagel in front of me. It was embarrassing laying out the intimate details, but I'd vowed to try harder at the friendship thing. So, I pushed through my embarrassment, since they'd made it clear they were in my corner, supporting me.

"We went back to his house, and..." I told my bagel, pausing to clear my throat again. "Well. We took our friendship to the next level. Multiple times."

Kylie slapped her palm down on the table. "I knew it.

And from the blush on your face, it was good too. No man with abs like his can be bad in bed. It's illegal."

Leah chuckled softly, shaking her head at Kylie. Relief flooded me for whatever silly reason I couldn't define. I only knew that there was a kindred connection with these ladies, and I was enjoying it.

"Kylie, settle down. Go easy on her, she's not used to your outspokenness yet."

I smiled gratefully at Leah and shifted my attention to Kylie, letting the grin turn sly. "He does have an eight-pack."

"You lucky bitch." Kylie said in awe and winked at me, flipping her hair over her shoulder.

I watched her while she chatted with Leah. Kylie was such a pretty woman, almost intimidatingly so. But under that beautiful package, she seemed...lost. Like her eyes held a forced light, like she was bright and bubbly for show, but deep down there was a darkness.

Conversation turned back to the topic of me and Nate, and I hedged as much as I could until Kylie blurted, "Jordan, you have to give us something. Don't break the girlfriend code."

"Things with Nate are..." I wiggled my eyebrows at them.

Kylie shot me a deadpan look, transferred it to Leah, then back to me.

"What? Athletic? Awe-inspiring?" Kylie arched a brow, while Leah cracked up laughing. Kylie's eyes went wide, and she gasped in horror, laying a hand on my arm. "Oh, girl. Is he bad in bed?"

I laughed at her antics. "No! I was going to say things are good. But you won't let me leave it at that. So just, know that I'm happy? Is that enough for you without details?"

Kylie and Leah both grinned, and Leah placed her hand on my arm. "That's perfect. I'm so happy that he's with someone who will appreciate him."

A throat cleared behind her and I looked up to see Bunny and a stunning blonde standing at the table next to us, as if they were considering sitting there. I hadn't seen her since I'd been back, but I hadn't thought much about her, because I didn't feel like she treated Thoren very well.

"Oh great," Kylie muttered. I wasn't sure what her deal with Bunny was, but obviously she didn't want them to join us.

"Hi, Bunny and Mary Catherine," Leah's voice was courteous, but not as open as she'd been with me. Seemed we all had our reservations with Bunny.

"Hi, y'all. Mary Catherine and I were just coming from the calendar committee meeting," Bunny said with false brightness.

This must be the woman who'd been calling and texting Nate all the time about doing the fundraiser calendar. Though, I hadn't noticed him receiving any messages from her since I'd been back.

Leah's eyes tightened at the corners at the mention of the calendar. "Mike mentioned that meeting was today. Did they come to a decision?"

Mary Catherine's gaze was shrewd as she eyed the three of us and I couldn't help but wonder how Bunny and she were friends. But as I watched, Bunny's gaze skated over Kylie dismissively and I realized, maybe Bunny wasn't being authentic after all. I'd tuned out the conversation as I studied them, when Mary Catherine's cool gaze drifted over me, and returned to Leah. She'd just totally dissed me. A little flair of bitchiness rose within me, and I wanted to call her out.

Looking down her nose at Leah, Mary Catherine said, "Tell Mike I'll call him later." Then the two sashayed out.

I was dumbfounded. "Did she...Did that sound like she was warning you?"

Kylie rolled her eyes, waving them off. "She's got it in her head that she's all that, and she uses the calendar as a connection to hit on our guys." For half-a-second I wondered if Thoren was Kylie's.

"It doesn't matter," Leah said. "Mike always makes sure he's on speaker and that she knows I'm listening."

"So, tell me how you landed the hunky Nate," Kylie said.

"I didn't do anything special. Nate is first my friend, and second hopefully something more."

"So, is this a friends-with-benefits deal then?"

"No, we haven't really defined what this is exactly." That we hadn't discussed it made me pause. My feelings for him were starting to run deep. Never had I felt so close to someone in such a short period of time.

Kylie and Leah watched me expectantly. Lifting my shoulder, I gave them a small smile. "I just know he is my favorite person. I was scared to move things forward because my greatest fear is losing his friendship. But now that we have, I'm a little..." I shrugged again, unable to define my emotions.

Leah smiled gently at me. "I get that. But don't miss out on a beautiful connection because you are afraid. Nate is a good man. He'll let you know if he's not on the same page."

"It's not just that," I said to my cup, afraid to meet their eyes. I gathered my courage and spoke to Leah. "Mike has a scary job like Nate. How do you deal with it?"

Leah tilted her head. "How do you mean?"

"Like, I keep remembering that fight at the concert, and

them just jumping right in the middle of it. That didn't scare you?"

"Not really." Leah gazed off into the distance, then back at me. "I guess I trust that Mike knows what he's doing and won't put himself in a situation he can't handle. I won't lie, it does make it easier that he's transitioning to the Fire Marshall position though."

"Plus, Mike is a badass," Kylie added. Kylie had a point, but I reflected on Leah's words. She trusted him. Was that what I was missing? Was it a simple matter of me not trusting Nate? He'd proven himself capable, so many times. But still, I couldn't seem to let go of how risky the whole thing was. Would I ever be comfortable with this aspect of his life?

Conversation turned to the Fourth of July party Nate was throwing, and they tossed out ideas for some fun games to play. Kylie suggested a drinking game called Sharts, exclaiming, "You put one of those mini liquor bottles in a Dixie cup with instructions and secure a napkin over it with a rubber band. Then you throw darts at the cups, you read the instructions and either take your shot or pass it. It'll be fun."

Leah and I laughed at the suggestions she was dreaming up. Kylie's wild-at-heart attitude was dampened only when she asked me if Thoren and Bunny would be there.

"I'm sure they will be. Why?"

Heaving a huge breath, she said, "I guess I'll have to play nice with her there."

"And you wouldn't if she weren't?" Leah asked.

"Ugh, I don't know. She's nice enough, I guess. There's just something about the two of them, together, that gets on my last nerve. And he's too great of a guy to be treated like shit or taken advantage of."

So, I wasn't alone in my misgivings about Bunny.

Leah pointed a finger at her friend. "Be nice. Jordan is nervous enough without you making a scene."

I lifted my brows. "I'm fine. I'm not nervous." I shifted my gaze to Kylie. It seemed like maybe Kylie liked Thoren a little more than she let on. Or maybe I was just happy with my guy and wanted that for her too. "Go for it, girl. Do your thing."

Eventually, conversation shifted to their yoga studio, and then shopping. I sat back and enjoyed spending time with my friends.

The brief twinge of doubt from earlier remained, but I shrugged it off. I needed to trust my gut with Nate. He was a great guy, he wasn't perfect, but so far, things were going well. All the rest would work itself out.

Plus, I had new friends.

Life was looking up for me. If I could come to terms with the whole risk-taking, dangerous job thing, everything would be perfect.

Chapter 21

Jordan

In the days before the party, I spent my time doing some deep cleaning while Nate was on duty. He hadn't asked me to, but I felt like it might be a nice thing to do. I'd gotten my work done early and had a couple of hours to kill anyway.

I made some dinner, but realized I'd made way too much and wondered if he'd eaten.

Jordan: Can I bring you food?

Nate: I would love that. How soon can you get here?

He was waiting for me outside the station when I pulled up in his truck. We were sharing a vehicle so that I wouldn't have to drive Pearl while running errands. I took him to work, and he'd catch a ride from one of the guys the next morning.

He opened the door as I turned off the engine, dragging me out of the truck and into his arms for a drugging kiss.

"Hi, beautiful." His eyes crinkled, matching his smile. "I'm starving, what'd you bring me?"

"Nothing fancy, just some meatballs. I thought we might have subs." I blushed, feeling silly.

"Are you going to stay and eat with me?" He looked happy, like me bringing him dinner was the highlight of his day.

"Can I?" I sounded so pathetic and needy, but I really didn't want to go home alone.

"Of course."

"I'd like that. Eating alone at your house makes me feel a little sad. Which is weird because eating alone never bothered me before."

Tender eyes met mine. "Well, grab the keys and let's go grub."

Nate carried the container in one hand and clasped mine with the other, strolling confidently through the bay of the firehouse and into the living quarters where he deposited me at a chair in the small dining area. I congratulated myself for not totally staring at his ass in his uniform pants. He got out two plates and filled them, coming to join me at the table. I couldn't stop my grin at his domesticity.

"What?" he asked, looking amused.

I tucked a strand of hair behind my ear. "Nothing. I just like seeing you like this."

"How do I look?"

"Happy."

He leaned over and kissed me. "That's because I am."

I ran my tongue over my lip, tasting him, watching his eyes flare as he tracked my mouth. "It's a good look on you."

"Don't tempt me into pulling you into the bunk room and having my way with you," he said quietly, eyes hooded.

Mine popped wide open. "No way. People do it at the station?"

He cracked up laughing. Clearly the man loved teasing me. "Only if they want to get fired."

I let my face fall in disappointment, enjoying the banter

with him. "And here I thought we might check out that cool ladder truck. See if those hoses make a nice bed."

He chuckled. "That stuff only happens in TV shows." He lowered his voice and leaned close. "But I will be visualizing that, now that you mention it."

A loud alarm blasted through the station, echoed almost immediately by the radio on his hip. I nearly bolted from my seat, my heart rate instantly skyrocketing, as a flurry of activity broke out at once.

"Shit. I gotta go, babe." Nate jumped up, pushing his chair back, then leaned over to kiss me.

Two other guys I hadn't met yet came running. I followed all three into the bay, wondering what I should do.

The speakers in the bay were blasting a dispatcher's voice. "911, Engine 4. Respond to the area of East Broad. Possible structure fire."

"Stay and hang out if you want. This might not take long, could just be a false alarm," Nate called to me as he stepped into his boots, pulling on his gear, slipping the suspenders over his shoulders. I took a moment to appreciate the vision of him in his work gear.

"Do I lock up when I leave?" I asked.

"Just kick that door closed when you leave and go out the side door." He climbed into the cab, looking down at me. "I'll call you when I get back. I'm sorry, Skippy. I really wanted to eat you."

I blushed to the roots of my hair.

"I mean, eat dinner with you," he corrected as the other guys climbed in the truck, laughing at his mistake.

The engine roared to life, big tires squeaking on the painted concrete floor and sirens blaring as they pulled out of the bay. Once they were out of sight and earshot, an eerie silence stole over the empty station. Left behind, I tried to relax enough to allow my heart rate to return to normal. The minute or two that it had taken from the tones ringing out to when they'd rolled out of the station had been controlled chaos, and I needed a moment to calm down.

I went back into the dining area and cleaned up our not-dinner, placing Nate's part in a container in the refrigerator. Radio traffic from the crew to dispatch kept me aware of what was happening. Listening to them call their location and status was fascinating.

I sat in the recliner waiting a bit longer, feeling out of place even though he'd said it was okay. Nate had said they might get cancelled. On the off chance that he did, I wanted to wait around for a few minutes. Until another crew arrived on the scene and confirmed that they did have smoke showing.

The kitchen needed some attention and they'd probably be tired when they got back, so I tidied the dirty dishes and wiped down the counters. The radio ran their conversations as I worked. Though I kind of felt like an eavesdropper, not understanding most of what they said, I was too invested to leave.

I stalled as long as I could. Eventually, I couldn't rationalize hanging around any longer, so I grabbed my keys and headed out the side door to Nate's truck.

"NFD...to command. We...man down...repeat...have a man down!" The broken transmission came across the radio as the door was closing, sending chills down my spine.

I reached out to grab the door, but it clicked shut on the rest of the conversation. The sheer panic in that voice. My stomach dropped to my feet and my heart stopped.

I tugged on the door frantically, slamming it against the metal frame. When it wouldn't open, I dug my hands into my hair and scanned the parking lot.

Breathe. You don't know that it's him.

On wobbly legs I made it to Nate's truck. I probably shouldn't have driven, not with the way my hands shook. But I couldn't sit there and wait, not knowing if it was Nate trapped in that fire, if he was the man down.

I dug my phone out of my back pocket and stared at it, mind racing. Could I call 911 and see if they would tell me anything? Oh, to be able to recall the address they'd responded to, then I could drive myself over there. Maybe if I just drove through town, I'd see the smoke. But I needed to get my shit together before I put anyone else in danger.

I unlocked my phone and went to my messages, ridiculously hoping for what? I didn't know. The last message I got was from Leah. It clicked then. Of course—she would be able to ask Mike.

I dialed her number, and she picked up on the first ring.

"Jordan." Her voice was high and tight, nothing like the soothing, chill yogi I needed her to be in that moment.

"Leah," I managed, my voice cracking with fear that threatened to consume me. I took a deep breath, still trying to get my shit together.

"Mike heard the radio traffic. He's on his way to the scene to see what he can find. Where are you?"

"I was at the station visiting Nate. I'm still here. I was just leaving when they called that a man was"—I swallowed against the tightness of my throat—"down."

"Okay, I'm coming to get you. Stay where you are. I'll be there in a minute."

Stupidly, I nodded at my phone and ended the call. Nate was probably fine. I was overreacting, just like my mom did.

I walked into the house to find mom sitting on the couch, tears streaming down her face, crumpled tissue in hand.

"What's wrong, Mom?" I said, my tone bored, as I dropped my bag by the door and grabbed the stack of mail off the table. My college acceptance letters should be coming in any day.

"Jordan, honey. Come here. We need to talk."

"Mom, whatever it is, can it wait?" I flipped the envelope with my name and my number one college pick return address adorning the corner. I slid a finger under the flap to open it.

"Honey, something happened to your dad. There was an accident today..."

I zipped my finger across the envelope, slicing the dry skin at my knuckle. I snatched it back, sticking it in my mouth automatically. I pulled the letter out and read the first line of my acceptance before her words sank in.

"Jordan. Did you hear me?"

"Yes, I heard you. I'm just waiting on you to tell me the rest of it before I get all up in a tizzy. Like the time you told me about the divorce and then him and Sandi getting married."

"Jordan." Mom's voice cracked on a sob.

I looked over to see tears streaming down her face while she shook her head.

"Honey, I know I sometimes overreact. But this time..." She visibly swallowed. "They don't know if he's going to make it."

A knock on the driver's side window startled me from the miserable memory. I looked up to find Leah standing by the truck, reaching for the door handle.

"Oh, honey, open the door." Leah's voice was calm but firm, in control, and reached that chaotic part of my brain, allowing me to finally take a normal breath.

I hit the unlock button and she pulled the door open, reaching in to hug me.

Wiping her thumb across my cheek, she gazed into my eyes, sympathy written all over her face. I hadn't even realized I'd been crying. "Grab your bag, come on. Let's go wait somewhere together until Mike calls."

Gently, she tugged my arm and led me to the passenger side of her car before tucking me in, reminding me to buckle up.

Surely Nate was fine. I swiped the remaining wetness from my cheeks and dug deep for some rational train of thought. I was not going to be my mother and overreact. Just because they'd said someone was injured didn't automatically mean that it was Nate. My mind and heart and experience were just playing tricks on me.

The landscape whipped by as I stared blankly out the window. Leah's gentle voice was soothing background noise.

We were stopped at a red light when her phone rang.

Leah hit the Bluetooth button. "Hi, Mrs. O'Malley."

"Leah, dear." An elderly woman's warbly voice filled the car. "The rumor mill is stirring about something going down in town. What can you tell me is happening? You know I need to beat Eunice with the most reliable information. I'm counting on you to deliver the goods."

"I don't know anything yet. I'm picking up my friend Jordan now. Mike has gone to see what he can find out."

"Where are you girls going?"

Leah glanced at me. "We aren't sure. Jordan dates my friend Nate. He's on that call. She was at the station when it rang out, I just picked her up. We wanted to be together while we wait to hear what is going on."

"Nate was one of the calendar boys, right? Which

month is he again?" Mrs. O'Malley sounded like she was moving, flipping pages. "You girls come here, and you can show me. I made some of my special brownies today."

Leah looked over at me again, eyebrows raised, tilting her head as if asking me.

I nodded stupidly, too numb to decide.

"Okay, we'll head that way."

"Excellent, dear. I'll get out the shot glasses."

The phone disconnected as Leah accelerated from the light. "That was my neighbor Mrs. O'Malley. She's a bit of a handful. But she's good as gold."

"Okay." My voice sounded as hollow as I felt.

Moments or hours later—time was a blur—Leah ushered me up the stairs of a quaint little bungalow. A sweet-looking, white-haired elderly woman greeted us at the top of the stairs, giving us each a hug after pushing a mug into our hands.

"Here you go, my sweets."

She pulled back, patting my cheek. "Hi, I'm Francis O'Malley. You sure are a pretty little thing."

"Thank you," I mumbled.

Leah opened the door and Mrs. O'Malley bustled us inside.

"You girls come on in here and tell me all about what you've been up to. I haven't seen you or Mike in an age, young lady. I hope that's because you've been taking advantage of that hunky man of yours." Mrs. O'Malley wiggled her eyebrows at Leah. To my surprise Leah flushed bright red.

"Mrs. O'Malley, play nice," she admonished.

The older woman harrumphed and tottered to a table, coming back with a calendar in hand. She shoved it in my direction demanding, "Which one is your beau?"

I set my mug on the table and thumbed through a calendar of public safety members, all of them shirtless. Any other time I would've appreciated the photos more. I turned the page and saw a photo of Mike with a precious puppy nestled in the crook of his arm. On the next page was Nate. One leg propped on the step of the fire engine, wearing his gear, smiling adorably at a golden retriever puppy.

Tears filled my eyes.

What if he was hurt right now?

The urge to bolt and run away and hide from this extreme fear was strong. But I knew I couldn't leave without knowing if Nate was okay.

What would I do if something happened to him?

The calendar was tugged out of my hands and Mrs. O'Malley's sad face appeared through my watery vision. She clasped my hands, giving them a squeeze. "Sweetheart, you find a way to go on."

"I'm sorry, I didn't mean to say that out loud. It's just..." I squeezed my eyes closed. The words wrestled forth painfully. "This is a lot."

Leah gathered close to us, wrapping an arm across my shoulders. "That's why we are together. It's too scary to go through alone."

I tried to let her comforting words sink in. Mrs. O'Malley pulled me to a couch where they sheltered me between them.

"Now dear, I'm sure that he is going to be quite all right. This town has had too much trauma lately to have to deal with more. I believe that to my soul. I need you to take a breath and tell me what this is really about."

I glanced up, meeting her kind eyes. She looked so concerned for me.

"When I was a teenager, my dad was in a plane crash. He was hurt very badly, brain injury. I don't think I ever fully processed that, and this feels so much like that terrible waiting period. Not knowing if he was going to live, or if he did, if he would ever be the same."

Leah rubbed my back, still offering me comfort, trying to soothe my fears. "That's terrible, Jordan. I'm so sorry. I didn't know."

Mrs. O'Malley reached forward to the short coffee table and plucked a tissue out of the dispenser, sitting back to wipe my eyes with one hand while her other held both of mine.

"My dear. Regardless of what has happened before, it's plain to me that you care very much about your Nate. Does he feel the same about you?"

I blinked. Did he?

"We've not said the words so much, but he makes me feel like he cares for me."

"Then have faith that he will do everything he can to make sure he stays safe. It's not a foregone conclusion that he's the one injured right now."

I took a deep, gulping breath, allowing the truth of her words to sink in. If something happened to him...I shoved the thought away. I couldn't go there. As excruciating as it was, now was time to wait.

Chapter 22

Nate

The building was a total loss. The whole scene had been a shitshow from the beginning. First the water source had been unreliable. Then the pumper had failed to engage. By the time we got inside, the fire had progressed unusually fast, and had become a monster before we could make any real headway.

To top it off, Rook acted like he was scared to death and had gotten himself cornered. I'd gone on a retrieval mission, trying to pull him out of a fucking burning building instead of fighting the fire.

Thoren and I worked our way to him, beating back the flames. We found him huddled in a corner, his oxygen tank bell screaming that he was running low on air. I tapped Thoren on the shoulder and radioed in that I had him. I slung the idiot over my shoulder, and Thoren and I retreated to the safety of the yard, where I dumped him then fell to my knees.

Medics met us and took over his care. I jumped up and ran back to Captain Collins at the scene command.

"Williams," Collins barked. "How is he?"

"Alive. Medics have him now." I ripped my helmet off and sloshed a bottle of water over my head, trying to cool my body temp down.

"Good. Take five. You and Thoren will be on the next crew in." Collins slapped me on the back and walked away.

I scanned the yard to find Thoren rehabbing at the ambulance, double fisting water bottles.

I walked over to him and grabbed another ice-cold water, slugging it back as fast as I could gulp it down.

"That's one hot mother right there," Thoren said, with a nod toward the fire.

"Yeah, no way that one got this hot without some accelerant."

"How's the kid?" he asked.

"Lucky. He was curled up in a little ball in the corner. Just waiting to burn up. How the fuck did he pass rookie school if he's that scared?" I shook my head in disgust. "Who was his partner?"

"Cal. But Cal wouldn't leave the guy. I don't know what happened, how they got separated. I'm sure we will hear all about it."

"Nate! Thoren!" Mike shouted from the other side of the road, where PD was huddled in a group, keeping onlookers at bay.

"What are you doing here? Isn't it a little early for you to be here?" Thoren asked, finishing the second bottle of water.

Mike hooked his thumbs in the pockets of his jeans. "Heard someone was down over the radio. I came to find out what in the hell is going on. Otherwise, yeah, I might as well be here from the start."

"The new guy got himself trapped in a corner. But as far as I know, everyone else is out of the building," Thoren replied, just as a loud crack sounded from the structure. The radio squawked with traffic for the crew inside to retreat.

Mike watched with his hands on his hips while Thoren tossed his empty bottle to the trash bag. "Won't be surprised if that roof collapses soon the way this bitch is burning."

The words had no sooner left his mouth when there was a terrible crashing sound and the roof lit up, the back side falling into the building as sparks shot high in the sky.

Fuck, that was a close call. We could've been in there.

Mike whistled low. "Glad y'all made it out first."

"I was just thinking the same thing." I said, a shudder running down my spine.

"I better call Leah and let her know I laid eyes on you two." He looked over at me. "She's with Jordan."

I nodded. "Thanks, man. I felt bad leaving her at the station."

"I'm on it. Thoren, do I need to call Bunny?"

Thoren scowled at Mike. "Fuck no. I don't owe her anything."

My head snapped around. First off, Thoren was normally the upbeat optimistic guy, and was never disrespectful, especially to women. For him to call her out as a bitch meant something major had happened.

Mike threw his hands up. "Sorry, man. I'm guessing that means it's over with her?"

"You could say that," Thoren growled, turning his back on us and heading back to the captain.

We cleaned up the scene, and finally, on the way back to the station, I broke the no-cell-while-driving rule and gave Jordan a quick call.

She answered on the first ring.

"Nate?" Her voice quivered like she might have been crying.

"Hey, Skippy. I'm headed back to the station. I'm sorry I had to run out like that. Did you stay and finish eating?" Just the mention of her eating reminded me that I hadn't before this clusterfuck call. My stomach clenched with hunger.

"Nate," she whispered, her voice breaking.

I pulled the truck into the station, and the guys jumped down. I stayed put so I could have a private moment with her because she sounded upset.

"Just got to the station. You okay?" My adrenaline had finally started to drop, and I could think clearly. I'd been going full out since I'd found Rook in the corner. Soon the exhaustion would set in and I'd crash.

"Not really. I was leaving the station and heard there was a man down over the radio. It was scary. I was so worried about you."

The drone of the diesel engine nearly drowned out her soft voice, but not before I caught the tremble in her words. I cut the engine as the tremble sliced through me. Outside the truck, the guys were being loud as fuck, bitching and yelling about who was doing what, since the Rook was stupid and got himself hurt, leaving more work for everyone else.

Someone banged on the window. My cue for getting off my ass and getting my truck back in service.

"Look, Skippy, I'm fine," I said quickly. "I can't talk. I've got to get the truck back in service now."

She sniffled on the other end of the phone while outside the truck someone banged the door again. "Give me a fucking minute," I barked.

"Sounds like you're busy." I barely heard her soft words.

"Uh, yeah. Just a little."

"Call me later when you get settled. It doesn't matter how late. Oh, and I put your food in the fridge."

"Thanks," I said and disconnected the call.

An hour later, I walked out of the showers and into the kitchen to see the rest of the guys at the table, huddled over their plates. Pulling out the container Jordan brought, I dished myself a huge plateful, heated it in the microwave and joined them.

"Everyone check in at home?" Collins said around a mouthful. Everyone around the table nodded. Collins eyed me. "Nate?"

"What?"

"You check in with your girl?" He raised an eyebrow at me, looking at me like I was stupid.

"Yeah, I'm good. I called her when we got to the station." I winced, remembering her tearful voice. "She sounded pretty upset."

"That's why I'm checking in. Families hear those words that someone is down, and they freak out. Rightfully so."

I nodded and pinched off a bite of the bread I'd been holding.

"I can't imagine I'd take it well if I got word that someone was down, and then had to just wait until my person called." He looked pointedly at me. "That would fucking suck."

Guilt crawled up my spine. I'd been too short with Jordan, too abrupt, too caught up in all the work to give her the care she deserved. Of course she would be upset. She'd been here when we got the call.

I reshaped the bread in my fingers, studying the way it mashed down into compact bites, before admitting, "Sounded like she might've been crying. I feel like a real jerk, because now I'm realizing maybe I should've taken a little more care with her."

The other guys got up from the table, leaving me and Collins alone. He forked up another bite and then spoke to his plate. "Boy, that girl cares about you. I saw it when she was here earlier."

I hadn't even known he was around when she'd stopped by. Not wanting to face his censure, I glanced his way but didn't fully meet his eyes.

"It's in the way she looks at you," he continued. He flexed his hand, before reaching for his water.

I didn't know if he expected a response, so I waited him out, studying the ink that covered every inch of his big ass arm.

"Let me ask you this," he finally said. "If the roles were reversed, would you have been waiting for a phone call?"

When she'd been on the road, I'd been a nervous wreck.

I met his eyes then. "No, sir. I'd be busting up this place, making sure I could lay eyes on her."

He nodded with approval. "So, put yourself in her shoes. It's a lot to ask of a woman—hell, it's a lot to ask of anyone, knowing you face danger of the could-be-life-threatening variety." He leveled his gaze on me. "Take it from me—not everyone has what it takes to be a part of a relationship when one of the parties is in our line of work."

He knew that firsthand, considering his fiancée had left him stranded at the altar a decade ago. I'd felt bad for the guy and respected the hell out of him for going ahead on the trip that would've been his honeymoon. No doubt about it, Mac Collins was one badass dude.

And he had a point. Jordan would be especially worried about something happening to me because of her father's accident. She'd had one close call that had changed her life forever, and here I was asking her to trust me with her heart, and I'd just dismissed that she'd even worry about me at all. But she had been scared, and she'd been waiting to hear from me.

And that feeling, although now was a weird moment to realize it, was something that I wasn't used to.

"I think I need to call her back."

Collins studied me for a moment more, his grey eyes gleaming. "She know you got it bad for her?" One corner of his mouth tipped up. If I didn't know better, I'd say it was a grin, but Mac Collins never grinned. "Hell, do *you* know you have it bad for her?"

"I don't know, Cap. But I think I fucked up and I need to take care of my girl."

He nodded. "Good call. Get the fuck out of here."

I shot up from the table, grabbing my empty plate, and dumping it in the dishwasher. I had my phone in hand as I entered the hallway. It was late and she might be asleep, so rather than call, I tapped out a quick message.

Nate: Hey doll, you up?

I waited a few minutes and got no response. I was a fool for not taking more care with her. She showed me she cared in so many ways, always willing to spend an extra minute with me, to listen, to just be with me. She took care of me in so many ways. Showed me she cared for me by listening, paying attention, being there even when I didn't want to admit that I needed her. And I'd been a heartless ass. With my heart in my throat, I wrote more, trying to convey all the emotions swirling inside me in a simple text.

Nate: Skippy, I need to apologize. I should've known you'd be worried. Hell, I would've been, if I'd been in your shoes. I can't stand the thought of you hurting or being worried. It's ripping me up inside. You're probably sitting here reading this message right now thinking I'm some kind of douchebag asshole, and you'd be right. I feel like one. I just wanted you to know that I'm sorry. Please say we can talk it out in the morning. Sleep well.

The next morning, I careened into the driveway and jumped out of truck, racing to my front door to find it unlocked. Like Jordan knew I was coming. She always did that, probably had a hot cup of coffee waiting for me too, because she was so sweet and always took care of me that way.

Guilt had bile rising in my throat as I busted through the front of the house, searching for her. Needing to see her, and still not trusting all these feelings coursing through my body.

I'd lain awake all night, thinking about all the ways things could have gone wrong in that fire. And all the ways things could have gone wrong on her trip. She'd made sure that I knew that she was safe. And what had I done? I'd discounted her. Made her feel like a nuisance, unworthy of a simple phone call.

Just like my parents had all the times they'd forgotten about me or left me home alone late into the night. Leaving me feeling small and unlovable.

I finally found her standing by the coffee maker, staring out the window like I'd found her countless other mornings. She held a mug while a fresh one brewed, no doubt for me. She must've started it when she heard the truck pull up. I halted at the edge of the room, unsure what to say. How to act.

Something clenched deep in my chest that would only ease if she turned around to give me one of her smiles.

But she didn't turn around.

Instead, she dropped her head, her mug clanking to the counter. She looked utterly defeated, arms hanging limp by her side. Then her shoulders shook.

Motherfucker, I'd made her cry. Again.

In two strides, I was across the kitchen and wrapping my arms around her, burying my face in her neck. Her hands landed on my arms, and her chest heaved as a sob broke loose, the sound shattering any composure I had left. She turned in my arms, and we wrapped each other up. Faces buried in necks.

Her tears coated the skin above my uniform shirt. I clasped the back of her head, holding her to me. Tears pricked my own eyes.

"Skippy, you're fucking killing me. Please don't cry," I begged, my voice as broken as I felt.

She hugged me tighter, squeezing me while she emptied her emotions all over me. I didn't fucking care. I'd take them. I'd take anything this woman would give me. Never had anyone made me feel so cared for, so important, so loved.

I hadn't even known how much I needed that until she came into my life.

And I'd hurt her so much that she was crying her heart out all over me.

Well, let her cry.

I'd be strong enough for the both of us.

I'd wipe her tears and hold her hands. And let her know every damn day how much I loved her. Because love was the only thing this feeling could be.

She finally quieted, just resting in my arms. She pressed kisses along my neck and jaw.

"I'm sorry I cried on you," she whispered.

"Baby, you can always cry on me. I will always be here for you."

She pulled back, meeting my eyes. "But will you?"

I looked deep into her beautiful eyes, seeing the swirling confusion and emotion shining there.

"Jordan, I'm telling you right now that I will always, always be here for you."

Instead of nodding like I thought she would, she pulled away with a sigh. Grabbing our coffees, she headed for the door, where she looked back and said the most dreaded words in relationship history.

"We need to talk."

My heart dropped to the pit of my stomach as I followed her to the deck, suddenly scared shitless that she was going to say she didn't feel the same way. That she didn't feel strung out at the thought of us not being together. That I wasn't worth the worry and fear she'd experienced.

She sat at the edge of the stairs, looking out over the yard and the garden beyond. I dropped next to her, making sure we touched from hip to knee, then pulled my coffee cup away and entwined our fingers, clasping them like a lifeline.

"Jordan," I started, but she held up her free hand, halting me. I swallowed hard, scared to hear what she was about to say.

"Nate," she started, her voice stronger than it had been mere moments ago. "Yesterday scared me to death."

I tamped down my fear, and my pride. "I know, baby. I'm so sorry."

She shook her head. "It's not your fault. It just is what it is." She was wearing her favorite cutoff shorts, fiddling with the frayed edge. Her face tilted down, watching as she tugged at the strips of material, so closed off from me, it felt like she was a million miles away. "It's your job and it's so much a part of who you are."

I put my hand over hers, stilling her fingers, needing that connection, holding on with both hands because it felt like she might be slipping away.

"Jordan, I can change jobs." I voiced it as a vow, and I meant every word.

She gave my hand a squeeze and looked at me with a sad smile playing on her lips. "I would never ask you to do that."

And she wouldn't because what she said was true. Helping people was part of my DNA. "But you don't like it." I filled in the missing pieces for her.

She looked out over the yard, as if contemplating her next words. The best thing I could do was be patient. So, I waited while my heart thumped in my chest and my guts roiled. I'd listen to what she had to say, then beg her not to go. Because that's what I was afraid of the most. I could handle the storms and running into a burning building. But I was terrified of her leaving.

Chapter 23

Jordan

Nate's hand wrapped around mine, as warm as the early morning sunshine bathing those mornings we'd spent looking out over his property. Each day we'd watch the wildlife, talk about his garden, happy and looking for the good in each day. Now though, the atmosphere around us felt desperate, heavy. His leg pressed against me, as if he couldn't bear us not being connected. And I knew he could feel me pulling away, so he was holding on tighter.

"Nate, last night scared me. But I don't know if you know all the reasons why."

I set down my coffee and let go of his hand to stand, taking the few steps down and pausing, turning back to look at him. He looked so sad and forlorn, as if I'd broken his heart. I hated being the reason for that sad look on his face.

I held my hand out to him. "Let's go for a walk."

He joined me, and I nestled my hand in the crook of his arm as we strolled through his property.

We headed toward the long fence, our favorite spot for resolving confrontations.

"I nearly lost my dad, and it broke something in me." It was harder to explain than I expected. "When he and my mom split up, when he had his plane crash, I just...pulled away, because that was easier than facing the hurt of the truth." I looked up at Nate to find his jaw clenched as he studied his feet. I tugged his arm to get him to look at me.

"But I realize now that I spent way too many years running from the pain of nearly losing him, and I wasted that time, grieving the dad I once had, when I could've been spending that time with him."

I locked eyes with Nate, letting him see all my emotions, all the pain and confusion. Not wanting to hide from him, not running.

"Please understand what I'm saying. Last night sent me back to that terrible time when I thought my dad had died. I was scared to death. And you called me, acting like nothing had happened. When I'd thought my whole world was ending."

His jaw clenched, but his eyes swam. He placed a hand on my hip, pulling me close. "Jordan." His voice was low and rough.

I laid a hand on his chest, needing to get the rest of this out. "I'll be honest. I stayed up most of the night, because my first inclination was to run. I even packed a bag."

He was shaking his head, gripping me with both hands now.

"But I saw your messages and stopped. Running away from that fear, and you, that's not the right answer."

"No, it's definitely not." His reply was swift. Adamant.

My lips lifted in a sad smile. "Do you know what happened to me yesterday while you were saving the world?"

He shook his head, still gripping me with his fierce gaze,

as if he couldn't look away for fear I'd be gone. As much as I hated seeing his discomfort, and being the reason for it, seeing that he was taking me seriously gave me the courage to continue.

"Leah came to get me. She took me to meet Mrs. O'Malley, who is hilarious by the way. They sat with me and took care of me. And later, Mike called Leah, because he knew we were together, and he talked to me and told me that he'd spoken to you, and you looked fine. That you weren't the one trapped." I turned away, resuming our lazy meandering. It was easier to talk if I didn't have to meet his gaze. I noted the pretty summer flowers we'd nurtured together, the pops of color vibrant in the morning sun.

"I was scared to death thinking that I'd lost you, and I had people around me supporting me. Telling me to keep the faith. And I know that if anything had happened to you, I wouldn't have been allowed to run, because these people would've wrapped me up in their love and they would've taken care of me." From the corner of my eye, I saw his nod. He knew how wonderful his friends were. Birdsong serenaded our stroll, and I paused to soak in how much I'd come to love this place.

Drawing strength from that, I turned to Nate to find his eyes swimming with emotion. I took comfort in seeing that emotion and forged ahead. "But I also realized that I don't *want* to run away. I need you Nate." I gripped both of his hands in mine, pressing them to my chest. "I care about you. But I need you to be gentle with me, and I need you to let me know that you are in this with me. And I need you to not take risks that you don't have to take. Because I can't lose you." My tears spilled over again. At what point did someone dry up?

He brushed away my tears with the gentlest sweep of

his thumb across my cheek. As more fell, he framed my face and kissed them away. "I'm so fucking sorry, Jordan." The ragged apology was whispered, tortured. "I hate that you were so scared. That it triggered a bad memory, and I didn't make things any better by being short with you." He kissed my forehead. "I'm not used to checking in. I've never really had anyone who gave a shit about me to need to do that." Another brush of my cheek, another gentle kiss. "Captain let me know I was wrong. He clued me in that sometimes we need to go gentle. And I wasn't with you. And I'm so sorry."

His eyes swam with remorse. He hadn't meant to hurt me.

I was the one with the issues. And poor Nate was beating himself up over it. It was time to face my problems because no matter how far I ran, I'd never get over Nate. So I needed to fix the real issue. "I think I need to go see someone to help me get past this trauma response," I admitted.

Nate slid his arms around my shoulders, my face pressed to the skin of his neck. I breathed in his comforting scent, cherishing the way he ran his hand over my hair. His voice, when it came, was soft and sweet and went straight to my heart. "Do you want me to go with you?"

Bless this sweet man. How could I have ever thought that I could run away and leave him? He was so much a part of me, I didn't know where I ended, and he began. "I'd like that."

He released me, letting me see all the emotion that he felt, before gifting me the softest, most heartfelt kiss of my life. Even if we hadn't said the words, I knew we were both in the same place. He showed me every day in all the little ways he took care of me.

I closed my eyes and kissed him back, needing to feel him in this moment. All of him. I stepped closer, wrapping one arm around his strong shoulders, and the other around his head. His hands went to the backs of my legs as he lifted me up. Automatically, my legs hooked around his hips and then he started moving.

I broke the kiss to ask, "Where are you taking me?" Not that it mattered as long as he was with me.

"I want you, Jordan." His voice was deep. The need in it sent my heart racing.

I pulled him back for another kiss, letting him know I wanted him too. My back crashed into the side of the van. In a flurry of movement, he ripped the hem of my shirt up, over my head, flinging it to the ground at his feet.

He latched onto my breast, sucking my nipple through the lace of my bra, and desire exploded in me. I flung my head back against the camper, holding him to me, needing more. I reached down and pulled his shirt up, panting as he reached back with one hand, breaking his kiss long enough to pull the shirt off over his back.

"Damn, that's hot." I whispered.

"What?" He grinned down at me, spanning my ribcage with a rough hand.

"I like that thing you do with your shirt—you know, the pulling it off like that."

The grin grew. "That's good to know." Then he was back at my chest, leaving a trail of heat as he licked the curve of my breast, running his tongue across my collarbone and up my neck, sending my heart rate soaring.

"I need you, Nate."

He pulled back a little and popped the button on my shorts. "Off" he growled against my lips, dropping my legs. I shimmied out of my shorts as he undid his enough to let his glorious cock spring free. He bent and hoisted me up again, while I reached between us, gripping the length of him and giving him a slow drag with my fist, my other arm draped over his shoulder.

"Oh God damn, Skippy, just like that." He groaned, his forehead landing on mine. But I needed more, so I gave him another tug as I lined him up at my entrance.

"Nate, baby, please," I begged.

He slid into me, in one long slow thrust until he was seated deep. He pulled back, meeting my eyes. "Watch us, Jordan. See how beautiful we are. How beautiful you are."

He leaned back to get a better view, eyes on where we were joined, his jaw gritted, face entranced. I looked down to see him pull out of me, pause, and then slide gloriously back in, and a moan burst from my throat before I could catch it.

In that moment, I felt so close to him. Watching the way our bodies moved together, completed each other.

"That's it, baby, let me hear you," he coaxed, watching us move together again. "I want to see you touch yourself the way you did all those times you teased me on the phone."

I lowered my hand, sliding it between us to grip him as he pulled out of me.

"Oh fuck, Jordan" he cried, slamming back into me. I slipped my slick fingers over my clit as he pounded into me.

"Baby, next time, I promise, I'll go slow and tell you all the ways that I love you. But right now, I need to fuck you hard." Nate's voice was a low growl as he slammed his mouth to mine. Our tongues danced, teeth nipped and the pressure at my core built. He shifted once, hitting me in exactly the right spot, and began moving in a punishing rhythm that left me gasping. My orgasm shimmered just out of reach.

He trailed his tongue down my throat, his hips pounding into mine. I reached up, raking a hand down his chest, and he went wild, thrusting into me, rocking the van I was pressed against. He clamped his teeth down on my neck and I cried out as my orgasm exploded over me.

Burying himself in me, he pumped hard twice, gasping his release.

He dropped his forehead to mine, trailing gentle kisses across my nose and cheeks before taking my lips. As he pulled out and released my legs, he wrapped his arms around my back, deepening the kiss.

Finally, he pulled away. My lips latched onto his to keep him close, pulling on his lower lip until it released with an audible pop.

He smiled at me as he let me go. The words he'd spoken played on repeat in my mind.

I'll go slow and tell you all the ways that I love you.

I grinned sheepishly at him as he stooped to gather up our discarded clothes. "Hand me my shirt, please, slick." I said, intentionally using the stupid nickname I'd given him so long ago.

A naughty twinkle lit his eyes. "I don't think I want to."

No way. He seriously was not about to leave me naked in his yard. Even though we'd just had wild sex in the wide open, running across his yard felt like too much.

"Nate, I can't run naked across your yard."

He grinned at me while he fastened his pants. "No one's going to see you."

I propped my hands on my hips and said sternly, "Nate, give me a shirt at least."

"You'll have to catch me," he teased, taking off at a sprint across the yard to the house, leaving me to chase behind him in my bra.

"You are so going to get it for this!" I yelled.

"I can't wait!"

Chapter 24

Jordan

I finished stringing the last of the twinkle lights across the yard and stepped down off the ladder to admire my work. Nate was going to love this, and making him happy, taking care of him, made me happy.

After his big idiot move and subsequent apology, I'd tried my best to get things back to normal between us, and he was making a bigger effort to keep me in the loop on what was happening with him as well. If the way he consistently sent me text messages and randomly called me throughout the day was any indication, I was constantly on his mind.

And we were happy.

It was the day of his big party. We had plans to go catch the parade, and then everyone was coming back to his place for a cookout.

Nate had burgers marinating, and I'd made two huge salads—one pasta and one cucumber. Everyone else was bringing their signature dish. Tables were set up in the yard, coolers were packed.

The excitement of hosting a party with Nate had me up

at the crack of dawn, and I'd done a bunch of decorating before he'd gotten home from his shift and had been waiting on him by the time he'd gotten home. I jumped him in the hallway, starting our day off right. Really, every day should begin with sex. Nate laughed when I declared that a rule and agreed with me that it was the best way to start the day.

We were walking hand in hand to the fire station, where we'd watch the annual parade, when my mother called.

"Hey, Mom," I answered hesitantly, a trickle of guilt making me grimace. It had been forever since my mom had called me. Usually, I was the one keeping up the communication.

"Jordan, I spoke to Sandi," Mom said without greeting. Great, this was starting off on a good note, with her already sounding anxious. It was unusual for her to talk to Sandi, and that should've been my first clue. Nate gave my hand a squeeze, asking with his eyes if everything was okay.

"How is Sandi?" I asked, not sure I wanted to hear her answer.

"Jo, Sandi says you are dating some guy." Mom's voice sounded incredulous, which should have been insulting, but I couldn't stop the smile that spread over my face as I glanced up at Nate.

"I am, Mom. His name is Nate," I said, earning a quick squeeze of his hand and an answering smile. If anyone was watching us, I'm sure we looked like two dopey teenagers.

"Why am I hearing about this from Sandi, and not my own daughter?" Her voice kept growing shriller, wiping the smile off my face. Of course she couldn't simply be happy for me, she had to make this about her.

"I'm sorry, but in all fairness, Sandi wouldn't have known if I hadn't gone to see Dad," I said, trying to keep my patience in check.

"Yes, I heard about that too. How awful that you had to see that on your own." Her tone turned on a dime. Sympathetic. "If you'd have called me, I would have been happy to go with you."

Irritation rolled through me at the thought of dealing with my mother, yet here I was, letting her bend my ear again. "It was something I needed to do on my own," I said, losing patience with the conversation quickly.

"I'm sure it was emotional for you, sweetheart. I could've been there to help you."

The sugary sweetness of her voice grated on my nerves that much more. I bit my lip to keep from saying something hurtful. Something like, I didn't tell her so that I could focus on processing my own thoughts and emotions without having to cater to her.

"I'm finding that sometimes I need to do things solo, Mom. So, did you need something? Nate and I are on our way somewhere," I hedged. It'd be great if I could end the conversation before she could launch her next round. Maybe I wouldn't have to suffer her usual hysterics.

"Yes, I do need something. I need you to think long and hard about what you are getting yourself into, young lady. Sandi says that this person is a firefighter." Her tone turned reproachful. "Jordan, that is a dangerous profession. You don't want to be mixed up with someone who works such a dangerous job. Haven't you been through enough?" Negativity and attitude laced her every word and pricked that tender spot I'd been trying so hard to heal.

I froze in the middle of the sidewalk, pulling the phone away from my ear to look at the screen, unable to believe what she'd said. How dare she just naturally assume that something bad was going to happen to Nate? And how dare she assume that I was so like her that I couldn't handle being in this relationship?

Nate stepped in front of me, blocking me from the foot traffic, concern written all over his face.

I slipped the phone back to my ear as Nate asked, "What's wrong?"

My mother was still spewing her attitude. "...is that him? Are you with hi—"

"Mom," I said harshly, cutting her off mid-sentence.

Gripping my phone hard, I lowered my voice, fighting for control. "Yes, I am with him right now. And I will continue to be with him. I am not letting you force your fear on me anymore. I can't help what happened to Dad. But I am so ashamed of myself that I wasted years, *years*, not taking the time for him, all because *you* thought I couldn't handle it." My voice vibrated with pent-up emotion. Hot angry tears burned my eyes, but I would not cry for her anymore.

She gasped on the other end of the line, but I was on a roll, my breath sawing in and out as my agitation grew. "I care about Nate a great deal. I would think you'd be happy that I found a man that treats me like I hung the moon, instead of trying to scare me away from him. He's a good man. So he has a scary job. I trust him enough to take care of himself, and he will, for me. And I am not about to let a day go by that I don't cherish every single moment I have with him."

My phone was snatched from my hand. I gaped as Nate put it to his ear, eyes burning a hole into mine. In a low, firm voice, he said, "Jordan has to go."

He ended the call and slipped my phone into his pocket and jerked me up into his arms, planting a deep, passionate kiss on me. By the time he was satisfied, I was panting for a different reason and he had me leaned back over his arm, every inch our bodies pressed close together.

"Thanks for standing up for me, Skippy," he said, his eyes roaming my face, and a slow smile creeping over his.

"Uh." My brain wasn't back online yet. "You're welcome?"

He gave me a peck on my nose. "You're adorable," he said, drawing me back to stand on my own. Tugging me along with a waggle of his eyebrows and a wink, he set off toward town. "Let's go find some ice cream."

My heart flipped at his ability to make everything okay. He was the expert at saving my day.

Leaving the conversation with my mother behind, I followed him. He was worth every harsh conversation, every scary call, because what I'd told her was true. He'd do his damn best to keep both of us safe and happy.

Chapter 25

Nate

"Hey Nate, I put another case in the cooler," Thoren called across the yard from the side of the house. The first of what I hoped to be an annual July Fourth party was well under way. Mike commandeered the playlist and had us vibing to some good tunes. Leah and Kylie were helping Jordan move food inside and desserts outside. Thoren was restocking drinks, and Cal was necking with his date on the far side of the shed. Mo and Theresa hadn't been able to make it. He was recovering well and was almost ready to come back to work.

"Hey, Cal! You know we can see you, right?" Thoren jogged up the steps to meet me on the back deck.

I chuckled as I drained the last of my beer. Thoren pitched me another and cracked the top of his own as he leaned against the deck rail.

"This has been a good day. Thanks for doing this, man." He tipped his beer up for a long chug.

"It has been fun. I'm glad Skippy went along with it." Aside from the call with her mom, she'd been smiling and happy all day, and that made me happy.

He fingered the little twinkle lights she'd strung. "You like having her here, don't you?"

"Who likes having who?" Mike stepped up beside Thoren.

I couldn't stop the dopey grin that stretched over my face if I wanted to. "I like having Jordan here."

Mike pointed a finger at me with his beer hand. "That's what being in love gets you. That stupid shit-eating smile."

Thoren frowned at his beer and looked out over the yard. He'd been in an odd mood all day. And he'd had a lot to drink, more than normal. Something was up with him. I'd need to check in with him later.

And then Mike's words registered, wiping the smile off my face. I ducked my head so they wouldn't see the heat creeping up my neck.

"I don't know what it's called, if it's got a name, or if it's just a feeling. I just know I like her being here. I like spending time with her. She makes the world a brighter place just by being in it." I swallowed thickly. "She makes me want to be a better man."

Thoren pushed away from the rail, started to speak, and paused. He looked down, studying his feet for a second. After a beat, he looked at me with haunted eyes. "I'm happy for you, man. I'm gonna go see if that other cooler needs more ice." He stalked off, chucking his empty beer can in the trash, and reached for the cooler, dragging out two more. Passing right by the cooler he said he'd check, he strode down the stairs and back around the corner of the house.

"What's up with him?" I asked Mike.

"He's been acting off since the whole Bunny thing happened." Mike said.

"What did happen with Bunny? He won't talk about it."

Mike shrugged. "Not my story to tell, man. I just know

it's not pretty. So anyway, you told Jordan how you feel about her yet?"

I shook my head. "Nah, dude. But I'm getting there."

"Well, don't be a chicken shit and assume she knows." With a tip of his beer, he left me to go drape his arm across Leah's shoulder.

A pair of arms wrapped around me from behind.

"Hi, stranger." Jordan's voice held a smile. I spun to face her, running my hand along her arm. She leaned in close, tilting her head back as our chests brushed.

Her hair was a wild mess around her head, her cheeks the slightest bit pink from the day in the sun, her full lips begging to be kissed. I watched my thumb as I traced it over her lower lip, along her cheek to her jaw, then met her eyes.

"Hello, beautiful." I leaned in and brushed my lips to hers.

"What was that for?" she said on a sigh.

"Because I wanted to."

"Will you do it again?"

I leaned close and brushed my nose along hers, giving her another soft kiss. "I will always give you kisses."

She sighed happily and snuggled close, laying her head on my chest. I closed my eyes and pressed my cheek to the top of her head. Something sweet filled my chest. There was no other place in the world I would rather be.

I ran my hands down her back, and felt her fingers slip into the back pocket of my jeans. I'd never been a snuggler before Jordan, but I didn't mind it one bit.

"This is nice," she whispered.

I pressed a kiss to her hair. "It is."

She turned her head, her tongue tracing up my neck, and gave my butt a squeeze. "As much as I love having everyone here, I can't wait to get you alone."

I chuckled, squeezing her tighter, pulling her against the growing bulge in my jeans. "I can tell them it's time to go home."

She laughed a little, leaning back to look in my eyes, then her expression grew serious. I could tell she had something to say, but for whatever reason, she kept quiet. She pulled her hand out of my pocket and cupped my cheek, her eyes traveling all over my face. I captured her hand and placed a kiss on her palm, wanting to get back to the light of her smile.

"Come on, let's go see if we can embarrass Cal. He's had that girl in that shed for far too long."

Hours later, Kylie had driven Mike and Leah home, Cal and his girl were shacked up in Pearl, Thoren was passed out in a lounge chair on my deck, and I finally had alone time with my girl.

"I had such a good time tonight," she said, standing in the bathroom doorway, wiping her face with a cloth. I was transfixed, watching her do her nightly routine of makeup removal, brushing her teeth, slipping out of her bra in that fascinating way women took it off without removing their shirt. Something about that intimate act of letting me see the real her had my heart pounding and my dick getting hard.

I was lying on top of the sheets in bed, one arm propped behind my head. I ran a hand across my abs, slipping it under my shorts to grip myself.

She paused, watching me, then leaned back and dropped her rag on the counter, not taking her eyes off me. The long slow tug I gave my dick under her greedy gaze ratcheted up my pulse another notch.

"Whatcha doin' there, slick?" Her lips tipped up on one side, and her tongue peeked out, running over the edge of her teeth. She paused at the foot of the bed, and bent over, bracing her arms as she cocked a knee to crawl in. God damn she was so sexy and having her eyes on me as I worked myself felt fucking amazing.

I sucked in a breath and bit my lower lip as my back arched involuntarily. "I was just watching the most beautiful woman in the world do her thing. I can't help it, watching you makes me hard as a rock."

The expression on her face grew devilish as she crawled up my body, her hands on the outside of my legs. At my hips she paused, glancing down to watch my hand. She cocked her head to the side, looking at me out of the corner of her eye. "You want some help with that?"

"Oh, I don't know if you can do it just the way I like," I teased, knowing that was the biggest fucking lie of all time. Hell, one touch of her hand and I'd probably blast off like a rocket.

"Oh really? You doubt my hand job skills?" she countered, straddling my hips, and slipping her fingers under the waistband of my shorts. She leaned forward, doing that thing with her arms where she pressed her tits together, teasing me with a glance down her tank top. "I'll take that as a challenge."

"I don't know. What if I told you I like it a little rough?" I squeezed my dick and gave another tug just so I could see her eyes flare.

She pulled my shorts off, dragging her nails up my thighs, bearing down as her fingers passed over my hips. I sucked in a breath—fuck that felt good. She sat up, a goddess looking down on her subject.

"I think I can handle rough." Her voice was a siren's

call, and I was a doomed man. My chest heaved as those nails scraped over my abs, then up my chest, clipping the edge of my nipple. Grabbing my wrist, she pulled my hand away and pressed it up over my head.

"But soft and tender can be good too," she whispered, altering her touch to just the barest caress. Trailing her fingers down my inner arm and across my chest, she left goosebumps behind her gentle touch. She shifted and pressed the softest of kisses to the sensitive skin below my ear, her soft breath hitching as she shifted, rubbing herself against my thigh.

"Close your eyes and just feel."

My dick pulsed at her breathy command, but I did as she asked. I felt her shift away, and then her feather light touch landed, first tracing the line of my collarbone, then alternating to the V of my hip.

She moved down my body, dropping kisses and brushing touches, everywhere except the one place I needed her most. A soft breath blew over my rock-hard dick, and my hips bucked, waiting on the soft touch I hoped would follow.

"Fuck," I gasped.

She paused for a moment and the bed shifted. I raised my head and cracked my eyes open to find her poised over my dick. With her eyes boring into mine, she took me in hand and lowered her lips to brush them down my length.

She gripped me, pumping up and down while her tongue left teasing licks on the tip, and I fought for control.

"Ah, so that's what they mean by a quivering member," she teased as I flexed my dick in her hand, wanting more, needing more, but loving the chase.

Her hot breath skated over my skin and my resolve crumbled. "Jordan, I need more, baby," I begged.

"Watch me then." She sank down, her perfect, lush lips wrapped around my dick. I couldn't stop my hips pumping into the warmth of her mouth. She gripped the base and sucked hard as she pulled back, swirling her tongue at the tip before diving back down. Over and over until my balls drew up and my toes were curling. I shifted restlessly, grinding my hips into her hot mouth. The intensity of the way she owned my body was staggering.

"Oh fuck, Baby. I'm gonna—"

She pulled off me with a wet pop, ordering, "Don't come."

I flopped back in the bed, slamming my eyes shut, chest heaving as I tried to gain some semblance of control.

The bed shifted again as she crawled on top of me. Her soft voice reached me through the throb of my heartbeat pounding in my brain.

"Look at me, Nate. See what you do to me."

I lifted my head up as she lowered herself over me, rubbing her pussy along the length of my dick.

I lowered my hands, gripping her hips, feeling her wetness through the thin material of her pajama shorts. She sat up, trailing her hands over her breasts, down her stomach to the hem of her tank. Ever so slowly she rocked on me, while uncovering the smooth expanse of her skin.

I sat up, placing my hands over hers. "Let me."

Her beautiful smile stretched over her face as she placed her arms over my shoulders and let me take over, sliding my hands up her ribcage, cupping her breasts before peeling the tank off her.

Her lips met mine in a languid kiss. I cupped her head, turning it for better access, delving my tongue into her mouth, until she was grinding herself on my dick and I was ready to blow again.

I slid my hand up her leg and across her hip, palming her sweet round ass, snugging her tighter against me, running my fingers along the crease of her ass, down to find her wetness. I swirled a finger through her wet folds and back up, loving the way her breath hitched.

She rocked back onto my hand and said with a gasp, "More."

I flipped her onto her back and landed on top of her, grinning. "My turn to play." She propped up on her elbows, watching me as I dragged her skimpy shorts down her legs, splaying her thighs wide as I crawled between them.

"Let me see you touch yourself," I said softly, leaning into her leg, opening her wider.

Her eyes blazed with desire as she reached down and trailed one delicate finger through her folds. I gripped her inner thigh, my fingers massaging the skin at the crease of her leg. When she withdrew her fingers to circle her clit, I drove a finger into her, feeling her tighten on me.

She gasped. "Oh damn, that feels good."

"Fucking gorgeous," I said, mesmerized by the sight of both of our hands working to bring her pleasure.

Her hips bucked and I couldn't take it anymore. I needed to taste her. I replaced my finger with my mouth and edged her hand away as I took over devouring her. Teasing her to her breaking point just as she had done me.

When she was writhing under me, I licked my way up her body, pausing to lavish attention on her breasts.

Finally, I sank into her in one deep push.

Her hands tugged at my hair, and she pulled my face to hers, kissing me in long, slow, drugging kisses that I matched with my thrusts.

I pulled away and met her eyes, watching her while I made love to her.

"You are everything I never knew that I needed. You are steady and sure, and you still let me be who I need to be," she whispered.

That feeling I'd had brewing in my chest spilled over. I buried my dick in her and lost myself in her eyes. "Jordan, I love you." I reached a hand down and ran my fingers over the small scar she had on her leg. "I love every little part of you, I think from the moment I first met you. You are my best friend. You take care of me, you see me."

Her palm landed on my cheek, and she lifted to kiss me softly. "Nate, I love you too."

I began thrusting again, holding her gaze, certain my whole heart shone through my eyes. I clasped her hands in mine, stretching them over her head, wanting every part of us to be joined. Her legs wrapped around my back, her feet digging into my hips, pressing me harder into her. I shifted, hitching one leg up the bed, so I could get deeper, pound harder, become one with her.

"Nate!" she cried. Her walls clenched around me.

"I know, baby, it feels so good. Just let go, come with me."

I caught her lips with mine, releasing her hands and sliding my arms under her. Hers wrapped around my shoulders holding on tight, as I felt those first flutters of her orgasm around my dick, tightening around me, sucking me into her. The sensation so overwhelming I emptied myself into her and gave her everything I had.

Chapter 26

Jordan

"I don't know how you guys talked me into this. I thought it would be fun. I didn't know you were going to try to kill me," I griped from the floor, staring up at a strange looking rack system on the ceiling of Leah and Kylie's yoga studio. "I thought you liked me."

Leah had invited me for a session during Nate's party, and I was excited to try it out. The remodeled home that served as their studio was in downtown, just a few blocks off the square. Our plan was to do some yoga and then grab a beer together. Nate was on duty and I was having fun with the girls, despite the way they'd made me fold my body.

"Oh, quit your bitchin'," Kylie said. I lolled my head to the side where Kylie and Leah were both sitting in a weird cross-legged pose that looked like their knees should be hurting.

"If I could move my arms, I'd flip you a bird right now," I declared.

Kylie chuckled while Leah shook her head, as if she couldn't do anything about Kylie.

They were both sadistic bitches.

I rolled to my side with a groan, thankful that we were the only three in the room and I could play it up without embarrassing myself in front of anyone else.

"You did great, Jordan. It's a practice, one you do daily and improve over time," Leah said.

I shook my finger at her. "Uh-uh, don't try to work your magic woo-woo positivity on me."

We gathered our mats and met in the front room, gathering our things. My phone buzzed with a missed call from Nate when I turned it off airplane mode.

"Nate's party was fun. Tell him thanks again for hosting," Leah said.

"Tell him next time to skip inviting Thoren though," Kylie grouched. "He was a total dick the entire night."

"Nate is worried about him. He won't say why, but I can tell," I said, stepping into my flipflops.

"Mike is too," Leah replied.

"Well, when they figure out whatever the fuck crawled up his ass, maybe they can work it out so he's not such a general asshole." Kylie snatched a t-shirt over her head, her words muffled, but laced with pissed-off female attitude.

My phone rang in my hand, Nate's name flashing across the screen. I swiped and put it to my ear with a smile on my face. "Hey there."

"Skippy," Nate's voice was full of gravel. He sounded almost like he was wheezing. Immediately, my heart started pounding. Something was very wrong.

"Nate?"

There was a rustle on the line, and then a different voice said, "Jordan, this is Captain Mac Collins."

My ability to stand leaked out of me and I sank to the bench at the wall. Something bad had happened to Nate.

That was the only reason they would call. I fought the instinct to panic. He was okay, I'd heard his voice. I had to repeat the mantra in my head a couple of times before I found my voice again.

"What happened," I croaked.

"First off, Nate is fine. Well, he will be. He has a little smoke inhalation from a house fire a little while ago. His throat is sore, and he's a little wheezy." His no-nonsense delivery settled me even further. "They've got him on oxygen now, if he'll just keep the damn mask on. I'm hoping maybe you can come down here and sit with him while they monitor him."

"Of course."

"I'll stay with him until you get here." Captain Collins's deep, gentle voice grew quiet. "I know this call is scary, and you are probably worried, but he's going to be just fine."

I swallowed thickly. "Okay, thank you. I'll be there as soon as I can. Was anyone else involved?" I tried but couldn't quite keep the tremor from my voice.

Captain Collins cleared his throat, and when he spoke it was gruff. "We had another guy get injured, but he's going to be okay as well."

He told me where to meet him, and I hung up, turning to face Kylie and Leah, who met me with wide eyes.

"I don't know what happened, but Nate is at the hospital. That was his captain. He says Nate's going to be okay, but I need to get down there."

They burst into action, gathering bags and shuffling me to my car. Leah went to hers to follow us to the hospital.

Kylie floored it as we pulled out of the gravel parking lot, tires squealing as we hit the pavement. "Was anyone else hurt?" she demanded.

I gripped the oh-shit handle to steady myself. "He said one other guy was injured but he's going to be okay."

"Who was it?" Desperation laced her words.

"He didn't say."

She cussed under her breath and sped through a red light.

"Um, maybe I should drive?" How was it that I was the calm one? And why was she so freaked?

"What? No, I'm fine," she argued, whipping around a car into the next lane without so much as a glance.

All calmness faded. If she didn't calm down, we'd be headed to the hospital, but for a different reason. "I appreciate you trying to get us there quickly, but maybe don't have a wreck in the process?"

She swiveled her head toward me, shock and fear written all over her face.

"Watch the road!" I screamed. Dear God, she was going to kill us.

"Sorry. Sorry. I'm not as chill as Leah in times of crisis," she said, finally slowing down to a decently safe speed.

We pulled up at the hospital, and I burst out of the car, running to the emergency room entrance. As a volunteer checked me in, Kylie and Leah closed in on either side of me. Leah gripped my elbow, and I clutched her hand to my side.

"Hey, is that..." Kylie trailed off.

"What?" I said distractedly, looking for the volunteer to appear back through the doors. Willing her to come take me to Nate. I just needed to lay eyes on him at this point. I knew Captain Collins had told me he would be fine. But I needed to see that for myself.

"Nothing. I thought I saw Thoren over there. But that

doesn't make sense, because he's on duty, and that guy wasn't wearing a fire department uniform."

The electric door leading to the emergency room section slid open and the volunteer walked out followed by a strikingly handsome older man in uniform. He was a big man with a head full of beautiful salt and pepper hair. He spotted me and a strained smile spread across his tan, weathered face.

Kind eyes met mine as he stuck his hand out. "Mac Collins, you must be Jordan. I missed meeting you at the station the times you've been by, but Nate talks about you a lot, so I feel like I know you."

His voice was gentle and reassuring, and his big hand engulfing mine set me at ease. Between the phone call and the steady greeting, he gave me the impression that he was solid as an oak. Open and polite but would definitely not take shit from anyone.

"You can come with me. I'll take you to Nate." He paused, looking at Kylie and Leah. "I'm sorry, ladies, but they are enforcing the two-visitor rule tonight. You'll have to wait out here."

I turned to see them both staring dumbly at Captain Collins. Leah broke her trance first, visibly swallowing before saying, "Yes, sir, we'll just wait out here in case Jordan needs us."

I followed behind Captain Collins, catching a whiff of his cologne as he held the door for me. He offered me a cup of water as we passed a small water station. Then he was pushing open a door and my eyes fell on Nate.

He took up most of the hospital bed as he lay there, eyes closed over the pasty pallor of his smut-streaked cheeks. An IV protruded from one hand and a blood pressure cuff wrapped around his other arm. An oxygen mask was blowing fresh, clean air into his lungs. His body looked strung tight, as if he were fighting for every breath, even in sleep. A rough cough shook him. As he struggled to get it under control, Captain Collins squeezed my hand and leaned closer to me.

"He didn't settle down until I'd told him you were on your way. He's looking rough right now, but the doc says he's going to be okay after he gets some oxygen. Look past all the contraptions to see the man," he said softly.

I tore my eyes off Nate to find Captain Collins studying my man. He looked tired and worried, and my heart squeezed. It was obvious that he cared about Nate.

"Can you tell me what happened?" I asked quietly.

Captain Collins stepped back into the hallway and motioned for me to follow. I pulled the door closed behind me to not disturb Nate. Following the captain, I focused on the graceful way he navigated the crowded hallway to a private consultation room. He ushered me in and sat across from me in a hard chair, leaning forward to place his elbows on his knees.

With a heavy sigh, he dropped his head to his hands, almost as if he was trying to decide where to start. The dejected pose was startling to see on a man who exuded strength and control. He scrubbed his hand over his face and sat back, squaring his shoulders, once again resembling a man able to bear the weight of the world.

"We were on a structure fire. We were making good progress, had one crew on the second floor and another on the stairs. I'm not sure exactly what happened, I've still got to debrief the rest of the crew and put the puzzle together, but Nate and another firefighter had their masks pulled away and were exposed to super-heated air."

"What happens when they get exposed to that? What

does it mean?" I asked, not sure that I wanted an answer, but needing to know the details all the same.

"They suck in smoke, chemicals, hot air." He paused and ran his hand over his head, then blew out a breath as he sank against the back of the chair. "I'm not going to lie to you, Jordan, and I'm not going to sugarcoat things. It could have been bad. We don't always have this many incidents in our department, meaning we don't typically have a lot of structure fires. But they do seem to come in cycles. We'll have a rash of them, and then not have any for a good long while." A frown marred his handsome face and he spoke as if to himself. "We've had too many already this year."

His attention shifted back to me. It was an effort to not fidget under his weighty stare.

"My guys are well-trained, and they know their shit. They risk their lives to do their jobs, and they take that risk seriously. But you need to understand that they will always risk their lives to save their brothers. And they will always do whatever it takes to come home to the ones they love. Always." He let that sink in for a moment. "I want you to hear me, really hear me, Jordan. Understand what I am trying to tell you." He leaned forward, elbows to knees and linked his hands as he watched me.

"Nate loves you. He will always do whatever it takes to come home to you. But he will not leave a brother behind. There are some that will. But Nate is not that man. Nate is the kind of guy that you want having your back on scene. You can trust him when shit hits the fan. There are a lot of women that can't handle that, knowing that their man puts his life on the line for others." The passionate delivery left me speechless. He'd obviously had this experience, and I wondered briefly who'd hurt this complex man.

He held my gaze, jaw clenched before his expression

shifted to something softer, ratcheting up his handsomeness. "Somehow, I think you are a woman who can handle it."

I nodded absently, letting his words sink in. Nate cared for his crew, but he'd fought to survive for me. My heart swelled with that knowledge.

"How did they get out?" I whispered.

"Thoren and Cal drug them out."

I nodded again and squared my shoulders. I wasn't entirely at ease with how close Nate had come to being seriously injured but understood what the captain was telling me. Nate was a trained professional who was passionate about his job. He'd do whatever it took to come home to me, and when he couldn't do it on his own, he had a team of brothers at his back that would do whatever it took to make sure he did.

"I'll make sure I make them a special treat to say thank you."

"You don't have to do that."

I gave him a little smile. "Yes, I do. They need to know how much I appreciate them. I'll make sure I include you on that too."

He clapped his knees and stood. "All right, let's go check on Nate then."

I stood and stepped into him, wrapping my arms around him. He froze for a moment and then hugged me back. He was a good hugger.

"Thank you, Captain, for taking such good care of these men I've come to care so much about. You've obviously done a great job at training them."

He patted my back and cleared his throat as he stepped away from me. He blinked several times as he turned to open the door, leading me back down the hall. Pausing at

Nate's door, he squeezed my arm. "I'll let you have some time with him."

Nate was in the same position as when I'd first entered the room, shoulders hunched, fists curled on his abdomen. I pulled the guest chair next to his bed and took his hand, easing his fingers open so that I could have some kind of connection to him. My mind drifted to Sandi. How had she handled my dad's accident? Because even knowing that Nate was going to be okay, seeing him connected to these machines broke my heart.

Having my independence had been my goal, and I'd achieved it. But it meant nothing if I didn't have Nate in my life. Yes, his job came with risk. And that scared the hell out of me. But if I'd learned anything about myself over the last few months, it was that I could handle scary things. I couldn't imagine walking away from him now. Not when I'd just found him. Found home. Found love.

A pull somewhere deep in my soul tugged at me, and I looked up to find his sky-blue eyes swimming with emotion, gazing at me like I was the most important thing in his world.

"Hi," he mouthed under his oxygen mask, searching my face, squeezing my hand.

"I love you," I blurted.

His throat bobbed on a swallow, and the oxygen mask fogged over his muffled voice.

I placed a hand to the chest that I loved so much, quieting him. "Just rest and heal. I'm not going anywhere." I stood up and ran a hand over the curls that were plastered to his forehead, drinking in his presence, and the love that shone in his eyes. Letting it flow through me and sending it back to him. "I might step out to let the others know you are okay, but I'll still be here when you wake up. It's going to be all right."

He nodded and his eyes drifted closed. The machines in the room beeped, and outside in the hall, voices carried. I found a rough paper towel and wet it, wishing I had something softer, and gently washed away the grime that covered his face. I fell harder for him with each pass of the rough towel.

This man was my soulmate. I knew it without a shadow of a doubt. Yes, he had a dangerous career. Yes, it was scary. But it was the core of who he was. He was born to help people, to save life and property. And when he looked at me with his whole heart in his eyes, I couldn't deny that I knew he would give it all up if I asked him to.

As I watched him relax, watched whatever meds they'd given him do their magic, I realized that I would take him any way that I could have him. I would support him and stand by his side.

All the mornings where he came home and shared his day, he needed me to help him process and stay centered, just as much as I needed him to stay safe.

Captain Collins's words finally sank in. He'd obviously had experience with not having support. I would not be the kind of woman who couldn't handle this. I would be strong. I would trust in Nate and in his brothers. And I would show him every day what he had to live for.

Fifteen minutes later, the doctor came in and gave us an update. With a kiss to Nate's forehead, I left him to find our friends and share the news.

In the waiting room, Mike, Leah, and Kylie were huddled together, Leah tucked securely under Mike's arm. Captain Collins stood by the long row of windows, staring out at the engine parked in the drive. Thoren and some other guys from Nate's shift were all sitting in chairs, everyone wearing worried expressions. My gaze traveled over the lot of them, and I wondered if Nate knew how loved he was.

"Hey, guys," I said as I drew near, getting their attention.

"The doctor just came in. Nate is responding well. He's going to be fine." I met Captain Collins's eyes and nodded. "Would someone else like to go back and see him?"

Chapter 27

Nate

Captain Collins was the first through the door after Leah left to update everyone. He clapped me on the shoulder. "Good job, son. Maybe next time don't scare the shit out of me like that."

Thoren passed through the door and came up on my other side, giving me a fist bump. "Yea, no shit, Nate. I'm too pretty to get scarred up for your sorry ass."

"I'm sorry, Captain. I don't know how it happened. One minute I was on the stairs. The next minute I was falling backwards. Rook and I tumbled together, and my mask was ripped off in the flailing," I croaked.

Frustration passed over his face. "I think I know what happened and it'll be dealt with once I get confirmation. Just know, that guy will not be on another one of my scenes. Two shifts back-to-back with fires resulting in injuries is not acceptable."

Thoren cleared his throat and said, "Hopefully we're done with our run on structure fires for a while anyway. We've had our yearly quota already."

Having multiple structure fires was not normal for our

town. True, with growth came more occasion for it. But with updated building codes, it was rare that we had multiple barn burners. And we'd had far too many recently.

I got Thoren's attention. "Thanks for saving my ass, man. I owe you one. That could've been bad."

"Anytime. You know I have your back. I love you like a brother."

I swallowed hard against the sudden tightness in my throat. For a man who'd never felt like he was enough, suddenly my eyes were being opened to all I did have.

As Captain and Thoren left and others filed in, my heart was bursting with all the love my friends were bestowing on me. They didn't have to be here. They could've simply waited at their homes or at the station for a phone call. Instead, they'd spent hours in the waiting room to hear about my condition because they wanted to be close by.

As Mike and Leah, then Kylie and all the rest of the guys filed in and out—every one of them wishing me well, and happy to see me—it took everything I had not to break down and sob like a fucking crybaby, all because my friends were worried about me.

Finally, Jordan pushed through the door with a smile on her face, and I couldn't hold back anymore— the fucking tears finally won and spilled over. She crossed the room to me in a quick blur. Then my head was in her arms, pressed to her chest and her soft hands were soothing my hair.

"Oh, honey, it's okay. You're going to be fine," she murmured to my head in between kisses.

"It's not that," I said, my voice trembling. I swallowed, trying to get control of my emotions.

"My whole life I've felt like I wasn't good enough, like I didn't matter enough for anyone to give a damn. My parents couldn't sacrifice their time to spend with me. I didn't rate high enough for them." My voice cracked. "Climbing the corporate ladder was always more important."

Jordan made a sound in the back of her throat and ran her fingers through my hair. I swiped at the fucking tears running down my cheeks.

"All I ever wanted was to be important enough. To be loved."

My emotions were bleeding all over the place. Jordan kept running her fingers through my hair. I slid down in the bed and managed to get my arms around her. She pressed my head to her chest, and I pulled my mask down and tilted my head, burying my face in her neck. In the safety of her embrace, I lost my shit, letting every hurt piece of me, every feeling of inadequacy, fade away.

"I don't deserve you," I whispered to her, pressing a kiss to her soft skin, tasting the salt of my own tears. "But I'm so grateful that you are here, and that you are mine."

She hugged me tighter, then pulled back, shifting and placing a hand to my cheek. "I love you, Nate Williams. I promise to show you every day just how much. Thank you for not dying today."

She kissed me tenderly, and I cupped the back of her head. Taking my sweet time exploring her mouth.

The door burst open, and my nurse walked in. "Well, it looks like you are feeling better. Ma'am, we ask that you not share the bed with the patients. Although I do appreciate the fact that the both of you are crammed into that uncomfortable thing."

Jordan pulled away, her face deliciously flushed. I decided that was my favorite look on her.

I swiped at my face once more and smiled at my gorgeous girlfriend.

The nurse fluttered around the room, chattering away, and all I could do was keep my eyes on Jordan.

"...soon as I get the paperwork signed."

Wait? What was she saying?

"What was that?" I finally focused on the nurse.

"The doctor will be back around shortly, but your vitals are good, and you'll be free to go as soon as he gives the all-clear."

The sun was high in the sky, streaming through my bedroom windows, when I woke alone. Jordan and I had made it home in the dark and crashed hard. I had no idea what time it was, or what day it was even. I just knew that I was alive and in love and had so much to be grateful for. I rolled over and hugged Jordan's pillow, burying my face in the scent of her.

The distant sound of my cell phone ringing, the tone being cut short, and then the murmur of Jordan's voice finally motivated me to move.

I found her on the phone in the den, huddled in the corner of the couch, one leg tucked under her. She shifted as I crawled to sprawl on top of her, laying my head on her belly, with my arms around her hips.

"He's going to be just fine. He just walked in if you'd like to speak with him."

Her voice was high and tight, anxious. The way she got when she spoke to her mother. I shifted to see her face to find her holding the phone out to me with wide eyes. "Your parents," she mouthed.

Fuck.

I shook my head at her and mouthed, "No."

She waggled the phone at me and mouthed, "Are you

sure?"

With a defeated sigh, I glared at the phone. Yes, I was sure that I didn't want to talk to them, but it was better to get it over with.

"Hello?" I croaked, my voice sounded raspy, and my throat burned.

"Nathaniel, sweetheart, how are you?"

"Hi, Mom. I'm okay."

"I'm here too, son." My dad's voice was loud as if he was yelling into the phone. Though I'd just gotten out of bed, I was still exhausted. I put them on speaker and laid my head against Jordan, who immediately began running her fingers through my hair. It felt so good, so soothing to have her hands on me. I never wanted to leave this spot.

"Sweetheart, we heard that you were in an accident at work," my mother said.

"Where'd you hear that?" Son of a bitch, my throat hurt like I'd swallowed glass.

"We follow the newspaper on social media. There was a big article, and your name was mentioned."

Of course. Disappointment, shame, something else—regret, maybe?—rushed through me. I hadn't heard from them in months even though they only lived an hour away. They hadn't checked in after the tornado. They hadn't checked in at all.

"Well, tell us what happened, son," my dad demanded.

"Dad," I started and grabbed my throat like that would stop the knives from stabbing me. Jordan snatched the phone away.

"Mr. and Mrs. Williams," Jordan said sweetly, "I'm sorry. I should've checked with Nate before putting him on the phone. He's not feeling well enough to speak now. He can hear you if you'd like to talk to him. But I'll have to answer for him."

I blinked up at Jordan and mouthed, "Thank you."

She reached down and picked up a bottle of water, taking the cap off and handing it to me. I took a tentative sip. The cool liquid eased some of the pain, so I took a few more before handing her the bottle. Then I laid back in her lap and she resumed running her fingers over my scalp.

"I hope those doctors down there know what they are doing."

"How long do you have to be out of work?"

"Will you be on paid leave?"

"You should come for a visit when you feel better. The leaves will be pretty in the fall."

"We heard there was a tornado down there."

"Is it still a mess?"

My parents droned on and on, talking over each other. Their questions layered on top of the other until I couldn't tell who was asking what, neither of them allowing Jordan a chance to respond. I closed my eyes, unable to keep up with them. Unwilling to even try.

"Um, excuse me, again," Jordan said softly. "We're going to have to let you go. I think Nate has fallen back asleep."

I wasn't asleep, but my eyelids weighed a thousand pounds and were too heavy to lift, so we'd just go with that excuse.

She said good-byes and ended the call, then shifted slightly beneath me. I groaned my objection to that.

"Honey, raise up a sec, let me move a little," she said, a smile in her voice.

I felt her leg adjust beneath me, making room for my shoulders, and I sank back into her. I needed to move. I was probably crushing her, but I needed another second of holding her before I did anything.

Her hands resumed their path through my hair, chasing away the discomfort of talking to my parents. Just this little act of kindness was more than they'd done for me in years.

"Oof, who knew a man's head could be so heavy?" Jordan mumbled.

My chest shook with silent laughter, and I drifted off to sleep with a smile on my face.

I woke to the rumble of Jordan's belly. She hadn't moved an inch. I pulled my arm from around her waist and ran my hand down her leg. My fingers brushed over a raised bump, and I paused to trace the line of the scar she'd gotten the night we met.

Memories of that terrifying night flashed through my mind. The tornado. Finding her trapped in her house. Working so damn hard to find people.

"We've been through a lot in a short period of time, don't you think?" Jordan said quietly, as if she'd read my mind.

The angle of the sun filtering through the windows gave the impression that it might be some time in the late afternoon.

I recalled all the things that had happened since that first night. Her moving in with me, building Pearl together, her leaving for her adventure, both fires, meeting the family of the man I'd saved. I nodded, rising on an arm to look at her. Her eyes were puffy from lack of sleep. Exhaustion was written all over her face, yet she still greeted me with her angelic smile.

"I'm so glad you are here. Thanks for taking over with my folks," I whispered, finding that my throat didn't hurt so bad if I didn't try to actually speak.

"I wouldn't be anywhere else," she said, cupping my cheek with one hand and lifting up to kiss me. "Are you feeling better?"

I nodded again, unable to drag my gaze away from her.

"I love you so damn much, Jordan. No one in my life has ever loved me like you do," I declared, catching her hand and pressing a kiss to her palm. I lowered my head, pressing a chaste kiss to her soft lips, and laid my head on her chest.

"Do you want to talk about the fire?" she asked quietly, running her hands over my shoulders, petting me. Just touching me, showing me that she loved me too.

I swallowed, still getting used to talking about the details of a scene with anyone other than my crew. "We were charging up the stairs, I was in the lead. The guy behind me slipped, and reached out to grab me, which made me stumble. I remember crashing into the wall, then falling backwards. My air hose must've gotten snagged on the banister, because the next thing I knew I was sucking in hot air."

"That sounds scary," she said softly. The warmth of her hands on my shoulders kept me grounded, kept me safe with her instead of in that dark building.

"It was. All I could think of was, 'Oh fuck, this is bad' and 'Skippy is going to kill me if something happens to me.' Which is a stupid thought, actually."

"It really is." She tried for a laugh, but her eyes swam, and her chin quivered. "But do me a favor and maybe let's not joke about something bad happening to you. I'm holding it together by a thread over here." Her words held the weight of the fear she'd felt.

The reality of the situation had not fully settled on me until that moment. I could've died and left behind this beautiful woman. "I was scared, Jordan. So fucking scared. All I could think of was that I had to make it home to you."

She tugged my hair, pulling my head up, before pressing her lips to mine.

"I'm so grateful that you are okay," she said against my lips, then pulled away, her eyes searching mine. "I love you," she whispered, her chin quivering.

My heart broke at the sight of her tears, and I gathered her in my arms. "I know you do, sweetheart." Her body heaved under me as a sob broke loose, and she buried her face in my neck.

"I was so scared." Her voice broke. Bless her heart, she'd been through hell, and she'd held it together. But she'd stayed. She hadn't run. I could handle these tears. She could cry a river, and I would hold her through it and dry every single last tear she shed.

When she finally exhausted herself, I turned us so that we were face to face and my back was to the couch with her head nestled on my chest. We lay there long into the evening, staring at each other, whispering *I love yous*, and being grateful for every single moment.

Jordan

I pulled Nate's truck up to the curb in front of Mrs. O'Malley's cute bungalow house. The quaint neighborhood was quiet in the middle of the day.

Two weeks had passed since that terrible call. Life was back to normal. Nate and I were still sharing a vehicle, seeing as how most days, I didn't have anywhere that I especially needed to go. I saved my errands for the days that he was on shift and focused on my editing business the days he worked remodeling jobs. Any other time we were together.

I'd been finishing up a grocery run when Mrs. O'Malley had called in a near panic and demanded that I come over right then to help her with an issue.

I jogged up the short stairs to find her standing at her door, wringing her hands, a pinched expression on her face.

"Thank you so much for coming, dear," she greeted, holding the door open for me.

"Of course," I replied. Not that I'd had any choice in the matter when she'd demanded, "I need you to get over here right now."

"I tried everyone," she said. "Kylie is out hiking somewhere, and I can't get ahold of Mike or Leah." She ushered me through her little house, past the den, down a hall to a wood door. "I've been hearing this noise since yesterday. I can't put my finger on exactly what it is, but it sounds like a distressed animal."

Pulling open the back door and pushing through the screen onto a small patio, Mrs. O'Malley stopped just beyond. Pointing in the direction of a small shed, she then brought her finger back to her lips, indicating for me to be quiet.

Her back yard needed cutting, the bushes needed a good trim, a bird bath sat dry in the middle of a flower bed lining a wooden privacy fence. Hummingbird feeders hung from iron hangers at the edge of the patio.

We listened quietly for a few moments, the songbirds in the trees providing a lull in the background noise. Then I heard it. A faint, high-pitched whine coming from beyond the shed.

Mrs. O'Malley whipped her head to me, brows high on her forehead.

I nodded. "I'll go check it out."

I set out across the back yard, heart hammering, adrenaline picking up. What if it was some wild animal stuck under the shed? As I drew near, I could see the fence needed some repair. Holes along the bottom of the wood would've allowed any type of small critter access to the yard.

Unsure of what I would find, and a little bit scared that whatever it was might not be terribly nice, I began investigating the shed. I paused as I drew near, inspecting the windows and doors. They were both locked up tight.

The whine came again, this time a little bit louder.

"I'm trying to find you, little buddy. Keep talking to

me," I crooned to the animal. The whining increased and I followed the sound to the back of the shed, where the bushes were even more overgrown. Kneeling, I spotted a hole leading under the building.

I got close as I could and squatted, shining the light from my phone into the dark space. With a thumping heart, I prayed that whatever was in there didn't have rabies and come rushing out to bite me.

"Hey there, little buddy, come out to the light." I sounded like a stalker. If I were a scared animal, I wouldn't trust me either. The animal shifted and whined again, as if in pain. My light passed over dark fur, but it didn't come out.

I stood and turned to find Mrs. O'Malley halfway across the yard. "Do you have any food we could try to coax it out with?"

"I've got some chicken we could use. I'll go grab it," she said, turning back into the house.

"We'll need a bowl of water too," I called after her.

I returned to the hole under the building and cooed to the animal some more. "You can come out. I'm not going to hurt you. I just want to feed you and get you unstuck."

The animal shifted closer, and a small muddy paw stuck out. The hole was rather small, and I wondered if it couldn't get out. I went into the shed and found a small shovel. Maybe if I dug the hole out a little whatever it was could get out easier.

I'd made two passes with the shovel, making the opening wider and deeper, when Mrs. O'Malley returned with food and water.

I crouched down, holding a bite size piece of the chicken out, waving it in front of the hole. "Come on, buddy, I've got some yummy chicken for you here."

That muddy paw peeked out again, followed by a black nose. Then the face of a precious puppy poked out of the opening, little nose twitching. With skittish eyes, the baby crawled from the hole and approached the food in my hand. Relief washed through me that it was a puppy and not a raccoon.

It was a little thing, short, with a long body, and covered in mud. I placed the chicken down in the bowl and sat back, giving it space to feel comfortable. Sitting patiently, I talked nonsense while I watched the puppy come fully out of the hole and approach the chicken.

"You're a mess, aren't you, sweet baby," I cooed. "Did you hurt your leg? It's okay, that chicken is all for you." The scruffy little mess of a dog took a tentative bite, then returned for more.

Once it finished the food, the dog sniffed around, inching closer to me, as if wanting to trust me but scared to death. I waited until it was close, and offered my hand to smell, eventually able to scratch its dirty head. The change was immediate. The baby crawled its muddy little body into my lap and curled up.

"Well, looks like you got yourself a dog," Mrs. O'Malley said quietly from behind me.

"This baby is a cutie-pie, that's for sure," I said wistfully. "I think it needs to go to the vet—looks like it has an injured leg."

"Come in the house and let's make some calls."

An hour later, I left the vet's office, puppy in tow, and headed to Nate's. I glanced at the dashboard clock, noting I had plenty of time to get her cleaned up. In the backseat was a loaner leash and a sample bag of puppy food and treats.

The pup—I'd taken to calling her Gracie—sat in my lap, wrapped in a towel.

I parked at the back of the house and gathered my precious cargo. The driver's side door swung open. "Surprise!"

"Oh my God!" I yelped, spinning to see a grinning Nate filling the space the open door.

As his gaze passed over me and fell to Gracie, his wide grin fell too.

"I can explain," I put up a hand to halt his objection, wiggling myself to the edge of the seat. His stunned expression had my defenses up.

"She was trapped under the shed at Mrs. O'Malley's. I rescued her," I sputtered, forced to quickly make my best argument. "Mrs. O'Malley got me in with the daughter of a friend. She's a veterinarian. She says she's about six months old. I couldn't just leave her there, Nate. She was starving and injured, but she's going to be okay, her little hind leg just has a little sprain. And she had a de-wormer at the vet's office, so she might poop a little, but otherwise she just needs a healthy diet and some TLC, and she'll be good as new. Oh, and we ran into Jules and Nelson from my old neighborhood while we were there, and she's already made a new friend and we have a playdate for next week."

My word vomit tumbled to a stop. Nate was staring at Gracie with wide eyes, and I couldn't read if he was angry, or upset, or stunned, or what, exactly, was running through his head.

"Don't be mad, please." I swallowed thickly, nervous that I couldn't read him. For as long as we'd known each other, he'd always been so open. I'd never seen him this stoic and impassive. "It's only for a little while, until I can find her a permanent home."

"No," Nate said gruffly, stroking a knuckle between Gracie's ears, his jaw working.

Emotion swelled in my chest, a mix of anger and heartbreak. I couldn't believe he wouldn't let her stay with us until we could rehome her.

"Fine—I'll keep her in Pearl until I find her a home." I huffed, jumping down from the truck, forcing him backwards.

Nate didn't give an inch as he glared into my eyes. "No."

What the hell was his problem?

"What? Seriously? I cannot believe you, of all people, would turn away a helpless, injured..." I snuggled Gracie closer and stomped past him, my voice rising with righteous indignation. "... frightened, innocent little puppy dog."

"Skippy, simmer down." He grabbed my elbow.

I spun on him, prepared to launch into how terrible this travesty was, when I noticed the expression on his face. My argument died on my lips at his expression of childlike awe. His wide eyes were glued to Gracie, and he reached hesitantly for the puppy bundle in my arms. Bringing her to his face, I stood fascinated as he booped her little nose against his in the most precious Eskimo kiss of all time.

Sweet Gracie licked him right on the nose, then began wiggling in his arms, licking all over his face. I couldn't blame her. I couldn't get enough of him either.

"So..."

"So," he said, "it looks like you trumped my surprise, and I need to rearrange my plans." Nate snuggled Gracie in an arm and took my hand, leading me to the house.

It registered then. "What are you doing here anyway? Aren't you supposed to be on duty? How did you get here? What's going on?"

He tugged me close, planting a kiss on my lips, a goofy smile plastered on his face. My heart flipped over in my chest at the sight of Happy Nate.

"Apparently, me and my girl are bathing our new puppy."

"Does this mean we can keep her?" Excitement spread through me.

Gracie crawled up his chest, tongue flicking out constantly and leaving dirty paw prints in her wake. "I'm scared not to. My woman has a vicious tongue when she gets miffed."

"Oh, he's got jokes now," I said, following him to the bathroom.

"What kind of soap can you use on a dog this small?" He leaned over to turn the water on and fill the tub.

I rummaged through his toiletries. "I don't know, probably none of this stuff. It might make her itchy."

He sat on the edge of the tub, pulling the towel off Gracie, and leaned to place her in the water. Her hind legs hit the water and she cried out, scrambling to get back to the safety of his arms.

"Aww, she's scared," I said. Poor little baby had been through so much in a single day.

Nate pondered for a second, looking around the room. He stood quickly and handed her to me, then toed off his boots and ripped his shirt off. He emptied his pockets and in one swoop, snagged Gracie from my arms and stepped into the bathtub, pants and all.

"Oh my God, you are an idiot, what are you doing?" I laughed at this crazy fool.

"She's had a rough day. No way am I going to scare her to death." He tucked Gracie safely under one arm and bent his head, pecking her little nose. "Who's a good girl? You ready for a nice warm bath?" His baby talk voice was kind of hot. I picked up his phone and accessed the camera, snapping a photo of my man in the bathtub with his puppy.

We managed to get most of the dirt scrubbed off Gracie, then got her towel dried and fed. She was snuggled in my lap snoozing when I remembered his reaction at his first sight of her.

Nate had a large hand on her, his fingers absently brushing her fur, as if he couldn't bear to not touch her. I laid my hand on his. "Why'd you tell me no when you first saw her?"

Nate shrugged a shoulder, avoiding my gaze.

"Seriously, Nate. We don't have to keep her. I didn't even know if you like dogs or not. I just wanted her to be warm and safe tonight." I didn't know what I'd say if he told me she had to go.

Nate turned his hand over, linking our fingers, brushing his thumb across my wrist.

"I have always loved dogs, but never had one of my own." His voice was low and soft, wistful almost, as he stared down at the sleeping baby. "My parents never wanted the hassle of a pet. Hell, most of the time they forgot they had a kid. So, every time I brought it up, they'd shoot me down, and tell me we didn't have time for a dog."

My heart squeezed at the longing in his voice. "Sounds like it might have done you some good to have a companion though."

He nodded. "When I started working at the fire department, I never considered it because of the schedule. Hard to take care of an animal when you're gone for twenty-four-hour shifts."

I frowned. "So, when you said no earlier..."

He lifted his eyes to meet mine. "I wasn't saying no to Gracie. I was saying no to her leaving, to you leaving."

This sweet, soft-hearted man. He did so much for others. How had I never realized that one of the things missing in his life was the unconditional love of a pet?

He shifted in the seat to face me, wrapping his arm around me and pulling me close. "I had this excellent surprise planned out for tonight. I was going to surprise you by coming home, and sweeping you off your feet, and asking you to stay here, for good. To move in with me, Jordan. To be mine." His eyes held no hesitation as he spoke the words.

"Nate..." I started, but he silenced me with a finger to my lips.

"You are everything to me. You make my life so much better in ways you aren't even aware of. Even when you aren't trying." He leaned in to press a kiss to my lips. "I love you, Skippy. I want to make this permanent."

My heart exploded with happiness. "Does this mean we get to keep Gracie?"

He cupped my cheek, tenderly. "We can even get her a friend." Then his arms were around me, his face buried in my neck. "Say you'll stay."

Gracie squeaked in my lap at being squashed between us. I caressed the line of his jaw. This man. My man. "Always," I whispered, and sealed the vow with a kiss.

Epilogue

Nate – Six months later

A low rumble of thunder crawling through the night woke me. Glancing at my clock, I found it was barely after midnight. At the foot of the bed, Gracie snored from her little doggie throne. Beside me, Jordan slept soundly with her back to me.

The thunder rumbled louder, the flashes of lightning illuminating my dark bedroom, and she never moved.

Not too long after my accidents, she'd called a therapist, and had been to several sessions. I'd been with her on the first few visits. We'd come up with a plan of communication and actions to help us both learn to deal with all that we'd been through. It helped knowing that we were in this together. Knowing that no matter what either of us faced, we could lean on each other.

So much had changed since she'd come back. My side business continued to grow. The gratification I got from doing odds jobs that positively impacted my customers had filled the void I hadn't even realized had been there.

Jordan's business was taking off and she was booked out most of the year ahead.

The therapist had helped her create healthy boundaries with her mother, but she and Sandi had begun weekly calls that eventually led to video calls with both Sandi and Waylon.

My parents were even making more of an effort, though sometimes it felt like too little too late. Through it all though, I had my girl, and she had me.

I rolled to check on Jordan after a particularly loud crash of thunder. She turned to face me, sliding a hand over my waist. Slipping my arm around her back, loving the feel of her warm, soft body snuggled to mine, I closed my eyes.

Sometimes I worried that she'd wake frightened of the storms, like the time I'd found her in the van, curled into a little frantic ball. But the last few storms we'd had, she'd slept right through. When I asked about it, she'd told me it was because she knew she was safe.

Hopefully the ring hidden in my bedside table would remind her that I'd do my best to keep her safe for the rest of our lives. She sighed in her sleep, a precious sound that I cherished. Pressing my lips to her forehead, I closed my eyes and let the sound of the storm lull me back to sleep.

The End

Want to see more of Nate and Jordan? Grab your bonus scene here!

Burn Point Bonus!

Ready to see how Thoren and Kylie handle being snowed in

a cabin? Keep reading for a sneak peek of this how a little forced proximity turns these frenemies to lovers.

Read Flash Point Now!

296

Want to stay in the know on all things Rae? Join my newsletter here!

Also by Rae Fields

Mike and Leah

Ignition Point

Thoren and Kylie

Flash Point

Mac and Liv - Coming July 2024

Anchor Point

Acknowledgments

First and foremost, thank you, reader, for taking a chance on me! I hope you loved Nate's story and my world of heroes. There's more to come.

This story originated after my own hometown experienced a devastating tornado, and to process my emotions, I poured them onto the page. I have so much respect for first responders and public safety, the people who see us on our very worst days. If that's you, thank you for your service.

To my hubs, thank you for being my personal hero all these years. I couldn't chase this dream without your love and support. To my family and friends, thank you for cheering me on, and for understanding when the writers cave calls. To my HEA Club friends, your knowledge, encouragement and support are everything. I heart you. And to Jessica, you're the real MVP- thanks for your wisdom, patience and endless support.

About the Author

Rae Fields is beginning her publishing adventure and hopes you'll come along for this journey. She feels weird talking about herself in third person and hopes you'll join her newsletter and socials where she can just talk to you, and not feel weird about it.

Find all my links and join my newsletter at

www.raefields.com

Want to stay in the know on all things Rae? Join my newsletter here!

Join Rae's Newsletter